Blood Revenge

Also by David Thor:

Non-Fiction
In Search Of Ubiquitous Computing

Blood Revenge

A NOVEL BY

David Thor

Cosacinco Press

Miami * Springfield * London

Published in the United States by Cosacinco Press
www.cosacinco.com
www.cosacincopress.com

ISBN 978-0-9824877-0-9

1 3 5 7 9 10 8 6 4 2

Printed in the United States of America

First Edition

For Maura

Prologue
April 1974
Xiamen Island, China

Tan Yi and his wife, Jin, bowed and smiled warmly as they greeted each guest. They were hosting the ruling party's minister meeting at Putuo Palace on Xiamen Island, China. Most of the attendees had less than four hours to live. In just a few hours, the East China Sea would become the final resting place for twelve of the fourteen gathered leaders; the planned strike for precisely 11:00 p.m. would leave only the ministers of agriculture and health sciences alive.

There were strong wind gusts from the southeast buffeting the island cliffs and toying with the direction of the driving rain. Even the local sea birds took refuge, their instincts alerted by the impending storm. At ten-thirty most of the palace staff was asleep. Only the palace guards were still on duty, patrolling the outer wall and gates of the palace.

Inside the palace, fourteen-year-old Ellen, the younger of the Yi's two children, fidgeted. She tried hard to keep from worrying about her older brother, Ren, who was on his maiden patrol with the palace guards. Ellen stared through one of the large windows of the stone palace. She could vaguely make out the shadow of a passing guard against the backdrop of lights that illuminated the long drive extending to the palace gates. Flashes of lightning added to her uneasy feeling, but against her instincts she tried again to get to sleep.

Tan Yi and his wife, Jin, were newly appointed; having served, respectively, as the ministers of agriculture and health sciences for less than a year. They'd politicked hard for the leadership roles for the better part of three years. Despite their longstanding and well-known opposition to Chinese economic and political reform-which positioned them as unlikely candidates for appointment to the new age Chinese ruling board—the pair had prevailed. Not only had the couple been appointed to the positions, they'd been the surprising choice to host the semiannual ministers' meeting.

Tan Yi, a Republic protector, believed that the government's gradual shift in politics would ultimately spell the end of traditional Chinese Republic rule and the end of one of the last successful Communist régimes. During a break in the proceedings, he whispered to his wife, "Of course, I am torn, but we have no choice. I could never exact direct revenge on our country. Tearing the Republic apart with civil action would be counterproductive and self-defeating."

Jin whispered, "Yes, Tan, I agree. The most prudent action is to shift the balance of power in the current bureau. We must alter the makeup of the ministry."

Tan nodded in approval.

Jin, a distant cousin to North Korean leader, Kim Il-sung, followed the career of the Great Leader closely. Both she and Tan recognized that Il-sung's rigid model for a communist society was not the model they wanted to reproduce in the Chinese Republic; they did however admire the Great Leader's continued strength in the face of continuous Western political attacks. Both also recognized that the

North Korean promise of equality for all fell short in one major way. Equality for all meant a meager existence for most, and that was far from their goal.

As Tan Yi often preached to his children, the battle against Western ideals was not new age but rather a continuation of a century-old battle—a battle that had begun in the mid nineteenth century when the forceful British practice of using opium to create a faux balance of trade for their export of tea prompted the Chinese leadership to enforce its prohibitions on the importation of the substance. Great Britain, looking for a way to end the Chinese restriction on foreign trade, responded by attacking several Chinese coastal cities, including Shanghai. China, unable to combat the modern British navy, was forced to sign a series of treaties. One of these treaties ceded Hong Kong to the British. Similar trade treaties were forced on China by other Western nations including the United States.

Tan's eyes narrowed and his mouth twisted into a grimace as he reflected on his hatred of the West. His anger, stirred by a history of Western aggressions, was further fueled by twentieth century trade embargos enforced against the Chinese Republic by the United States and their allies—trade embargos that Tan viewed as an illegal and unethical form of forced democracy.

———

Just before 9:00 p.m., the first of three small launches left the port of Jimei for the nine-mile trip to the southern cliffs of Xiamen Island.

Guard in training, Ren Yi, patrolled the sea-facing outer palace wall. Ren, like most other young, elite Chinese males, was required to spend at least six months as an apprentice in the Republics defense services before turning fourteen. His parents' connections were invaluable; he'd spent most of his six months of service stationed close to home.

Ren paused when he heard what he thought was the sound of a diesel engine. Cupping his ear, he cocked his head in the direction of the sound then wrote off the sound as a trick of the wind. No merchant marine ship or fishing rig would be out in this storm. He moved on to his next checkpoint. An hour later, his superior would not be so lucky.

———

They came over the wall just before 11:00 p.m. Two by two, the hired killers stealthily moved toward the palace inner walls, quickly and quietly slitting the throats of three guards who were taking cover from the storm under the palace eves. Ren Yi emerged from the shadows just in time to view the sickening tragedy. Stepping back into the shadows, Ren bent over and vomited. Ren quickly regained focus. He needed to protect his sister and parents. He forced himself to turn his attention away from the massacre, and a fast walk turned into a sprint through the palace courtyard toward his sister's room.

Following less than fifty yards behind, a small army of black-clothed soldiers turned on a right angle and charged into a hallway leading to the palace meeting room.

The wall of fiends entered the room and, with rehearsed movements, stationed themselves, one behind each of the twelve seated ministers. Tan Yi stood as his wife Jin left the room. With the movements of a symphony director, the minister of agriculture gave the signal that quickly sealed the fate of his twelve guests. The trained mercenaries slashed the throat of each minister and left each victim to bleed to death on the marble floor. The killers ran from the room and headed back through the courtyard toward the outer palace wall and their waiting transportation.

―――

With the horrible image of his murdered comrades still in his head, Ren tried in vain to convince his sister to find refuge elsewhere in the palace.

"Come, we must go!" Ren pleaded.

"No," Ellen said. "I want to find the men who killed our guards."

"We can't!" Ren shouted.

Ellen crossed her arms in defiance. "What about Mom and Dad? We must help them."

"We can't help them if we're dead," Ren insisted. "Come with me to the basement. Now!"

Ignoring her brother's pleas to take refuge, Ellen tugged at Ren's arm. "Help me get the weapons from the slain guards," she said.

The young soldier and his sister were only a few short steps from the bodies of the fallen guards when they met with the retreating killers. Noting Ren Yi's guard uniform, the killers moved quickly to complete what they thought was unfinished business. They moved in on the siblings, knocking both children to the ground. Ellen embraced her brother and lowered her head as the lead soldier raised his sword. In concert with series of shouted commands from the background, a figure stepped from the palace shadows and calmly waved the swordsman off. The group bowed in unison before completing their retreat.

As the palace chaos settled and the dead ministers' bodies sank to the bottom of the sea, the Yi family's brief stand in the ministry was about to come to an end. The parents realized that they could no longer put off the inevitable. This was their war, not their children's. They needed to remove their children from this place, this era in Chinese history. They had long planned for and in fact had expected the day for relocation would come. Only the pain of family separation stood in their path.

What Tan and Jin Yi did not know, could not know, was that, at almost the same instant, another family drama was playing out almost one thousand miles to the north.

1974 - Vladivostok, USSR

Lieutenant Suan Moon was a young man and an old one at the same time. Those who had occasioned the steam rooms of Vladivostok during the past six months would have seen the body of a strong fit young man. It was his face that was old. His face showed pain and wear, not from the climate but rather from an agonizing life as a young adult. A perpetual biology student, he was coerced, like many skilled North Koreans, to practice his trade within the ranks of the government. He was an especially attractive candidate in the eyes of his superiors. He had been married and fathered two children before the age of twenty-five. His wife and second child had died during childbirth, leaving a vulnerable young man and his son at the whim of a very persuasive government. He'd been offered, and had agreed, to exchange his surviving child's future for his own dedication to a national weapons program.

In an unusual deal for the Communist regime, Moon had agreed to an assignment as an army biologist. In exchange, his son would be sent to the United States to be cared for and educated by a Western child welfare association. This association specialized in what it called the rescue mission for children of the Far East. The program was initially designed for war orphans but often used as an escape route for sons of the elite.

———

Jutting south from the eastern extremities of Russia, the Vladivostok Peninsula represented a unique geographical base of operations for the Soviet Republic Military Intelligence. The area shared a border with both China and North Korea and, for a brief moment in time, it had also been the home to The Korean People's Socialist Vacation retreat. It was not much of a vacation retreat; for most of the year, the climate matched the vast wastelands of Siberia and was inhabited by a hardened people who had never been completely free. In fact, it was not really a retreat at all, rather the secret headquarters for what was once known as the Supreme People's Assembly of the Northern Peninsula.

During the late 1940s, the peninsula had been used as a joint planning and staging area for the efforts put forth by a surging and ambitious Soviet- and Chinese-sponsored North Korean government. In the years since the formal end of the Korean conflict, the port area of Vladivostok had become the central staging ground for the Soviet's Cold War naval buildup.

In the spring of 1974, the North Korean minister of defense approved a plan that would fund the acquisition of a credible weapon of mass destruction. The North worried that a continuing relationship between the United States and the South Korean government would result in a buildup of tactical nuclear weapons along their negotiated demilitarized border. The North was seeking to offer a credible deterrent to the presumed buildup of nuclear weapons by their neighbor—a weapons buildup that the North could not counter. The Great Leader Kim Il-sung engaged the Soviet regime in discussions.

The Soviet government no longer viewed the Korean Peninsula as strategic and would not offer any direct support to the North

Korean government. The Soviets had been set back once before while playing chicken with the United States over its nuclear arsenal and didn't intend to make the same mistake again, especially in an area so close to home. The Soviets did offer a compromise to the North Koreans. The compromise agreement called for a trade. In exchange for access to credible weapon technology and an adequate testing environment, the North Korean government promised to wage a series of spot aggressions on the South. The intent was to ensure that the Korean Peninsula remained, at least somewhat, a player when it came to the mind-sets of the other world powers.

—

Lieutenant Suan Moon was nearing the end of his assignment in Vladivostok. It had been nearly eighteen months since he had traded his life for his young son's future, and he was nearing the end of his tour of duty. His mission had been a success in the eyes of his superiors. He'd successfully designed, produced, and tested a virulent biological weapon. He knew this from his six months of live subject testing of a uniquely human virus.

Lieutenant Moon prepared to leave the Vladivostok lab for the last time. His head pounded at the thoughts swirling through his brain. He was not conflicted by memories of a place that would haunt him for the rest of his life; nor was he tortured by recollections of a mission filled with pain and death. Rather, his mission would result in a lethal weapon that could only be used in a war that no one would win. It was a time of death, and no matter how often Lieutenant Moon would come to face death, the face of death would never be far from his thoughts.

He prepared to lock his viral recipe book in his briefcase for the last time and tried to rationalize his role in the People's government. He could not. His whole life had revolved around his wife and children, and now they were all gone. He prepared to make one last human sacrifice. Neither he nor his infamous recipe book would ever make it home to Pyongyang.

———

With his last action, Lieutenant Moon attempted to put both his own pain, and his new creation to sleep. He was successful in ending his own pain but his government's invisible eyes would keep his work and legacy alive. Suan Moon could never have fathomed the frequency with which death would eventually be born from his work.

———

September 1980
Leyden Academy
Northfield, Massachusetts USA

Ellen and Ren Yi returned to the Leyden Academy for their fourth and final year. Each fall when they returned to the academy from their adopted summer residence in Yakima, Washington, it seemed to Ren as though his younger sister, Ellen, and their classmate, Doug Moon, demonstrated an increased passion for inflicting harm on others. This fall was no different. Both Ellen and Doug had reached a new level of excitability, a level that Ren often worried would be their downfall.

One day in the lunchroom, Ren sat beside his sister and said in a hushed but stern voice, "Listen, Ellen, stay cool. You take too many risks. Why do you risk being the focus of attention?"

It wasn't the first time that an argument like this had broken out over lunch.

"You can't go around poisoning the student body whenever you feel like it. Save it for your pets."

Ellen knew that her brother was referring to the cage full of rats that she kept in her dorm room. Ellen never viewed her rats as pets. They were breathing, four-legged incubators for her biology and chemistry experiments.

Ignoring the unsolicited comments, Ellen Yi turned and exchanged an odious look with her brother. Sitting nearby, Doug Moon just looked away. His dark, straight, shoulder-length hair fell into his eyes. His face showed no expression.

A young boy sitting alone at a nearby table bent over and wretched on the floor. Ellen knew that any other members of the student body who opted for hot chocolate at lunch would meet a similar fate. She took a small notepad from her breast pocket and made a quick tally. "Another boy. Fascinating," she said, arching an eyebrow. "That puts today's success rate at 80 percent for boys and 70 percent for girls. Interesting demographic, don't you think?" She spoke out loud but no one was listening.

Ellen, slender with a pale complexion and black, short-cropped hair, possessed a certain amount of evil cleverness. She was by far the most intelligent of the three, and her tortoise-shell glasses helped portray that image. She didn't find her studies at all challenging. In fact, she rarely studied at all, often mocking her teachers as nothing more than talking heads. She viewed the artsy, self-enrichment curriculum at the academy as stifling and a waste of time. Her real interest was in biological sciences.

Her placement at the academy was not of her doing. It was mostly out of family necessity. She viewed her years at the academy as nothing more than a slow drain of time.

Her parents used her brother as a proxy for determining the

duo's ultimate fate. Ren's reputation as a communicator limited their search to institutions that would cater to his creativity rather than her logic-based strengths. Her parents had enrolled her and Ren in a liberal arts preparatory school in the northeastern United States, hoping that over time, she and Ren would become assimilated into American society without losing their heritage.

What the Yi family could not have planned for was the terrible confluence of personalities and events that would meet and feed off each other and, ultimately, strike a blow to society that no one could have predicted. The most dangerous kind of breeding that could happen did. The adolescents spent years together, devoid of any family influence. There were no adult mentors after which to pattern themselves or with whom they could exchange ideas. They only had each other. The trio's interactions were fueled by a deadly combination of hatred and cunning. The lack of any family influence and the isolated environment of the academy fed the children's emotions and turned a casual unhappiness with American culture and politics into a blinding hatred.

Ellen and Ren had met Doug Moon two years earlier during a homecoming weekend event. They'd spotted him hiding behind a large oak tree during an evening bonfire. He held what looked like a homemade blowgun to his mouth and was targeting the buttocks of a passing coed.

"Hey, what are you doing?" Ellen had called to him.

"Mind your own business," Doug had said, lowering the blowgun and stalking off.

"That's odd," Ren had commented. "For a freshman, that's kind of funny. For a sophomore, that's just stupid."

Only later did they learn that Doug had coated the ammunition with a rather quick-acting skin irritant that caused the victim to do everything short of disrobe to get at the source of the irritant.

The Yis were not immediately sure what to make of Doug. One thing that they did know was that he was not quite right. A dry personality, he showed little or no emotion toward anyone or anything. The only thing the Yis could tell about Doug was that he, much like Ellen, did not like the academy, its student body, or its faculty. Moon, like the brother and sister pair, was attending the academy in forced seclusion from his birth culture and geography.

Doug Moon was quiet and reclusive during his days as an academy student. It was only in the later years at the academy that he reached out to the Yis—a period that coincided with his own realization that he had not been placed in exile by his father and government but was instead strategically separated until a time when the North Korean government strategists felt he could be most useful. He felt no attachment to the country that he had lived in for the past five years. As far as he was concerned, his only true allegiance stood with his homeland and the government of North Korea. This allegiance was reinforced during visits with his welfare counselor, the same counselor that he had been placed with as a young immigrant from North Korea.

Doug looked forward to his twice yearly visit with this counselor, who often recounted Moon's heritage, a family tree that was strongly rooted in North Korean history.

Recently, the counselor had taken their conversations in a different direction. "You were assigned to me on purpose," the counselor had told Doug during their most recent meeting.

"Tell me more," Doug had replied, his face devoid of emotion.

Staring directly into Doug's dark brown eyes, the counselor said, "I cannot reveal much. But trust me, you were sent to me as part of an elaborate intelligence effort."

"How so?" Doug asked.

"I cannot say," the counselor said, "but it involves your young friends, Ren and Ellen Yi."

Doug Moon smiled for the first time in weeks.

Over the years, the visiting counselor had recounted stories of Doug's father. His father was often referred to as "the Great Scientist," the man who had ensured the Peoples' future. Doug never asked what the moniker literally stood for, but he was fairly certain that he would find out in the years to come.

Through the years, Doug relayed, almost preached, his messages from the homeland to Ren and Ellen, and over time the threesome became convinced that it was their destiny to inflict a cataclysmic strike of revenge on the Western world. They believed they would be protecting their homelands from further Western oppression.

They set a course for themselves that would ultimately scar the world.

———

June, 2003—San Francisco, California USA

Working from a suite at the Ritz Carlton Hotel, Ren Yi awaited the arrival of his former classmate, Doug Moon.

Yi spent the afternoon talking on the phone with fellow board members, investment bankers, and his sister in Massachusetts. The afternoon discussions proved quite helpful. The classmates, Ren Yi, Ellen Yi, and Doug Moon were two decades removed from their days at Leyden Academy. Ren was five years into his role as the leader of a medium-sized software company, and life was good. A few gray hairs and a few extra pounds did not detract from his handsome facial features and friendly demeanor.

During the past year, Ren had purposely distanced himself

from his sister. He realized her passion and understood her allegiance to their youthful promises. However, time had taken its toll on his enthusiasm for martyrdom. He rather enjoyed his position as evangelist and entrepreneur. His business was flourishing in the face of an aging economy and a business plan designed to rework geopolitical history. Ren was quietly removing himself from the activities of Moon and Ellen Yi. It was only a charade meeting that brought Moon and Yi together. Both knew the situation, and both understood the needs and wants of the other. Intending this meeting to be the last face-to-face between himself and Moon, Yi hoped that a posture of concerned cooperation would help further position him as an outsider with regards to his sister and Moon's plans.

Moon arrived at the hotel suite exactly on time. He was cordial but not overly animated as he exchanged greetings with Yi. Yi made quick work of the meeting. He delivered a promised briefing on the status of his company and its extracurricular efforts on behalf of the Moon's project. After the briefing, Doug Moon stood, bowed, and politely thanked Ren.

Moon passed through the hotel lobby and exited the hotel, turned right on Stockton Street, and walked the few short blocks to China Town. It was late evening, but he could see his way by light of the city streets and an unusual glow from the nearly full moon.

Anyone catching a glimpse of Moon would likely take a second look. Dressed like an ordinary businessperson, perhaps someone working in the financial district, his short dark hair, jaundice skin tone, and sharp facial features created a rather sinister look. Most passed off his neat dress and somewhat emaciated features as those of a local restaurateur.

It was only when you looked into his eyes that he seemed different than his projected stereotype. His eyes were a magnetic, soft brown that revealed an active mind but also showed the strain of years of pain and determination.

He paused under the overpass that marked the entrance into the blocks of Chinese storefronts that, by day, were filled with passing tourists. This evening, the only sign of life was a cry from a kitten lodged under the arm of a comatose homeless person. Satisfied that he hadn't been followed, Moon quickly made his way down a side alley. He stopped in front of the third door on the left.

A stone plaque hung next to the doorway. Moon stood motionless and stared into the center of the plaque. A burst of red flashes emitted from its center, and after a brief silence and the sound of an electronic latch, he exited the alleyway into the building.

His presence did not stir either inhabitant. Moon walked to the center of the room and stood beside a slender, fair-haired woman who was busy confirming inbound messages via her headset. Oddly, Moon thought, the woman was dressed in a business suit and was wearing a Berkley baseball cap. He moved across the room to where the woman was standing. They both took up a position behind the male operator of a large video and data equipment console. The operator was tracking a GPS receiver/locator signal. All communications were either delivered or received via a series of low-profile antennas hidden on the building's roof. The antennas were capable of secure communications anywhere in the world via satellite and shortwave signals.

"We're ready, Mr. Moon. Please move over to the video panel on the left," the female offered before dimming lights with a handheld remote. She took a step back to ensure Moon had a clear viewing angle of the raised display panel.

Moon leaned forward and observed the imagery on the screen. It was an enhanced digital satellite image. He recognized the image type by the clear but rigid transfer from frame to frame.

"Where are they?" he asked.

"They're in Maryland, exiting the terminal at Frederick Municipal Airport," answered the woman after quickly conferring through her headset.

Moon recognized the location. He had been on many exploratory listening missions at nearby Fort Detrick. The targets were leaving the airport terminal. It looked as though there were two groups of figures walking across the parking lot. There were three in the front group. All were clad in army dress uniforms. One carried a metal briefcase secured to his wrist. The trailing pair wore street clothes.

There was a brief spark from the rear group. Understanding what was taking place, Moon thought it was strange to see the action without any sound. The trailing group of two remained still as the front group collapsed in unison and fell to the ground.

The female standing next to Doug held her hand to her ear, cocked her head, and listened. "Three have been disabled," she commented without emotion.

Moon nodded and watched as a van emerged from the side of the picture. The three incapacitated figures were quickly dragged into the van. Moon bowed slightly to the woman, turned and disappeared into the alleyway.

1

October, 2007—New Orleans, Louisiana USA

The wind continued to intensify. It was now blowing steadily out of the northwest at 25 mph.

Dr. John Roker, chief meteorologist for the U.S. Coast Guard Eighth District in New Orleans, planned to stay in the communications center for the duration of the storm. But just as he was about to receive a new batch of satellite photos, he was interrupted.

"There's a team of NASA people here to see you," stated his assistant, Penelope.

"What do they want?" asked Roker with a tone of curiosity.

"They want to know if you have any interest in hitching a ride with them?"

Roker immediately understood. He had petitioned for years to participate in NASA's hurricane hunter program and now, with one moving into his quadrant, he just might be getting the chance.

Roker rose from his seat. "She's all yours," he told Penelope as he pointed to the main console.

"Gee, thanks," Penelope said, rolling her eyes.

Roker patted her on the back. "You can do it. Just keep me informed." He winked and then sprinted out to the communication center's lobby to greet the visiting NASA team.

After a short briefing in the hangar, the NASA team, accompanied by John Roker, headed out to the specially outfitted McDonnell Douglas DC-8 for the flight into the heart of Hurricane Pablo. This storm was the fifteenth named storm of the season. Dr. Roker was briefed on the mission as they taxied out to the end of the runway.

This mission would be especially important to the science of hurricane management. The DC-8 was carrying a newly installed moisture measurement device designed to study hurricane growth. The flight path took the NASA crew, plus one, due south at low altitude over the Gulf of Mexico.

U.S. Navy Captain James Wesson and Lieutenant Bill Emory were piloting the NASA DC-8. The flight was minutes old, and the plane was being bumped around by low-altitude turbulence when Lieutenant Emory noticed movement below. Captain Wesson sighed and reached down to adjust his radio frequency. "NASA 47 to Coast Guard Station New Orleans, over"

"Coast Guard Station New Orleans to NASA 47, go ahead."

Captain Wesson replied with their location and a brief description of the deteriorating weather.

"NASA-47, do you request alternate altitude, over?"

"No, we are looking for assistance with … um … um …"

"What's the problem, NASA 47?"

"We're are just passing over an offshore platform at complex 20685 with winds approaching seventy-five knots, and some joker is dancing around on one of the oil rigs."

Captain Wesson's message was relayed to the Coast Guard Search and Rescue duty officer, Wayne Lernski.

Coincidentally, Dr. Roker had sent the SAR desk an update on the storm earlier that day. His projected path for hurricane Pablo took the storm just to the south of the Gulfport Mississippi and just to the east of New Orleans.

Based on Dr. Roker's earlier communication regarding the storm, the SAR Duty officer in charge, Wayne Lernski, had issued a mandatory evacuation of all offshore oil and gas platforms. As an added safety measure, he'd proactively dispatched two coast guard patrol boats to ensure compliance with the offshore evacuation order.

Lernski cursed the message from the NASA flight. It meant that his evacuation mission had not been completely successful. He was sure that word of this would get back to his commanding officer. Sending a SAR team out now would draw attention to his team's apparent oversight during their earlier evacuation. After studying a U.S. Energy Department resource map, he was fairly confident that this particular platform had been mothballed over two years ago. He wondered whether the NASA flight crew was mistaken.

Mistaken or not, Lernski was certain that the ramifications associated with ignoring the NASA message were far greater than the mild embarrassment he would face if he had to pluck someone off the rig.

———

Brian Walker relaxed and slouched in a chair. He was resting his legs on the large, oak desk belonging to the commander of the United States Coast Guard Eighth District. His boss, Commander John Pierce, was late for their meeting. Walker yawned and leaned back for a few moments of rest. He was already regretting barhopping in the French Quarter until dawn.

Walker was one of the Coast Guard's more unusual intelligence directors. No socks, no tie, and often no shoes, he liked to drink, often in the company of his peers. He was rarely seen in uniform, leaning more toward the faux academic look of faded jeans, long-sleeve button downs, and Polartec outerwear. He had recently turned forty-one, but, fit for his age and activity level and with dark brown hair and fair skin, he could easily pass for thirtysomething.

Walker was a very competent operator in intelligence operations. He was particularly capable when it came to the implementation and use of advanced technologies. He was not introverted like many of his technology alumni at the University of Virginia. He rather enjoyed mixing with a crowd and was especially adept at extracting information during the course of casual conversation. A planned short tenure with the coast guard, a quid pro quo for tuition reimbursement, had turned into a two decade engagement. The coast guard seemed an odd choice for a man who was more at home behind the wheel of his 1979 Toyota Land Cruiser than any seafaring vessel.

Walker's appearance at the Eighth District office was not that unusual, but the catalyst for this meeting was. Walker had been unceremoniously summoned to the New Orleans location via an encrypted e-mail message from the base second in command, Lieutenant Commander Leonard McLeod. This was the first time that he could remember being summoned by McLeod and not by Commander Pierce.

Both Brian Walker and Commander Pierce were in their last days as officers in the U.S. Coast Guard. The freshly minted Secretary of Homeland Security and close friend of Commander Pierce had tapped the commander to head up the newly formed National Intelligence Agency. Lt. Commander McLeod would be assuming the base command later in the month.

The commander's office was a square room with air, sea, and personal memorabilia covering most of the free wall space. On one side of the office was a full bar complete with taps representing his favorite microbrews. Walker thought about testing one of the levers but held off due to the unpredictable nature of the participating McLeod.

Commander John Pierce exited his barrack-style home for the short walk to his office and the scheduled morning meeting with his friend Brian Walker. Commander Pierce was a tall, lean man, standing over six feet four. He was in excellent physical shape and had the frame that you would expect from a man who ran six miles a day. With a deep tan and rough hands, he looked like he preferred the outdoors over a halogen desk lamp. His gentle, built-in smile, light hair, and hazel eyes were part of a package that had attracted many females over the years.

Base Lieutenant Commander McLeod silently joined Pierce as the commander passed by one of the many administrative buildings at the Eighth District complex. Pierce and McLeod, walking in lock step, entered the main administration building and quickly traversed the short entrance hallway that led to the commander's anteroom and adjoining main office. McLeod held the door open for his superior, announced his presence, and stood stiffly by the door. Brian Walker merely removed his feet from his boss's desk.

The commander glared then smirked as he looked across the table at Walker. "What new information do you have on our eavesdropper?" he asked, reclining in his chair.

Pierce was happy to be able to relax in the company of his protégé. This meeting, while serious in nature, took on a less formal tone, thanks to Walker's casual demeanor.

"Someone was shadowing our alternate frequency during the

Chinese visit yesterday," Walker said, quickly examining notes on his iPhone and ignoring the lieutenant commander's peering eyes just off his left shoulder. "We picked up the remote signal just before the end of their tour. At first pass, the signal does not seem to come from a member of the touring dignitaries but rather from their stationary protection detail, probably in or near their transportation." Walker glanced up at Lieutenant McLeod, who seemed to glare back at him. "We implemented video and direct surveillance," Walker continued, but other than a clumsy driver who tripped when opening the door for the Chinese prime minister there is nothing special to report."

"What do we know about this shadow signal?" McLeod broke in.

"The signal was of burst nature rather than a continuing shadow monitor, and it seems that it was shutdown soon after our first detection, a coincidence, we hope," answered Walker.

"Maybe you can take the information you've collected and get together with our new field intelligence colleagues at the NIA. You can brief them on your findings and maybe find some similarities with transmissions that they intercepted during a recent visit by the North Korean ambassador."

An electronic tone emanating from Lieutenant Commander McLeod's wireless phone interrupted Walker's response.

McLeod turned to Commander Pierce and requested permission to acknowledge the summons from the small device mounted on his hip. The commander nodded. McLeod picked up the desk phone and, after a brief exchange, returned the receiver to its cradle. He grinned. "You guys want to take a chopper ride out to an oil platform?"

Commander Pierce bolted upright in his chair. "What?" He blinked rapidly.

Lieutenant McLeod filled him in.

"Do we have someone on the base that has experience handling an HH-60 rescue helicopter in a tropical storm?" asked Pierce, looking at both his subordinates.

"I'm certain that we can dig someone up. Do you have someone in mind?" the lieutenant commander asked.

"How about if I take the land lubber here and show him how it's done?" suggested Pierce, gesturing in the direction of Brian Walker.

"If I were in charge, I wouldn't take the personal risk. An Air Force has-been, out in this weather with twenty thousand pounds of taxpayer technology could land all of us on an ice breaker. However, since you're still in charge for another day and most of the heavy lifting will be done by one of our patrol vessels, I'll go along with it," responded Walker, directing his attention to the lieutenant commander for support.

Commander Pierce looked over the top of his glasses, stared straight at Walker, and smiled. Commander Pierce knew that Walker hated to fly in helicopters, particularly those not piloted by him. Walker was generally against any form of travel that he was not personally in control of. For his part, Walker realized that Commander Pierce's role as head of the Eighth District afforded him very little time to stretch his wings, and the pending transition to the National Intelligence agency would make this sort of side adventure a near impossibility. Walker quickly moved around to the chair side of the commander's desk and pulled up a recent weather chart on the commander's workstation. He wanted to be certain that the real weather was still a safe distance away.

"I don't think the heavy stuff's gonna come down for quite a while," Walker stated with a look of apprehensive agreement, while attempting his best Bill Murray imitation.

While Commander Pierce left to set up a pre-mission meeting

with members of the water-based patrol vessel *Cobia*, Walker made a quick call to the Washington headquarters of his new agency to coordinate an intelligence briefing on the mysterious communication intercepts. He arranged a meeting for two days out. Walker would be dealing with Kate Jensen, formerly of Naval Intelligence and now a fellow member of the National Intelligence Agency. He was anxious to see her again. They hadn't seen each other in months, but he still remembered her soft lips, the curve of her cheek, and her exceptional body. Their planned meeting was serious with national security implications, but he couldn't help but remember their past encounters.

Brian Walker and Kate Jensen had first met over fifteen years ago during a joint agency, new technology training session while she was still serving in the navy. Since then, their lives had been on different paths, but both had found time for an on-again, off-again romance that was dictated more by their career schedules than anything else.

Walker was ready to head home for a few days of rest and relaxation before beginning his new assignment at the NIA. He hoped that he would be able to convince Kate to drag herself out of the DC rat race and meet him at his home on Hilton Head Island, South Carolina. Maybe they could combine work and a little pleasure.

Commander Pierce was all smiles as he returned from his mission briefing. The earlier all-business demeanor was replaced by a loose and playful persona now that he was solely in the company of Brian Walker. He was excited to be able to fly again. He didn't know when he would get another chance. He looked over to Walker. "I owe you one."

"You most certainly do!" Walker shot back. "You can start by renting us a car for our ride home tomorrow."

Pierce nodded in agreement. The duo was scheduled for a two-day leave before reporting for their new assignments at the NIA.

Pierce had accepted Walker's invite to spend the time at his seaside home.

What the commander didn't know was that earlier that day Walker had unsuccessfully tried to commandeer the unit's HU-25 Falcon Jet for his flight home to Hilton Head. His request had found its way onto the desk of Larry Escobar. Escobar was the Eighth district's top asset officer. He was a good friend and resource for Walker, but this request had been met with a sarcastic laugh. The asset officer was quick to remind Walker that, for the time being, he was not on his favorite person list. Last time he'd lent Walker a transport jet it had had to be retrieved from the Gulf with a lift vessel.

Walker and Pierce walked the short distance from the hangar to the waiting helicopter and, after a brief but thorough preflight check, the pair strapped in and prepared for takeoff.

The pulsing sound generated by the blades of the Jayhawk helicopter quickened. John Pierce piloted the craft to a controlled hover before banking south and heading out over Grand Isle, Louisiana toward the Gulf of Mexico.

The flight out to the platform was uneventful. Walker was quiet and a little pale but otherwise physically intact. For Pierce, the flight had been like a walk in the park.

Pierce had been in the air force for over fifteen years prior to his transfer to the coast guard. In his career as an air force pilot, he had flown just about every prop or jet engine aircraft and helicopter in the force. His experiences as a test pilot were storied, only exceeded by the legendary retired Brigadier General Charles E. Yeager.

They arrived at the platform site just in time to meet the fast-moving *Cobia* out of Mobile, Alabama. Due to the high-rise nature of the oil platform and the visible increase in wave height, the *Cobia*'s captain, Jack Foley, preferred to get a top-down view of the situation from the boys in the Jayhawk before trying to come alongside. He radioed to the helicopter. "Any sign of life up there?" he asked.

"Yeah, we're still alive up here," shouted Walker through his headset.

"Hold on while I get a closer look," interrupted Pierce, flashing Walker a cold stare.

Pierce and Walker both saw them at the same time: two bodies lying face up on the platform while a third tried a feeble wave as he attempted to stand in the gale force winds. John Pierce was reporting his findings in real time to the *Cobia* below.

"The other two still haven't moved, and I'd swear this guy is trying to wave us off."

"Maybe he's the killer, and he doesn't want to be found out," shot Walker sarcastically.

"I know this was supposed to be a sea rescue with air support, but there is a nice big X in the middle of the platform and, given the swells down there, I would bet that the *Cobia* won't mind us touching down for a quick pickup," Pierce spoke into his headset.

"You'll get no argument from down here," replied the vessel captain.

Pierce quickly glanced toward Walker, half expecting some sarcastic comment. Walker saw the gravity of the situation and offered only a silent nod.

"Like riding a bike," shouted Pierce over the increased rotor noise generated by the landing chopper.

"Don't look now, but I think you were right; this guy doesn't want us here," alerted Walker, pointing at the deck below.

"What's this guy trying to ..." Pierce stopped in mid-sentence.

There was a brief silence as both he and Walker tried to recover from the initial shock of the unconscious victims' appearances. They stared at the two bodies in horror. Their faces looked like barnacle-encrusted rocks; their exposed skin was almost entirely covered with a combination of dried and broken sores.

The upright victim was saying something. He seemed to be repeating the same thing over and over.

"I think he's saying, 'They're dead. They're dead'," offered Walker.

"I agree, but this guy is still kicking, and by the looks of him, we should try and get him back to the base before he joins them."

Before Walker could answer, the obviously distressed victim ran across the platform and threw himself off the multistory platform into the angry sea below.

Noting the increased wind velocity and the lack of any live victims, Pierce radioed the waiting patrol vessel.

"We'll try and take it from here. Looks like you had better head back home," responded the *Cobia*'s captain.

"Good luck, *Cobia*," closed Pierce before heading back north.

———

Dr. Bali was head of the emergency trauma unit at Providence Hospital in Mobile, Alabama. Sixty-one years old, with black eyes and matching hair, he managed to keep up with most of his younger recruits but was tiring of the long shifts that accompanied his years as an emergency room physician. His five-foot-seven-inch frame and plump body gave him a Buddha-like appearance.

James Bali was just beginning a twelve-hour shift when the call came in. The local coast guard base had radioed ahead that a cutter had rescued victims from an unknown tragedy. They reported that one survivor was recovered from an oil platform in the Gulf. In fact, the radio message included a brief description of the survivor's vitals, along with the survivor's saga, beginning with his odd behavior and ending with his less-than-acrobatic dive into the Gulf. It was a miracle he'd survived at all. What the message had failed to relay was the abnormal skin condition of the two dead bodies that were also recovered.

Fifteen minutes later, an HH-65A Coast Guard Recovery helicopter hovered over the hospital rooftop staging area. Tropical storm winds had made their way inland and were hampering the aircrafts landing efforts. After a brief adjustment, the helicopter's pilots agreed to put down hard.

Dr. Bali and a hospital nurse moved quickly to the helicopter. Bali briefly consulted with one of the coast guard pilots. With the help of the pilot, the doctor climbed into the aircraft to check on the patient. His first thought was that he was staring at some kind of rubber corpse and that this was all some kind of joke, or possibly a coast guard training scenario. But he quickly discarded that idea. Dr. Bali stood silently and shook off a confused stare before touching the exposed wrist of one of the deceased. The skin was clammy and had no pulse. Bali confirmed the obvious. The victim stared back at Bali through lifeless eyes that could have easily been those of a stuffed animal. The whites of the eyes were completely gone, giving the eyeballs the appearance of two glass marbles. Horrific lesions covered the victim's face and forearms. "Oh my God," Bali muttered.

Bali had not seen this terrible condition in real-world practice, but his decades of experience and visions of a textbook disease told him that neither the corpses nor the lone survivor were going to be admitted to this hospital or any other medical facility. He motioned to the hospital nurse to head back inside.

Bali walked forward to the pilot's seat. "You can't leave these people here," he ordered.

"But sir," the pilot protested, "my orders are to …"

"I don't care what your orders are," Bali shouted, getting up in the pilot's face. "Take them to the old Navy hospital on the east side of town."

"But … but, sir," the pilot stammered.

"Do it!" yelled Bali. "Get the hell out of here!"

2

Brian Walker drank more coffee and ate more beignets than ever before. He had spent the last 10 years enjoying the city of New Orleans and this would be his last morning, and last chance to consume the sites, sounds, and tastes of the French Quarter. He sat silently and stared out the window of his favorite café. The Saturday morning crowd was light.

New Orleans was not an early riser as cities go. Most of the time, life had to be chased into the streets by the mid-morning sun. The few who braved the morning were gathered at one of the Quarter's many bakeries, their faces all but invisible. Most were hidden behind the morning paper trying to catch up on the aftermath of the storm.

The *Cobia* made the front page with a full-color photo. The coast guard cutter was shown cruising the Gulf during the storm. A file photo of the captain and first officer were just below the article. There were no pictures of the accompanying rescue helicopter or of its crew. The article included a passing reference to Hurricane Katrina and made note of the eerily similar path that Pablo took, sans the carnage.

Pierce's regular morning regimen would be canceled today. There would be no early morning run through the Quarter. He was having trouble recovering from a comatose sleep.

Pierce entered the bakery just after 8:00 a.m. and sat directly across from Walker. He nodded at Claire, his favorite waitress.

"Hello, Commander. How are you feeling this fine morning?" poked Walker, knowing full well that his travel partner was desperately in need of a large cup of coffee.

"Terrible. What was in those things?"

"Are you referring to the large blue drink that you grew fonder of as the party wore on?"

"Yes."

"I don't think you want to know."

The waitress brought Pierce his coffee. "Commander, I hear you're leaving for good."

"Yes, after twelve years and one wild bon voyage party, I'm ready to move on."

"We'll be sorry to see you go."

Thirty minutes and nearly three cups later, Pierce stood and pronounced himself fit for the journey east. He straightened his collar and checked the bakery for any familiar faces. There were none. He followed Walker out of the bakery and down the street to retrieve their transportation.

———

The estimated driving time to Hilton Head was twelve hours in the rented Toyota Corolla, which was ninety minutes longer than Walker thought it would be if he were allowed to drive.

Walker suggested that they check their messages before heading northeast into the L. Z. (Luddite Zone). Pierce smiled. Walker was referring to an area where wireless service providers had not invested in cellular towers, primarily due to local population demographics.

Walker spent about fifteen minutes interacting with the diminutive keyboard on his mobile phone before sliding the device into his back pocket. Likewise Pierce had finished replying to the last of a dozen e-mail messages on his Blackberry before putting it back in its holster.

After a short disagreement over who would drive, Walker climbed into the driver's seat and buckled in. Pierce mirrored Walker's actions, closed the passenger side door, and shoved something into the glove compartment.

"What was that?"

"My 1934 Beretta."

"Your what?" Walker asked incredulously.

"My gun, sidearm, pistol, or whatever you call it when you're in a civilian agency."

"Why is it in the glove compartment?"

"I didn't trust the shippers to move it, so I am personally transporting it to Washington. Besides, I will have to trade it in for the standard issue Glock when we arrive."

"Then make sure you keep that thing locked up. I have no use for guns."

"Whatever you say. You're the boss for the next three days," said Pierce.

Walker was reaching into his pockets for the keys when he spied John Pierce locked in a stare. Walker redirected his eyes to a similar heading.

They watched her, and it was very exciting. She moved with

elegance, clingy shorts, tight shirt, exposed legs, and olive-colored skin enhanced by summer exposure. Her long, smooth hair was the color of a sandy beach, and it danced behind her as she walked. Her eyes, Walker assumed, were certainly the brightest blue he had ever seen. The two men watched her closely as she moved quickly along the street before disappearing around the corner onto a quiet side street.

Walker, suddenly dry-mouthed, unbuckled and exited the car.

"I'll go buy us each a bottle of water for the trip," he said, moving in the general direction of the girl.

———

The man was still a good thirty yards away, but Gwen Saunders could tell he was headed her way. It was difficult to make out all his features; his hair was shrouded in a turbine, and much of his face was covered with short, pubic-like hair. He seemed to be of Middle Eastern or possibly North African descent. She thought it odd that, in these times, he wouldn't have toned down his native features or dress. She quickly dismissed the idea of turning and moving in the opposite direction as being overly paranoid. She continued on course to pass the man on her left. Just as they were about to pass, he grabbed her.

"Let go!" were the only words she was able to muster before he plastered her mouth with a strip of heavy tape. The large man deftly tied the girl's hands behind her back before tossing her over his shoulder so that her only view was his waist size.

He quickly moved down a nearby French quarter alleyway and toward a windowless van parked behind a trash dumpster. Unceremoniously, he dropped her body onto a large sheet of plastic that lined the back of the van. She noticed no emotion on his face. He made no attempt to touch her. She tried again to scream but was only able to conjure a muffled sound. Gwen Saunders made an attempt to look for some other sign of life. There was no one visible.

The bearded man reached over her head for something hanging on the van wall. Through the terror of the situation, Gwen suddenly realized that the man intended to kill her. The item he had retrieved was a gun, and it was lowered in her direction.

She was paralyzed with panic, unable to muster any mouth noise; she could not even summon her legs to kick at the gun.

Gwen closed her eyes in an attempt to lodge her brain out of this seeming nightmare. She reopened her eyes to face the realization that the end was near. With a pop, she heard what she was sure was the sound of her abductor's gun. Confused by the lack of any sensation of pain and overwhelmed by the situation, she rolled to her side and blacked out.

———

Brian Walker stood over the young woman's attacker. The attacker had blank eyes; not human-like at all, they were dark and seemingly two-dimensional. They just stared at him—or perhaps through him. They did not betray their owner; they gave no clue as to what he was thinking or to his next action. Walker had always wondered what it would feel like to come face-to-face with a fanatic. He knew the danger associated with stereotyping a person based on race or dress, but this dude just oozed evil. He had real misgivings about not completing what Pierce had started with his Beretta, but killing a man was out of his league. Even the more experienced Pierce stood back and watched as the bearded one lay silent, with wounds in the groin and shin.

———

Pierce held a cold towel to the forehead of the unconscious woman. Gwen woke to the feel of something damp on her face. She stirred and sat up suddenly, her eyes wide in fear, haunted by the recollection of her recent near death experience. She began to wonder if she had been dreaming.

"Hello," spoke a man's voice softly. "For awhile there, I thought you were going to sleep through the night.

Gwen looked at the gentle smile of John Pierce.

"Where is the man that tried to kill me?" she asked in a broken voice.

"We called him a ride," Walker chimed in.

She looked at Walker with anger. "You let him go?"

"I wouldn't have, but Quick Draw here shot him in the wrong head," said Walker nodding in the direction of Pierce.

"Who …? Where did they take him," she stammered.

Both Walker and Pierce could see that she was still disoriented and not ready to deal coherently with the events of the day.

"Let's just say that you won't see him again, except maybe in a courtroom," said Pierce.

"I guess I should apologize for acting so callously. I probably owe you my life, and all I can do is question your actions. Do you have a name, besides Quick Draw that is?"

"It's John Pierce, and this nut here is Brian Walker."

"I'm Gwen Saunders." She felt flushed as she looked into John's gleaming hazel eyes. She saw only warmth in return, and most concerns left her.

"Where did you come from, and how did you find me?" she asked curiously, having noticed only her assailant's van in the alley.

"Brian and I were going to the corner store to get some water for a car trip. We saw you come out of the store across the street. Brian, actually I, commented on one of your assets and suggested that we might get a better glimpse of the pretty young woman if we closed the gap, so we crossed the street and followed you for a few blocks," stumbled Pierce.

"Do you have any idea who Igor was or why he would try and kill you?" Pierce quickly changed the subject.

"No idea, maybe a serial killer who would rather get lucky with a corpse," she said dryly.

Pierce shook his head. "I don't think so. He didn't seem the Dr. Lecter-type. The way he tossed your body around and had already protected the inside of his van, I would guess that he was going to toss your body right back into the alley dumpster. Someone wanted you dead and made the mistake of hiring Igor to do his or her bidding."

"I can't believe any of this has happened. I'm a communications programmer for a semiconductor manufacturer. Who would want to kill me?"

"Having now had the opportunity to view you from both the front and the rear, I can't fathom anyone wanting to kill you. Do you live or work in the area?" spoke Pierce

Gwen Saunders ignored Pierce's off subject comments and continued with the facts. "No. I arrived yesterday with my boss. We both flew in from San Jose. My boss offered to accompany me to a developer's conference at the convention center." She flicked away a few blonde strands of hair from her face and massaged the corners of her blue eyes. "I have to give a presentation tomorrow, and she offered to tag along for moral support."

After conferring with Walker and promising to catch up with him in a day or two, Pierce turned and offered to ride with Gwen back to the police station.

"Okay, thanks," she said, eyeing him suspiciously."

He thought he might be able to convince Gwen to join him

for dinner and maybe, in exchange, the semiconductor engineer might help him brush up on short burst communications.

It took two phone calls and a personal visit from the local sheriff to vouch for him before Gwen Saunders was comfortable that John Pierce and his companion were legit. After a little more prodding from Pierce, she agreed to the dinner engagement.

3

John Pierce was standing at the bar of Emeril's Delmonico Restaurant. He wore a bright green linen shirt with tan pleated Dockers. Pierce leaned casually against the bar while he waited for Gwen Saunders to make an appearance.

The last twenty-four hours had been draining ones for Gwen, both emotionally and physically. Pierce hoped that a venue diversion for food and relaxation might help her better cope with the recent events. Given the circumstances, he had no trouble convincing Walker to drive to Hilton Head without him.

Pierce was worried about Gwen. She would receive more bad news this evening. It was Pierce's unhappy task to inform Gwen that her travel companion and boss had been found dead that morning. She'd been found in her hotel parking garage, shot in the back of the head while sitting in her rental car.

There was not any obvious motive or any real lead for either the murder or the failed attempt on Gwen's life. The only real chance for an answer had died with Gwen's assailant. He'd managed to swallow a cyanide pill on the way to the hospital. The pill had been concealed in a ring on his left hand. Even with the seriousness of the crime, Pierce couldn't seem to get images of Underdog out of his head.

Pierce caught her out of the corner of his eye. Gwen Saunders moved across the restaurant lounge with an unrehearsed grace, a motif usually limited to practiced heads of state. There was a hint of new color in Pierce's face as he followed her sleek body navigating nimbly toward him. She was wearing a short but simple black dress that clung to her as if it were designed expressly for her. Pierce was taken and intrigued by a woman who could stand the kind of mental trauma she was exposed to and still carry herself with an air of calm confidence. This confidence attracted Pierce—so much so that he thought another day or two together before joining Walker wouldn't hurt. He knew Walker would understand once he was briefed on Gwen's situation.

"You clean up very well," started Pierce.

"Thanks. You don't look too shabby yourself," she stated, mildly distracted by his hazel eyes. "You seem taken off guard," she continued.

He quickly looked around the room. "I guess it just hit me that I'm dining with such a young and attractive woman."

It was Gwen's turn to look flushed. She looked around the crowded restaurant. "This restaurant is packed. We'll be lucky to get a table."

"I have an in with the owner," said Pierce, raising his eyebrows.

Gwen looked up at the oversized image of Emeril Lagasse with a curious smile.

They we're interrupted by the maître d'. He showed them to

a table in the back corner of the restaurant. Their waiter appeared almost as soon as they had been seated. He gave them each a menu and was just about to hand John the wine list when he noticed Gwen's outstretched hand.

Gwen flashed the waiter a quick smile and said, "I think you can leave the wine decision to me, being a California girl and all. I'll leave the bland seafood decisions to my date for the evening."

Pierce smirked, knowing that there was nothing on Emeril's menu that could be classified as bland. "Fine with me," stated Pierce as he crossed his arms and sat back in his chair.

Saunders spent a few minutes offering additional information on her employment background before interrogating Pierce. He spent a few minutes offering his own story, ending with the previous evening's going away party.

The brief personal exchange was interrupted by the coordinated return of their waiter and the sommelier.

She had barely studied the wine list before ordering. "We will have the 2004 Levy & McClellan Cabernet."

Pierce spoke up, grinning. "The young lady and I will be having parallel courses this evening. We will start with the seared yellowfin tuna appetizer, and for an entrée, we will have the hickory roasted duck.

"Couldn't find 'chicken of the sea' on the menu?" poked Gwen.

"Were you expecting a less sophisticated selection for dinner," he fired back thinking that they were genuinely hitting it off. He decided to hold the bad news for as long as he could.

A few minutes later, the wine arrived. They raised their glasses in unison and toasted Gwen's longevity.

Gwen's face took on a more serious facade as she sipped her wine. After a brief pause and a swallow, she looked straight at Pierce.

"Why did that man try to kill me?" she asked.

"Anybody's guess, but I think there is a little more information I should share with you."

Pierce briefly related the stories of her colleague's murder and her assailants' suicide. He watched the color leave Gwen's face as he relayed the details of the two deaths. Pierce finished and paused. He leaned forward, expecting to console her. Instead, he was somewhat taken aback when her first question was about her former aggressor, rather than her boss.

"I understand that he failed in his job, but why would he kill himself?" asked Gwen.

"He probably felt more comfortable controlling his own destiny. You can bet that, if he hadn't done the deed, someone would have been along shortly to take care of it for him. You'll have to face the situation. These guys are brewing some real evil. They went to a lot of trouble to take you and your boss out of the picture, and I'm sure that they will not be happy to learn that you are still alive and well."

Lowering her head, Gwen looked away and bit her lip. The sparkle in her eyes had disappeared. She looked like she had just been told that she only had a week to live.

"Why would they try and kill me?"

"The only obvious link is your boss and/or your work. Maybe we should start there? What kind of projects were you and your boss working on?"

"You could hardly classify what I do for a living as project work. Most of my time is spent handling maintenance code for embedded chipsets."

Pierce's eyes glazed over.

"Maybe a little background might help put this in context," Gwen offered.

"My job is to update short pieces of code used to control a

cellular or radio device. I was originally hired to update all the code in a chipset to handle the year 2000 fiasco, a wasted work effort in hindsight. Since then, I've been doing mostly maintenance work to ensure that products using our chipset are able to handle new data functionality like global positioning, presence awareness, and streaming media."

"Sounds simple enough to me," smiled Pierce sarcastically.

The yellowfin tuna arrived just in time. Pierce knew this conversation was going over his head, and he welcomed the opportunity to change its direction.

"I think you'll find seasoning unnecessary," quipped Pierce in an obvious jab to his companion's earlier "bland" comment.

He continued. "Can you think of any part of your work that might have an impact on your company's international business or that maybe was a source of controversy?"

"I can't stress enough the low-level at which I sit in our company hierarchy. My job function and ..." Gwen paused. "We did have a little debate recently with the CEO from one of our partner companies. It seemed that he was a bit miffed that we were removing a portion of our developer API set with the next release of our chipset."

"Another quick techno speak lesson would help," smiled Pierce.

"The gist of it is that our chipset's embedded programming includes a set of program access points or commands. These access points allow a third-party programmer, usually an employee or contractor for the end-user equipment company like Nokia, Research In Motion, or Motorola, to request data or build in additional functionality for a particular product implementation."

"How's your tuna?" Pierce broke in, stalling so he could try and absorb what Gwen was saying.

"It's pretty good," she said. "Needs more thyme and a touch

of lime, though."

Pierce sighed.

"Anyway, back to the chipsets," Gwen continued. "The access point in question was merely a diagnostic access point that allows the final product, usually a wireless phone or two-way radio, to send a message to the owner acknowledging that it was in need of repair. But this product had been in the market for a number of years and almost never fails. Combine that with the fact that we have limited space on the chipset for our program, and we determined that the diagnostic access point was a logical candidate for removal," Gwen finished.

"Did your boss play a role in the decision to remove this access point?"

"As a matter of fact, she did. She is usually rather passive, but she did back me up in a product planning briefing that turned a little ugly."

"How so?"

"About a month before we were due to send the new code to development we held a product update meeting to coordinate the final product release. The release of code was considered minor, and the meeting's attendance was sparse. In fact, the only other attendees were two guys from our internal development group and the CEO I mentioned earlier. I remember my boss commenting on how she thought it odd that such a high-level official was attending this type of meeting." Gwen fidgeted nervously with the linen napkin in her lap.

Pierce interrupted, "You were getting to the ugly part"

"Sorry, the CEO—I can't remember his name—he was an Asian fellow. He pressed hard for the diagnostic access point to remain in the code. I stood my ground and Shelley, my boss—did I ever tell you her name was Shelley? I can't believe that she's dead. I didn't know her very well, but she was always kind to me." Gwen apologized again for digressing.

"That's okay," Pierce replied gently, noting her distant stare away from him and toward nothing in particular.

"Anyway, she, Shelley that is, was fairly strong-willed in defending our position during the meeting. When all was said and done, she told the visiting CEO that if he could document and deliver to her, within two weeks, a valid business reason for the code to remain in, we would include it," Gwen paused.

"And …" pressed Pierce.

"And nothing. That was the last we had heard from him. His answer was due by the end of this week." Gwen suddenly went pale again. "You don't think that argument was linked to her death, do you?"

"I doubt it, but I wouldn't repeat this conversation if I were you—at least not before I let Brian Walker in on our conversation. I'm sure he'll want to do a little digging on your behalf."

The waiter returned with the dessert tray. Both Gwen and John waved him off but not before politely asking for two espressos.

John stared at Gwen. He could see a look of remorse in her eyes. "Why don't we head back to the hotel so you can get a good night's rest. Maybe we can get in touch with my new work friends tomorrow and get a start at unraveling this mystery."

Gwen felt a strong attraction to John Pierce. She briefly mulled over the idea of inviting him back for a nightcap but decided instead to try and put this horrible experience behind her and clear her head before getting further involved. She did, however, stand, walk over to John's side of the table, and offer her hand for the walk back to the hotel.

4

Brian Walker was exhausted. He stretched his legs and groaned. His head was pounding. A long, lonely drive from New Orleans to Hilton Head, combined with running in a 10k race on the sand, was just too much for him. The muscles in his legs felt as though they were caked in cement. His shoulders and lower back were almost stiff enough to prevent him from reaching the six inches forward that was necessary to pick up the Jack Daniel's that had just been delivered to his table. More importantly, he wondered if he would have the energy to stand and greet Kate Jensen when she arrived. He made a mental note to train just a little bit before running next year's Hilton Head Island "Beach 5K and Back."

Kate Jensen stepped off the boardwalk and kicked off her sandals before walking across the hundred feet of beach that separated her from Brian Walker. She was an attractive thirty-five-year-old wearing tight fitting pants and a less-than modest-cotton sweater that would make even the most confident blush. Kate maneuvered deftly across the beach to Brian's table. She flashed a quick smile to the bank of young men straining for a better view and bent down to kiss Brian on the cheek.

Kate knew more about Brian than most any other person on the planet. Her many years in intelligence at the Department of the Navy and now with the National Intelligence Agency gave her access to unique intelligence on all members of the U.S. intelligence agencies. Not to mention that she had personal carnal knowledge of Brian through their occasional nonbusiness interactions.

"I thought we would be meeting with the boss," she said with a smile, referring to the obvious absence of newly minted NIA Director John Pierce.

"They say the average man falls in love six times in his lifetime. I think our boss is skewing the average."

"If I didn't know better, I would have thought you had some ulterior motive by not having Pierce join us."

"Well," paused Walker, "there might be something to the motive thing, but not by design."

The pair finished catching up over the post-race seafood feast before heading down the beach to find a quiet spot for some shoptalk.

Brian Walker and Kate Jensen had both been summoned to work on the same project. Now that they were both under the same governmental agency it would be easier for them to discuss work without having to walk the line between personal and work tracks. Their common employer, the NIA, was the branch of government responsible for domestic spy and terrorism investigations. The recent capture of unauthorized RF transmissions in and around government facilities was now a Priority 2 NIA project.

Brian and Kate traded initial findings regarding the source locations of the recent defense channel, communication interference.

Both had taken electronic notes:

1)   Atlanta, GA: Secret Service Detail, Vice Presidents Visit to the CDC

2)   Frederick, MD: Near Fort Detrick, no details

3)   San Jose, CA: Secret Service Detail, First Lady – Source Unknown

4)   Sunnyvale, CA: Moffet Field – Source Unknown

Other than the radio signature of the short burst shadow transmissions, they had very little to go on. Walker surmised that the transmission was some sort of test message. A message sourced in the 1710MHz–1850MHz frequency range, a restricted frequency range used only by defense agencies. Walker managed a little research time before leaving the district office in New Orleans. He was able to determine that the signal was a direct request for cache data from the targeted device. However, without the target device schematics, it was difficult to determine what, if any, information was stored in the device's cache memory. Having little more to go on, Kate and Brian decided to head back to Walker's house before making next step plans.

It was a few minutes past six in the evening when Brian and Kate turned off the beach and stepped onto a beach walk. The path traversed a barrier of sand and sea grass before being consumed by the island's unique, dense subtropical vegetation. It was just over a hundred yards to Brian's bungalow-style house. The house was modest compared to the posh community of vacation estates that all but blocked his porch view of the Atlantic. The neighborhood was a perfect escape for Brian, a private community where many of the neighbors were in residence only a few weeks a year.

Walker felt lucky to call Hilton Head his home, especially given his limited government salary. He'd taken possession of the land when he was in his late teens. His only uncle had willed the acre parcel to his parents, who in turn gifted the property to their only child.

Walker liked to do things for himself. He'd moved to the island after graduating from the University of Virginia and begun construction of his permanent home. His original plan had called for a four-room cottage, but it wasn't long after the completion of his original project that the property had become a perpetual construction site. As recently as last year he had added a new four hundred-square foot media room.

He opened the front door for Kate and walked around to the back of the house to rinse in the outdoor shower. After washing the coat of fine sand off his lower legs and feet, he entered the house through a rear sliding patio door. He was pleasantly surprised by Kate's soft sing-along to an Elvis gospel CD. He went to work mixing them both a cosmopolitan as Kate continued her gospel rendition of "Amazing Grace."

She took a turn rinsing in the outdoor shower. Walker stared wistfully as she pulled off her sweater to reveal a brief orange bikini top. The suit top looked to be made of a latex material and clung to her body like paint. To his eyes, her figure was near perfect. He focused on her ample breasts, which if memory served him, were equally as firm as her flat stomach. Brian continued to reminisce as Kate removed her ocean-dampened pants. Her legs were long with a visible tan line where her suit had worked its way up her inner thigh.

Kate looked up just as the song ended and caught Walker's stare. "You're supposed to be mixing us a drink," she said with a playful smile.

"I can mix a cosmopolitan in my sleep, but never in my dreams do I get a vision like you." Walker could see her visible glow enhanced by his compliment.

Content with a half day's work, they adjourned to the media room, vowing to continue in the morning.

The morning came quickly, too quickly for Walker. His evening rendezvous with Jensen had been tamer than he'd planned. Halfway through the viewing of a rented movie, Kate had fallen asleep. He'd had all he could do to get her to go to bed.

She emerged from her restful sleep and sat at the breakfast bar, watching as Walker proudly produced a gourmet breakfast consisting of a shrimp omelet, fresh peach slices, and homemade grits.

"I heard from Pierce this morning," spoke Jensen as she watched Walker fumble with the omelet pan.

Walker admired Jensen's tight, white T-shirt and denim shorts. "Good, I was beginning to wonder whether his newfound romance had permanently distracted him."

"Actually just the opposite seems to be the case. He and the girl have made some remarkable progress regarding our electronic intruder. It seems that the girl and her employer might be indirectly linked to our investigation. Pierce sent us both an e-mail late last night. In the message, he outlines a plan hatched by Saunders. I assume Saunders is the girl that you rescued in New Orleans."

"Correct, Gwen is the other half of her name."

"Well, from the tone of his e-mail, she must be a very bright individual. He extols her efforts as almost superhuman. She seems to have put on quite a show for some of the electronic experts at the base yesterday. She managed to get a digital copy of the schematics and the microcode for a military handset produced by Motorola."

"Sounds like she may have had a little help from Pierce if she was able to get detail on a military device."

"Actually not; that's the strange part. The information she received came right out of one of her company's unrestricted databases. Pierce did a little research on his own and was able to determine that all three electronic intercepts were from a handset used exclusively by the army. With that piece of information, it was only a few minutes before the girl was able to produce the schematics for the device and, except for a small piece of encryption code, the device is remarkably similar to the two-way walkie-talkie device that Motorola manufactures for the consumer market."

"I guess that's a good start," mumbled Walker through a mouthful of omelet.

"Actually that's not the best part. The girl went to work and dissected a couple of the army handsets right in front of your electronics experts. Unknowingly, she gave a clinic to the entire Eighth District Intelligence Department on field electronics. Using an Intelligence Department notebook computer and a homemade cable, she was able to update the EPROM on a pair of Motorola handsets and immediately demonstrate how the electronic eavesdropper was able to stealthily gain access to secure army communications and …" She paused for a slice of peach.

"And, and what?"

After eating the peach slice, she licked her lips and pulled her brown hair into a ponytail with a hair tie that she conveniently kept on her left wrist. "The message ends with a P.S. It says to tell Walker to call the director before 0900. I guess he's used to your tardy e-mail habits."

"That goes along with my tardy phone habits," Walker glanced at his Timex Ironman, still counting away in chrono mode from yesterday's race.

"It's 9:15," smiled Kate.

On cue, Walker's phone rang. It was Director Pierce.

"What's up?" asked Kate after Walker finished his brief conversation with Pierce.

"I'm not sure, but something is wrong. That was not the composed John Pierce that I know. He said that he needs to meet with us right away."

"Did he say why?"

"Yes, he said that he thinks it has been contained but they're not sure of the source," stated Walker in a dazed and dull voice.

"What are you talking about?"

Walker paused briefly.

"You and I are officially on loan to the CDC."

She stopped, peach slice midway to her mouth. "The CDC, as in the Centers for Disease Control and Prevention in Atlanta?"

———

The message went out at 6:30 in the morning. A special wireless messenger carried by a CDC biohazard specialist received the message. The message read "HSZ," an acronym used to inform the team to report to the Hartsfield Security Zone. Atlanta's Hartsfield airport was often the receiving zone for CDC test samples. The CDC maintained a safe area in a remote building complex at Hartsfield for staging contaminated deliveries. Over the years, they had received hundreds of sealed packages containing a variety of blood and organ samples from around the world. The one thing that the HSZ did not accept directly was the corpse of an infected subject. The facility did not function as a morgue. If the CDC director felt that a particular situation warranted a field operation, a team could be sent to perform a local autopsy.

Robert Tumi had been a member of the CDC mobile biohazard team for three years. During his tenure, he had never been called to the HSZ. The HSZ was used primarily as a local drop point for secured packages. These secured packages were almost always overseas field samples that would have been properly prepared and packaged in the local environment prior to being shipped to the CDC. This time it was different. His entire message was encoded, an oddity given the nature of his team's work. The decoded message implied that two human corpses were being delivered from a navy hospital in Alabama. The message went on to emphasize that the integrity of the packages was suspect.

It was almost eight o'clock when Robert Tumi's team arrived at the HSZ.

Tumi approached the security desk. "I'm Robert Tumi," he said, showing his ID. The attending army corporal stood and came around the desk. Tumi noticed the corporal was sweating profusely.

"Corporal Jones, sir," he said. "This way."

Tumi followed his escort through the deserted facility to a dark loading area. The corporal stopped and nervously pointed to a shadowy figure standing beside trash bags on the loading platform.

"Can we get some lights turned on around here?" asked Tumi.

The corporal moved quickly; a bank of fluorescent lights slowly came to life. Tumi's eyes took a few seconds to respond to the new environment.

"Holy shit … Shit, shit, shit," repeated Tumi. "This isn't good."

The sheepish corporal stepped further back. There were two oversize plastic bags lying on the ground; a disfigured white male stood three steps to the left. Tumi took a deep breath. He could see the outline of a body through one of the bags. It was not orderly at all. A prepared corpse usually lay flat with the arms either by its side or folded across the chest. This body had obviously been packed quickly. Its outstretched arms were positioned at unnatural angles to the body, and the head was face down. These packages were anything but secure. Tumi moved closer and inspected the bags.

"They're triple bagged," spoke the anonymous man standing next to the bags.

Tumi nearly jumped out of his skin. "Who are you?" he demanded.

"I'm with them," he said looking down at the bodies.

"What kind of joke is this?"

"No joke. Somebody needs to take my friends to the CDC facility in Cedar Grove."

"How do you know about the Cedar Grove facility?"

"I've worked there before. We've all been there before," he said pointing to the bodies. "Can you please take us to the lab and inform Dr. Bekins that we are coming in."

Tumi only managed a resigned nod.

5

Many years had passed since Ellen Yi's days at the academy, and much had changed. The world was a different place from when she was a student. Ellen Yi had changed also; she was more mature, more patient, though no less determined. Her physical appearance was the same. Her tall lean figure and pale complexion combined with short-cropped hair and tortoise-shell glasses helped complete her professorial image. Many living or working in the college town of Amherst, Massachusetts, would have easily placed her as a nerdy professor, researcher, or even student at the nearby University of Massachusetts.

Her bland appearance was moderately offset by her weekend drives. She often escaped her dry research persona with an overly aggressive back road trip in her 1968 MG convertible. The car itself was not atypical for a college town; what was unusual though, was the car's lack of personal markings. There were no stickers to indicate any particular political affiliation or social agenda, no university parking emblem; she didn't need one. She always walked the two miles to her part-time research job at the university lab.

She lived alone as the landlord of a converted two-family structure on Kellogg Ave just a block from the center of Amherst, Massachusetts. The building, a modest two-story dwelling, was neatly kept, similar to many other houses on the tree-lined street. Some years ago, before Ellen had purchased the property, it had been converted from a two-family to a single-family home with a first-floor office. The office portion of the house was completely separate from the private residence. It encompassed the entire first floor of the structure and was accessible by two entrances. The main and most trafficked entrance was the front door. A second side entrance emptied into the driveway and offered access to the single off-street parking space allotted to the tenant. All other office parking was street side.

For the last seven years, the office had been home to Toothless Wonder Dentistry—a strange name for a dental practice, but in this case appropriate. The tenant, Chester Gray, was a local boy and graduate of Amherst College. He had followed a short-lived dream by playing for the Albany River Rats of the American Hockey League. However, a few games into his rookie season, a postgame bar fight cost him many of his front teeth. Taking a cue from his newly engineered smile, he went from the injured reserve list back into the student ranks and continued his education, earning a degree in dentistry. His business's unique name was often a conversation starter for new patients. When asked, Gray happily removes his top front teeth before recounting his version of the story—a version that leaves out the bar fight and relies on hockey's reputation to fill in the blanks.

Gray worked fixed hours, usually 7:00 a.m. to 5:00 p.m., five days a week. He never returned to the office in the evenings or on Sundays. He was an ideal tenant for Ellen. She could rely on consistent private time when working in the evenings and on weekends.

Ellen lived in the building's private residence. The lone entrance, save a metal fire escape, was via a side door to the building. The entrance opened to a short hallway and two staircases; one led up to her residence, and the other led down to her low-profile research suite.

Ellen returned home from a weekend afternoon walk, indulging herself with a little fresh air before retreating to her windowless basement lab. She was more upbeat than usual. Her weekend work would be a little less stressful than usual. This weekend would be spent in front of her personal computer studying test results rather than working in a bulky protective spacesuit inside the room she referred to as "the chamber."

Her home lab was a suite of three rooms, an anteroom, a decontamination shower, and a working lab. The anteroom was used mostly for storage and study. In the anteroom she housed the row of cages that contained her test animals. They were mostly crab monkeys now. Originally she had been working exclusively with mice, and even though not susceptible to the human strain of her test virus, the mice did offer her a good testing model to build and rehearse a methodology for working with the human virus. The anteroom also housed most of her technology and research equipment.

The decontamination room was a simple Lysol shower that protected against bacteria or other contaminants, which might hitch a ride on her space suit when she entered or exited the lab.

Ellen's job was thankless. She had on-again, off-again communications with Doug Moon and her brother, Ren. She knew where Doug stood but worried about her brothers' allegiance. Doug often communicated his positive attitude regarding her work, though never in person. He believed that her work was the single most important piece of their plan. He kept himself, Ren, and their intelligence efforts separate from her work in an attempt to protect the Amherst lab from any undue attention.

Ellen worked long hours between her efforts as a researcher, focusing on genetically modified vegetation at the university lab and her stressful afternoon, evening, and weekend efforts in her private Kellogg Avenue lab. Ellen had been working with the awakened virus for over three years now and had become emotionally and visually immune to the images of disfigured and dying animals. She was working with the live variola, a virus commonly known as smallpox. Smallpox is an exclusively human virus that she had been able to adapt for testing in a variety of lower-level species.

Over the years Ellen's research into the history of smallpox offered her a wealth of information into the heroism of those fighting to eradicate the disease. But she was most intrigued by the stories relating to the use of the virus as a weapon. Coincidently, the namesake of her adopted hometown, Lord Jeffery Amherst, had used the smallpox virus in a battle with Native Americans in 1763. While commanding British troops during the siege of Fort Pitt, he'd ordered his troops to send smallpox-infected blankets and handkerchiefs to the Indians surrounding the fort in an attempt to wipe them out.

Her research also offered insight into one of the more visually destructive plagues of both historic and modern times. The disease had been chronicled throughout much of the twenty-first century and only declared fully eradicated in the late 1970s. Smallpox, a terribly disfiguring ailment, is fatal in 30 to 40 percent of cases. Ellen hoped to exceed that level. Survivors often seemed worse off than those succumbing to the disease. Their bodies were scarred beyond recognition, and in some cases, the victim was left blind by the scabbing associated with the disease.

Ellen had started with a base strain of the virus acquired by Doug Moon during a late 2003 pilgrimage to somewhere in Maryland. He never spoke about the trip; she never asked.

She was fortunate to have had access to the university lab at the time Doug had returned with the virus in 2003. Though she had finished outfitting her own lab in early 2002, she was not equipped to maintain the live virus for any length of time. The university lab provided her with access to a liquid nitrogen freezer. The freezer would become the home for the original test virus and, ultimately, a resting place for the enhanced strain of the virus should she succeed in her experiments.

Her research efforts were unique. She was fairly certain that no official experiments of this kind were in progress anywhere in the world. For over two decades, the World Health Organization had formally banned any experiments using the live variola or, for that matter, any smallpox DNA. It was widely assumed that the only viable smallpox samples were housed at the Centers for Disease Control and Prevention in Atlanta and somewhere in Russia, though most intelligence experts acknowledged that viable samples of the virus probably existed elsewhere.

Ellen clearly understood that she had smashed through any moral and ethical barriers by practicing with the live, definitely lethal virus in the basement of a house on a residential street. That fact never bothered her. She was, however, frequently bothered by the task of being chief cook and bottle washer when it came to working with the live virus. It would only take a small lapse in her concentration to expose the neighbors and their extended acquaintances to the deadly virus and derail the entire project.

Ellen Yi's research efforts were, on one hand, difficult, but many of her processes were fairly straightforward and repetitive. Her task to create a virulent virus meant creating a genetically modified version of smallpox that would be resistant to currently available vaccines. Her experiments were designed to expose the virus to a variety of antibiotics, enhancing it to the point where it would be difficult to fight with any known resources. This process, as documented in her partner Doug Moon's deceased father's research diary, would, in theory, create a virus that would easily spread from person to person and be uncontrolled by currently available vaccines or antibiotics.

Her biggest challenge, the same problem facing anyone working with a deadly virus, would be testing the virus itself. No one could know for certain the effectiveness of either a virus or a vaccine without some level of human testing. She or Doug would have to infect a series of humans to test the modified virus. Disposing of the test participants without infecting the general population would be, at best, difficult. They had already failed at this once in the Gulf of Mexico.

———

Ren Yi turned his new Porsche Boxster-S off the Seattle city street and into Regatta Park. A sculpture of a Giant Asian Pond Turtle sat in the middle of the cul-de-sac framing the elaborate office complex. The statue's arched carapace matched the building's atrium lobby entrance.

The three-building complex was completed almost seven years earlier by a high-priced construction firm imported from the San Francisco Bay area. The complex stood alone on Regatta Peninsula in northwest Seattle. In its offices and meeting rooms, Ren Yi's company designed, developed, and implemented secure transmission protocols for consumer and military communication applications.

Yi, now in his forties, a few pounds overweight, and sporting gray highlights near his temples, pampered his employees with luxurious surroundings and lavish holiday galas. Every season he added another extravagance to the upscale parties. He pampered the building as well. Each year, he upgraded the level of sophistication of his personal monument. This past year, he added Italian marble to the atrium floor, a luxury spa to the health center, and a private dining room to his personal office suite. The entire west façade was reworked to promote a less obscure view of Puget Sound and the Cascade Mountains. In less than six years, Yi had built a prosperous and well-known technology concern.

Ren Yi parked his car in a lone space just a few yards from the building's main entrance. Building One, the largest of the three structures, had been designed by Yi. It was shaped like a great Chinese palace, similar to the one in which he had grown up on Putuo Island, China. The two-story building contained a state-of-the-art conference center and twenty-five private offices. Large underground passageways connected the main complex to the remote structures, one with a state-of-the-art data center and a private underground apartment, the other a high-end electronics and engineering lab.

Yi boarded the clear elevator that ran exclusively to his private second-floor office retreat. He exited the elevator and walked toward the three spacious sitting areas surrounding his assistant's desk. Each was decorated in a unique motif representing a distinct era in Chinese history. He passed through the sitting areas, walked around the deserted clerical area and entered his office suite.

Moving across the cavernous office to an inviting high-back leather chair, Yi sat, stretched his legs, and sighed. He longed to be skippering his yacht on Puget Sound, but instead had to keep up the façade of cult terrorist. Yi picked up the lone item on his pristine black lacquer desk, an exotic looking remote control. He pushed a series of buttons, and the top of the desk slid away from him, exposing a 3-D map of the United States. Yi stood and stared at holographic images of little aerosol cans scattered around the map. The three-dimensional images were stationed near major population centers; one hovered near an east coast military establishment, another near Orlando.

Yi closed the desk then closed his eyes. He rubbed his temples and realized he hadn't slept well in days. The stress was getting to him. He could still recite verbatim his sister's scenario:

> *About ten days after the attack, the first of many visits to local medical facilities will begin. Patients will arrive complaining of a high fever and body aches. Victims will be routinely diagnosed with a viral infection and sent home with little support. The elderly or those with other chronic ailments might be held for testing and observation. At this stage of the infection, any lab results would be unremarkable and the patient would be discharged.*
>
> *Within a few days, many of the infected will return to their local emergency room or health clinic. The infected will demonstrate moderate blistering on the face and appendages; the usual diagnosis will be adult or child chickenpox, and the patient will be sent home. In a worst-case scenario, an alert physician will call in an infectious disease specialist to examine the patient. The true diagnosis will most likely be missed; most, if not all, of today's practicing health care workers are too young to have seen a case of smallpox. If an attendant does swab the skin rash, we might see the beginning of the fireworks. The lab would identify the specimen as being consistent with smallpox and the patient would be transferred to an isolation unit.*
>
> *From this point forward, the notification process should be viewed as unpredictable. There is little that can be done by authorities short of immediate mass vaccinations. That scenario is less than*

likely to play out. Local health officials will be brought in; ultimately the CDC will be informed and will probably cast a doubtful eye on the findings. It will be at least another twenty-four hours before samples are received and verified by the CDC as smallpox.

A carefully, previously drafted response will be delivered to the media by the parent agency of the CDC, the Department of Health and Human Services. Care will be taken not to mention the symptoms; the populous would fall into immediate disrepair if every body ache, skin blemish, or elevated temperature were viewed as the onset of the virus. This is where it gets interesting.

It will be general consensus that anyone having been vaccinated prior to or within days of coming in contact with the virus should be immune. Remember, this is not our fathers' smallpox; this was the Moon family variola.

It will take many days of testing in the CDC labs before it is realized that this strain of the virus is resistant to current vaccines. A new vaccine would need to be developed and produced. This process could take months. In the meantime, the infection rate and death tolls will rise.

If we assume a scenario whereby we are able to infect 5 to 10 percent of the target audience or approximately three to four thousand people, we should be able to project the follow-on cases. Approximately two weeks from the initial infection, the first casualties will occur. We are projecting our strain to have an ap-

proximately 60 percent hit rate as compared to the less than 30 percent casualty rate that will be projected by the CDC and public health officials. Using the CDC's own projections for spread, the initial infection base should grow exponentially every two to three weeks. By the end of three months, the number of cases will grow to over five hundred thousand with more than two hundred thousand deaths.

Ren Yi opened his eyes. He could still hear Doug Moon and his sister's chorus. "Our parents and our nations will be proud of us. Good fortune will follow us always."

Ren Yi slammed his fist on his desk and scowled. He wasn't proud and he wasn't happy. *In order for good fortune to smile on me, Doug Moon would need to be discovered and maybe, just maybe, Ellen could disappear into the population*, he thought to himself.

Yi sat back down in his high-back chair. With a push of his foot, he spun the chair and faced the office wall behind his desk. Exchanging a quick look with himself in a large mirror hanging above his credenza, he committed to ending the teams adolescent promises once and for all.

He picked up a small digital recording device, set the mode to voice modify, and dictated a simple message to an agent at the National Intelligence Agency.

Within an hour of the disguised transmission, a text transcript of Ren Yi's voice message appeared in former schoolmate Doug Moon's e-mail inbox.

6

CDC Virologist Mark Bekins was tired and confused. Maybe the combination of caffeine and no sleep was finally getting to him. Nothing was making sense. Unlike the other victims that had been brought to the secret Level 4 CDC lab, this one did not exhibit the same disease signatures as the two that had already been autopsied. None of the tests that he performed on victim number three matched his expectations.

At first, Bekins had worked in two-hour shifts, alternating with two other colleagues, but with mental momentum and a bit of adrenaline on his side, he'd begun to work four-hour shifts with only a two-hour nap and the occasionally caffeine break in between. He wanted very much to just lie down and sleep. Being a few pounds overweight was not helping. Though only thirty, Bekins did not have the same stamina and energy level as his younger colleagues.

He had taken nearly every experiment to a logical end, yet

none of his work had yielded any insight into the inner workings of the virus. Each test resulted in the same thing—an end that included a pitiful animal body bleeding to death from the inside out. Every path he pursued, every new idea he had come up with had ended in the same way—as a total failure. Time was of the essence, yet like so many other projects that he had been involved with, time was not on his side.

Bekins looked back at victim three lying naked on the autopsy table. He knew all the victims personally. All three had been co-workers at the Cedar Grove CDC lab for a short period of time in 2002-2003. Bekins shook his head.

"How did this group become infected with the virus?" he thought to himself. They had put it back to sleep over two years ago.

Victim three had still been kicking when he'd been brought to the CDC facility, and Bekins had tried to speak with him before he'd expired. The victim had offered no explanation for his condition. He'd spent the last hours of his life lying in bed, saying nothing.

Bekins's analysis suggested that victim three had expired from a different form of the virus than the other two. He could tell by the internal organs. There was plenty wrong with all three victims. They had all obviously died a very painful death, but victims one and two exhibited identical symptoms and internally were very similar. In fact, the genetic profile of the virus cells taken from the first two identically matched a previously cataloged strain of the smallpox virus. Not surprisingly, it matched one of the strains kept in the center's locked liquid nitrogen freezer.

Could it have gotten out? wondered Bekins. He already knew the answer.

Corpse three was puzzling. The organs were in much worse shape than the other three. A healthy liver is normally smooth and reddish brown in color, but corpse three's liver was anything but healthy.

It was almost black, it drooped like a wet newspaper, and the usually smooth outer skin felt bumpy, almost like a sack of marbles. A normal liver would weigh in at about three pounds; victim three's liver weighed twice that.

He knew that victim three had been infected by a different means. There was no sign of an injection wound, a mark shared by the other bodies, but beyond that he had little more to go on.

An audible signal diverted his stare to a nearby monitor and away from the deformed corpse that lay on the stainless steel bed in front of him. Dipak, his assistant, put up a new image. The high-resolution image was magnified over thirty-five thousand times by a high-powered electron microscope and looked almost real on the large, plasma overhead display. Bekins loved having the monitor in the lab; it allowed him to view his work in real time, and while on slow days, he could pipe in satellite TV.

"Can I have a split screen?" Bekins asked Dipak.

Bekins spoke to Dipak through a wireless, line-of-sight communications system that was embedded inside of his blue Chemturion protective suit. Each suit at the highly secure CDC lab contained two discrete communications systems. The line-of-sight system that the pair was currently using provided secure communications, allowing only those within the Level 4 chamber to participate in the conversation. The other system relied on a more traditional form of radio communications that allowed the lab workers to communicate with those outside the immediate lab area and to landline systems through a communications bridge.

"I'll use victim two for the split screen?" Dipak responded as he prepared to put up a magnified side-by-side comparison of the virus samples. One side displayed the image of the virus from victim three while the other side showed a similar image from victim two.

It was only a matter of seconds before the dual image appeared on the flat panel monitor. Both images shared similar charac-teristics. The entire frame on both sides was filled with a dense pop-ulation of the rectangular, brick-shaped virus. Bekins was unable to discern any difference in the images.

Victim three had died from a different strain of the virus, and he needed to understand this new form. He needed to know where it had come from.

Bekins was one of those stubborn people who refuse to give up. He was the kind of person who stays up all night to finish a book or to make final plans for a future vacation, but he had already been in the blue space suit for over five hours, and his bladder had gotten the best of him.

7

For only the second time in his life, Brian Walker was traveling to the CDC in Atlanta. The first visit had been for a retirement party. The mother of a fellow University of Virginia alum had been retiring as the assistant to the director of the center. This time, the invitation to the CDC was more order than invitation. It had come with an explanation from boss and friend, John Pierce, in his new role as NIA director. The short note made mention that the bodies they'd discovered on the oil rig were army officers and their facial disfigurements were the result of being infected with the smallpox virus.

Walker knew very little about the disease. He and Jensen were given twenty-four hours to prepare for the briefing.

———

The NIA team regrouped back at the Eighth District Coast Guard base in New Orleans before their trip to the CDC. They were all present—

Jensen, Walker, and Pierce, with Gwen Saunders in tow. They gathered in the officers' lounge for drinks and reintroductions.

Walker handed Kate a cocktail and said, "Let me introduce you to Gwen."

They found Gwen staring out the large window.

"Hi, Gwen," Walker said, "good to see you again." Gwen turned and looked at them. She wore a sleeveless, white top with pants to match that showed off her tan. "I want you to meet Kate Jensen," Walker said. "She's with the NIA."

"Nice to meet you," Kate said.

Gwen shook Kate's extended hand but seemed a bit distant.

"I was sorry to hear about Shelley."

"Thanks," Gwen murmured.

"Don't worry; we'll figure out who is behind this and make sure nothing happens to you," Kate reassured her.

After a brief interface with Larry Escobar, the Eighth District asset officer, the second such debate in less than a month, Walker requested access to a Coast Guard Guardian Surveillance plane. Recognizing the uncharacteristically serious tone in Walker's voice and the background presence of the former base commander, Escobar quickly capitulated.

———

Pierce gently dropped the twin engine Coast Guard Guardian Surveillance plane's nose. The plane touched down smoothly and taxied to a secluded corner of Atlanta's Hartsfield airport. A uniformed army sergeant met the plane. He moved to unload the luggage but was quickly waved off by the able-bodied passengers. The four occupants of the plane climbed aboard an army Humvee for the trip to the CDC; Brian Walker's sense of trouble was heightened by the presence of the army transport and accompanying security detail that met them at the airport.

"Why are we headed west, Sergeant Walters?" inquired Walker, interpreting the sergeant's name badge via the Humvee rearview mirror. "The last time I visited, the CDC was northeast of the airport."

"The popular access to the CDC, the visitor's center, and low-security lab facilities are adjacent to the campus of Emory University. However, most of the national security work takes place in a lesser known, more secure location southwest of the city," stated the sergeant with a meek look but stern voice.

Walker glanced back at his fellow passengers and shrugged.

Walker was not surprised to see that Kate Jensen had fallen asleep on their short trip to the center. The other passengers seemed content to stare out their one-way windows at the increasingly more rural landscape.

Jensen awakened when the army transport swung hard off the road and onto a long, neat, nondescript private drive. Sergeant Walters presented appropriate credentials and negotiated two security checkpoints before being escorted through a two-story, reinforced tunnel entrance. The parade of vehicles traveled downhill for another three hundred yards before stopping at an underground cul-de-sac. The only visible egress from this point was the road in and an elevator door at three o'clock. The visiting team was directed toward the elevator door.

Inside the CDC facility, the team met another uniformed officer who silently escorted them to a nearby conference room. The large conference facility could comfortably accommodate thirty people. Today's meeting would be limited to Walker, his companions, and two CDC workers who were already seated in the room.

A dialogue was already in progress when the team entered the room. An overly animated CDC employee Mark Bekins was engaged in a debate with the Center's Director.

"I think the idea of hiding the discovery stinks," blurted Bekins, a plump young man dressed in surgical scrubs. "The virus has been confirmed. I did the work myself. Why should we wait? The center's rules of engagement are clear. Directive V5 calls for definitive action when smallpox is confirmed domestically. We vaccinate and vaccinate hard. V5 calls for a massive ring of vaccinations surrounding any and all known discoveries."

The CDC director glared at Bekins.

"There is just too much uncertainty surrounding the discovery of the victims," spoke Director Baum in a calm tone. "All three victims were discovered on an abandoned oil rig far from the mainland. We aren't even sure if they came from this country."

"Yes we are," exclaimed Bekins. "They're U.S. soldiers!"

"We need to learn more," the director cut in with an angry tone. "The public reaction to this can't be predicted. We have models that suggest the number of casualties from a contained viral outbreak would be dwarfed by the fatalities from the ensuing public unrest." Baum spoke with a calmer voice this time, trying to play down his subordinates' anxiety-filled statements.

"Do those same models offer casualty numbers for an uncontained outbreak?" challenged Bekins.

Walker spoke for the first time. "Can we have a few minutes alone with Dr. Bekins?"

Director Baum smiled and introduced Walker. Baum and Walker had met on more than a few occasions. The mildly overweight, slightly balding middle age director of the CDC was a childhood friend of John Pierce and a frequent guest at coast guard ceremonies and other more private functions at the commander's private residence.

"Mark Bekins, meet Brian Walker," spoke the retreating director.

"How do you know my name?" Bekins asked.

"It's my job to know your name. I'm working with the NIA team assigned to unravel this mystery."

In the uncomfortable silence that followed, anxiety appeared in the eyes of the young CDC virologist. He stared steadily at Brian Walker, as if attempting to ward off an evil being.

Walker waited until the door closed behind the CDC director before he confronted Mark Bekins. He started by making the rounds. He introduced Pierce and Jensen, intentionally leaving out Gwen Saunders, who sat quietly at the end of the table. Bekins nodded in return.

Pierce jumped in. "We have all read the WHO doctrine on smallpox, and it obviously forbids any laboratory experiments with the smallpox DNA. It states that the disease is now exotic to humans, lethal, and nearly impossible to cure. We understand the secrecy behind the existence of the virus in Russia and here in Atlanta. What we don't understand is how three U.S. military officers became infected with a virus that has been in locked hibernation for over twenty years?"

"That's not exactly true," spoke Bekins sheepishly.

Every face in the room turned and stared at the now pale and shrinking figure at the end of the conference room table.

Bekins was not going to be cagy. He could tell that this group meant serious business and regardless of how many people he'd sworn an oath of secrecy to, it was time to tell all. He began the lengthy story of how he'd come to work at the CDC and, ultimately, with the fiercely guarded virus.

When he'd started, he'd been on loan to the CDC for eight months, and four years later, he was still in Atlanta. After securing his PhD in epidemiology and microbiology from Johns Hopkins, he'd accepted a position with a private biotech institute in Maryland. His acu-men in a lab setting combined with his lack of any social life made him a perfect candidate for the long hours of seclusion required to work in a Level 3 or Level 4 lab environment. Working for the insti-tute, he had only been allowed to work in a Level 3 environment. His interest in working with more volatile, Level 4 viruses had worried his employer; the company worried that he might leave for another opportunity.

His employer had been experiencing fiscal pains, brought on in no small part by a downturn in the economy. Much of the institutes' funding had dried up, and to make matters worse for Bekins, the in-stitute had not been involved in any projects that would require the use of their Level 4 lab. The lab had been dormant for over a year. In the past, in order to retain quality employees during project downtime, the company had turned toward loan programs. The loan model was simple; retain good employees while offloading the burden of salary and benefits to another organization. In Bekins's case, the United States government was the other organization.

When the institute proposed his loan to the CDC in 2001, Bekins had jumped at the opportunity.

Soon after Mark Bekins had arrived at the CDC, he'd voiced his interest in working in a Level 4 environment. In a Level 4 envi-ronment, he would be able to work with much more dangerous and exotic viruses than in the Level 3 lab. Level 4 viruses were usually life threatening to humans and often had no vaccine or therapy.

Like those of most new inductees, Bekins's request fell on deaf ears. He was assigned to a challenging but unimpressive program researching an unnamed virus brought in from Southeast Asia. The virus was considered a Level 3 virus and was harmless to humans but deadly to rodents.

Mark Bekins had spent six months working with, as he called

it, "the rat's disease." His work had been productive and fruitful. He'd spent long hours in the lab working within the Level 3 room. He loved his work but longed to take the next step. His daily routine was wearing thin. Each day he would arrive at the CDC lab shortly before 7:00 a.m., fill out a sign-in log, and don a scrub suit. When he was ready to enter the lab, he looked like a surgeon prepared for an operation. The main difference between Mark Bekins and a surgeon rested with the end result. Most surgeons entered an operation with the ultimate goal of healing the patient. Mark Bekins did a lot more killing than healing in his work.

He watched day after day as teams of CDC employees working in blue space suits, technically known as Chemturion suits, prepared for their work in one of the several nearby Level 4 labs.

Bekins's big break came in the spring of 2002. The World Health Organization had been under pressure from the United States Army to allow some kind of testing on the smallpox virus. Smallpox, less commonly known as variola, had been exclusively quarantined to freezers at a small research institute in Moscow and the CDC in Atlanta. As far as anyone knew, these were the only known samples of smallpox left on earth.

The army did not feel the same way. It believed that stockpiles of the virus were stored in Russia, North Korea, and possibly several other locations, including Iran. Army intelligence was certain that, prior to the end of the Cold War, there had been any number of discrete experiments to weaponize smallpox. The Russians had in recent years as much as acknowledged their success in the area. The army felt that work needed to be done to ensure that the world had a credible defensive program in place if the threat of bioterrorism via smallpox arose.

In the spring of 2002, the World Health Organization blessed a controlled study on the disease to be performed exclusively at the

CDC. Mark Bekins got the nod as the CDC representative. He finally got his chance to work in the Level 4 lab, albeit side by side with a number of U.S. Army virologists.

Bekins trained with a number of co-workers at the CDC. They showed him how to put on the Chemturion suit, how to check it for leaks, how to enter the Level 4 lab via a series of airflow barriers, and how to exit through the decon shower. The one thing he was not taught was what to expect from the smallpox testing. No one actively working at the CDC had ever worked with the virus. It had been asleep in a freezer for over two decades.

The army was in a bind when it came to testing the smallpox virus. The only known hosts for the smallpox virus were humans. The three army virologists teamed with Bekins—all from the United States Army Medical Research Institute for Infectious Diseases, headquartered in Maryland—were tasked with producing an animal model of the disease as a base for testing. The team began the experiments by infecting a variety of animals with the human virus. The results were not surprising. Most of the animals showed no serious effects of the virus, save a short-lived rash on a few of the monkey participants.

The testing had gone on for almost a year before the WHO informed the army and CDC virologists that time was running out. The program director for the army was becoming increasingly frustrated with the CDC oversight and, on a number of occasions, had suggested that the work should continue—possibly at his base in Maryland.

The CDC and Mark Bekins played little more than a supervisory role in the process and could have been best described as babysitters to the army virologist. Needless to say, the WHO announcement was a relief for Mark. It meant that he would get a new assignment, almost certainly in the Level 4 lab and definitely under his own management.

The early winter of 2003 was supposed to be the end of testing with the awakened virus. The army team had shown every sign of ca-pitulation. They had packed most of their equipment and euthanized all of the test animals. The only act left was to destroy the remaining experiments, put the virus back in the freezer, and send the army staff packing.

Having finished his tale, Bekins looked around the room for a reaction.

"The same army workers are now flat on their backs in the level 4 lab?" Walker questioned bluntly.

Bekins closed his eyes, nodded his head, and sighed.

Walker stared again at Bekins. "I guess all of this new infor-mation would explain your own working familiarity with a virus that was supposed to have been permanently put to sleep over twenty years ago."

———

At 4:00 p.m., the meeting at the CDC came to an end. Walker and Jensen were satisfied that Mark Bekins was on their side. During the course of the four-hour meeting, Bekins managed to paint the army as the enemy, a renegade division of the military that didn't always place a priority on protecting the nation's citizens.

Jensen whispered to Walker on the way out of the meeting. "I need to see you, alone." She tugged at a strand of hair and quickly shifted her brown eyes from side to side.

"What if I'm busy?" joked Walker. A quick look at her and he wanted to retract the comment; she was visibly bothered.

"We'll meet the rest of you at the restaurant," Walker said to the exiting group.

Jensen slid a small digital voice recorder out of her pocket and handed it to Walker.

"You taped the meeting?"

"No, this was handed to me by my taxi driver on the way to the airport yesterday. He knew my name and said that I would be interested in the contents."

"Have you listened to it?"

"Yes."

"And?"

"I'm not sure what to make of it, but I think someone is trying to help us find the eavesdropper."

Walker looked down at the small recorder. Across the back of the device on a handwritten orange post-it note, were the words: "For Ms. Jensen's ears only, please!"

The voice on the tape was significantly disguised and difficult to understand, but after fifteen minutes and a dozen rewinds, both believed they'd heard the same message.

Jensen turned off the recorder and slowly placed it back into her pocket. She realized the importance of remaining calm in her line of work, but she was anxious to follow the new lead.

There was a knock on the conference room door. Pierce and Saunders were standing outside.

"You're still here?" asked Walker

"They won't let us leave this CDC campus separately. It's a security thing; we all came in together, and we all have to leave together. Are you almost done?"

"Can you give us five more minutes?"

"I guess so. But try and finish up soon. This place gives me the shivers."

"Why is that?" asked Walker

"I'm not comfortable hanging around this place," Pierce answered. "It doesn't seem possible that a man-made, controlled environment can contain a microscopic virus."

"You're worried that the disease is blowing around in the air space?"

"It might sound silly to you, but every breath feels like it's loaded with toxin."

"Can we finish up in the car on the way to dinner?" Walker asked Jensen.

"I thought we were going to get a tour of the facility first," she said, toying with Pierce. She returned to a serious voice. "I think we can finish up on the way to dinner."

CDC Director Baum caught up with them in the hall. "Ah, there you are," he said. "How about if we all go into the city for dinner?" Baum collected the group, and the foursome, now a six-some with Bekins and Baum in company, prepared to depart for Atlanta. Evidently, along with the title of director came some perks. Baum stepped off the elevator and nodded to the guards stationed at the door. He led the group through each of the three security checkpoints without a second glance by the guards. While this facilitated the group's trip to dinner, Walker found the practice a bit disconcerting. It was akin to policemen being allowed to skip the metal detector at the courthouse or pilots being passed through security at the airport without the full scrutiny given to other travelers. It just didn't make sense.

————

The toast to the NIA's new ally, Mark Bekins, was a little subdued. Through the background chatter of the crowded restaurant, the group talked and smiled to one another. It was difficult. Everyone at the table had a different agenda. Jensen and Walker were biding time until their next contact with an anonymous tipster. Bekins's head swirled with thoughts of a tricky virus back in the lab. And John Pierce hoped that Gwen Saunders was thinking the same thing he was.

Each poked at his or her food and a few passed the occasional wink, but mostly the diners squirmed and glanced at the wall clock. The dinner was short. By seven-thirty, they had finished desert.

After a round of coffee and espresso, at exactly eight fifteen, Jensen and Walker asked to be excused and gracefully backed away from the table and exited the restaurant. Kate Jensen walked hurriedly to a street-side taxi stand and, as instructed by the mysterious recording, she waited for a signal. An odd-colored, red limousine pulled up to the curb. All the windows were open. She leaned forward to inspect the interior cabin. It was empty except for the female driver. Kate opened the limo's front passenger door.

Walker watched Jensen's every move from his perch inside a dark phone booth across the street. "Don't get in," he whispered to himself. To his surprise, she did not.

Kate reached into the limousine and extracted a package. No words were spoken between Kate and the livery driver. None were needed. A large manila envelope emblazoned with her name said it all.

Walker smiled, breathed a sigh of relief, and stared at the red limo as it pulled out into the traffic. He waited for Kate's all-clear signal and then joined her on the street corner.

It was an innocent walk down a city street, partners holding hands and wandering aimlessly through the steamy Atlanta evening air. They stopped in front of CNN Center and gawked at the overwhelming display of streaming and screaming media.

Kate held the envelope tightly, waiting for the right moment. She managed to peek at least twice during the evening walk, and she was certain the envelope was empty.

Finally, Walker broke the silence. "What's keeping you from tearing that thing open?"

"The driver warned that the contents were for my eyes only

and that she would be watching."

"I'm willing to take the risk. Besides, how can you hide a putrid red limo on a quiet night like this? She's nowhere around."

She handed the envelope to Walker.

"You don't want the honors?"

"You seem to be getting more of a kick out of this Jack Ryan stuff than I am, so you go ahead and open it," Kate replied.

The envelope was indeed empty, but a carefully penned message was written on the inside wall of the paper container.

The message was simple. An anonymous source was directing them—or Jensen at any rate—to a U.S. Army base in Maryland.

After a repeated analysis of the contents, Jensen and Walker agreed that she should track down Saunders and follow up on the edict by booking a weekend stay in Frederick, Maryland.

Coincidentally, Walker had his own orders to follow. Director Pierce, on Walker's behalf, had managed to set up a friendly intelligence briefing with the senior commander of the United States Army Medical Research Institute for Infectious Diseases' also located in Frederick, Maryland.

8

At about the same time the plane landed at Fredrick Airport, Kate Jensen woke up. The three-hour flight from Atlanta, which was a non-event for Jensen, had been a living hell for travelers Walker and Saunders. The turbulence had been particularly bad, and the landing wasn't much of a relief. The government pilots were both retired navy airmen and had done nothing to calm their passengers concerns. Unlike commercial pilots, passenger comfort was not one of their priorities. Their mission was to deliver the cargo to its destination in the most cost effective manner possible. The pair of white-knuckled flyers had spent most of the trip conjuring up images of spiraling descent to the ground.

Kate and Brian were being supported by Gwen Saunders on their trip to Fredrick. It was an unusual support procedure for NIA agents to be joined by a civilian, but Gwen had already been exposed to sensitive information regarding the security breach, and she possessed the requisite skill set to help identify the elusive radio signals.

Once safely on the ground, the group separated. An army private met Walker almost as soon as he emerged from the terminal and whisked him away to nearby Fort Detrick.

Meanwhile, Walker's female travel companions meandered across the small municipal airport, eventually finding the lone rental car counter.

———

Walker's meeting had been arranged through the Department of Defense. Director Pierce pulled more than a few strings to get Walker in.

"Now, listen, Walker," Pierce had said, "this group at Fort Detrick keeps a very low profile. They're very serious and very touchy. Do you know how many favors I had to call in to get you in there?"

"No, but I'm sure you'll tell me," Walker had responded.

"A lot, buddy, a lot. So behave yourself, okay? No arrogance; no wise guy comments; just don't make these guys mad. I want you on your best diplomatic behavior. Got it?"

"Okay, okay," Walker had said. "Best behavior." But Walker had had his fingers crossed. He wasn't interested in diplomacy.

Two uniformed army Officers met Walker just inside the Fort Detrick main gate. From his research, Walker recognized them as Colonel Charles Reynolds—second in command at the fort and a senior medical officer within the infectious diseases group—and Barry Stelz from public affairs. They began by offering Walker a quick tour of the campus. He politely declined. He didn't bother mentioning that he'd already been over the facility plan a dozen times and that he could name every above-ground building and its tenant, as well as a few facilities that were not visible from the air.

"Well then, what kind of information would be helpful to your intelligence gathering effort?" asked Stelz, as he led the group into a nearby conference facility. Once inside, the men settled into comfortable leather chairs around a small, round conference table.

"I'm interested in anything you can tell me about the army's capabilities in the event of a biological event."

"The infectious disease group at Fort Detrick investigates naturally occurring infectious diseases that require special containment and provides a critical capability to the army as the only Department of Defense laboratory equipped to study hazardous viruses at biosafety Level 4. The institute also operates a reference laboratory for definitive identification of biological threat agents and diagnoses of the diseases that they produce."

Sounds like a PR pitch from the Institutes Web site, thought Walker to himself while the public affairs representative cleared his throat.

The pitch continued. "While the institute's primary focus is on protecting military service members, we also actively collaborate with the CDC and the World Health Organization."

Walker smiled. He hadn't expected them to outline their efforts to design biological warfare agents, but the generic PR spiel was aggravating him. He needed to be careful. The Department of Defense knew nothing of the eavesdroppers; nor did they have any knowledge of the smallpox victims at the CDC, and he wanted to keep it that way. The military had a way of screwing up when finesse was called for.

"Do you have any ongoing intelligence gathering efforts in the area of bioterrorism?" asked Walker

"No, that kind of work is up to intelligence agencies like yours. We want to play a support role when and if it is needed."

"Under what scenarios would you see that occurring?"

"A good example is the Anthrax scare that occurred a few

years ago. The army was instrumental in securing and sterilizing the contaminated buildings, as well as developing a therapy for those exposed."

Walker began to worry that he was not going to get anything useful out of the meeting. He decided to float a red herring.

"How about Level 4 viruses? You mentioned before that you have a Level 4 lab on site?" asked Walker.

"I'm not aware of any current projects in the Level 4 lab."

"The lab is dormant?"

The public affairs officer looked at Colonel Reynolds, who said, "I thought we were here in the spirit of building a stronger homeland security plan?'

"My fault; I guess my own curiosity took over."

The public affairs officer smiled and leaned back in his chair. He was looking comfortably smug with the colonel's rebuttal.

"How about the plague or smallpox?" blurted Walker.

Both parties looked equally surprised by the question.

"What about them?" responded the colonel.

"Have you had any experience in your lab working with vaccines or therapies for either disease?"

"I thought we just went over this," quipped the senior officer, visibly bothered by Walker's line of questions. He drummed his fingers on the conference table and scowled at Walker.

"Just wanted to know if the army felt either of the diseases were real threats to national security?"

"You tell us. You're the intelligence officer," Stelz shot back.

Walker could tell that the meeting was deteriorating quickly. He needed a fast recovery.

"My division is more worried about the plague at this point. Smallpox seems to have fallen off the face of the earth." Walker floated the response.

"I guess you have your answer then," interrupted Reynolds.

Walker continued to press. "We did, however, hear some chatter down in Atlanta about a smallpox reawakening."

Colonel Reynolds nodded toward the door but said nothing. The public affairs officer stood and left the room.

Reynolds slammed his fist down on the table. "You realize that you just divulged classified information to a public affairs staffer. What kind of crap are you trying to pull?"

"No crap, just the truth," Walker continued, standing his ground in the face of the sergeant's red-faced glare.

"I can't talk about any projects that we have worked on or plan to work on."

"Then can you comment on your two missing virologist, their assistant and illegal cargo?"

Reynolds looked like he had just walked in on his wife and another man. "You tell me how you know about that," he said in a state of forced control. His angry eyes looked like they were trying to penetrate Walker's skull.

"Because I have a pretty good idea what happened to them."

———

The morning was less than perfect for Jensen and Saunders's open-air eavesdropping mission. A strong breeze combined with a light drizzle made the temperature feel a lot cooler than the 61 degrees displayed on the dashboard thermometer. Kate shivered as she drove their rented red Mustang convertible with the top down. Gwen needed to be able to clearly pick up radio signals on her wireless, handheld device, and she wouldn't be able to do it with the top up. Problem was, Kate hadn't thought to bring a jacket. To complicate things a bit more, a Veterans Day parade was due to pass the 7th Street gate to the Fort Detrick Base. Crowds of nearly three thousand were expected to attend.

Camp Detrick, a small base nestled in the foothills of western Maryland's Catoctin Mountains, had become a permanent installation for peacetime biological research and development shortly after World War II, a status that was solidified in 1956 when it was renamed Fort Detrick. The base covered over seven hundred acres, catered to thirty plus tenants, and maintained a special helicopter landing area that served as an emergency landing site for Marine One in the event of an onboard emergency while in flight to Camp David.

Unlike that of many army bases, the area surrounding Fort Detrick did not provide a distinct land buffer zone between the adjacent civilian areas and the base perimeter. The parade attendees could congregate along the route only a few yards from base facilities.

Kate Jensen was frustrated by her own lack of planning. She had not taken the time to refer to a local community calendar before dragging Gwen Saunders out on another in a series of dead-end eavesdropping missions. This was their third location of the morning. The two previous venues had not been at all productive. Jensen was beginning to wonder if her anonymous source was for real. She was ready to call off the plans for the day and try again tomorrow when Gwen offered a small bit of hope.

"There is some level of chatter going on."

"What does that mean?" asked Kate Jensen.

"It could be nothing, but this is the first time I have been able to collect any information at all. Somebody nearby is having a voice conversation on one of the altered wireless devices."

Jensen looked over at her busy partner. She could understand why Director Pierce had taken such a liking to her. Gwen was a very attractive young lady and, by all accounts, a very bright one also. She wore her sandy blonde hair in a simple ponytail held together by a floral scrunchie. Her round, blue eyes and strong posture gave her a look of determination as she monitored her handheld display.

Jensen broke her stare and looked away from the seemingly meaningless characters streaming across the small screen. A broad smile came to her face as she gazed into the nearby pedestrian traffic.

Gwen Saunders looked up at nearly the same instant. She noticed the smile on Kate's face and saw the catalyst for the smile. Brian Walker appeared out of the morning crowd.

"Looks like a retired veteran out to take in the parade," poked Jensen.

"Nice day for a convertible," he shot back sarcastically, gesturing toward the visible cloud created by his breath.

Jensen reminded him that the top would interfere with the range of their communications equipment.

Walker moved toward the car and, a minute later, was sitting on the folded convertible top with his feet resting on the minimal rear set area.

"How did your meeting go?" asked Jensen.

"It was interesting. I think I found the colonel's breaking point, but beyond that nothing else useful. Can I hang around and hitch a ride back with you guys when you're finished?"

"You can, but let's not distract our wireless scientist here. She was just saying that things might be looking up."

"Indeed they are!" interrupted Saunders. "The intercepts are coming in with increased frequency now."

"Glad you think so," replied Walker as he struggled to understand the incoming transcript. The text appeared in real time on Saunders's handheld monitor. The characters that did appear were not in any sensible sequence; in fact, most were intermingled with odd characters and symbols.

For the first time, we seem to be in the right place at the right time, thought Saunders. They had been blindly moving between the main gate and another more obscure entrance to the fort in an attempt to stumble on the electronic eavesdroppers.

Neither Jensen nor Walker had any idea of what to make of the less-than-coherent text that was appearing on the monitor, but whatever it meant, they could tell by Saunders's reaction that they were on to something.

"I've got something!" stated Saunders triumphantly.

"Got what? All I see is a bunch of words minus the required number of vowels," said Jensen.

"The entire text is here. You're looking at the diagnostic stream rather than just the message stream. If you give me a few minutes, I can strip out the diagnostic information, and it will begin to make sense," noted Saunders.

"I hope so. Director Pierce warned me that you might slip into nerd mode."

"Hold on one second. I just need to make sure I save a copy of the original stream, and then I'll explain," she said, ignoring Jensen's comment.

After a brief pause she continued. "We've been chasing up and down the coast looking for information that could lead us to the electronic eavesdroppers. Your anonymous tipster may help us find the source for one of the electronic attacks, but the abstract conversations by themselves won't lead us to the source. They might give us some indication as to what kind of information the eavesdroppers are after, but it won't provide us with any information on their exact location."

"So how do we get the location details?" Jensen asked.

"What we're really after is the message header information from one of the communication device's requests for transmission. That's the main reason they've been able to elude us for so long;

they're not always listening. They only seem to electronically request data when the circumstances suit them. We need to be listening before their signal goes out. Today we got lucky. With just a little work, I should be able to trace the request for data stream to a particular manufacturer's device." Saunders took an excited deep breath.

"Okay, let's pretend I completely follow you. What's next?" asked Jensen.

"First, I need to strip out the message header and then compare it to the different cell phone, point-to-point, and defense contractor device information that I have cataloged. It shouldn't take long, but I'll need at least a few hours to see if we have a match."

"Then I guess we should get you back to the office so you can get to work."

"Actually, I should be able to work on a piece of this right now. Maybe you two can chase down a cup of tea and a slice of dry bran toast while you're waiting," smirked Saunders.

Jensen returned the smile and exited the car, showing no deference to her young partner's healthy request. She pointed Walker in the direction of a nearby Krispy Kreme, hoping that the light would be on.

———

Walker and Jensen were only in the shop for a matter of minutes when a skirmish in the parking lot drew their attention. A dark-colored van was parked just a few spaces away from their red Mustang. Their first understanding that something was wrong coincided with the kicking legs of Gwen Saunders disappearing into the van. Jensen and Walker charged out of the store to the realization that they were the next intended victims. The occupants jumped out of the van and moved to cut off their path to the Mustang. Jensen and Walker were just about to retreat to the relative safety of the store when a recklessly driven car piloted by a male teenager and his seemingly uncaring female companion screeched to a stop in the parking space next to the Mustang. Taking advantage of the momentary confusion, the NIA pair lunged toward the Mustang. Jensen jumped in the driver's seat, and ignoring his urge to drive in favor of the most efficient retreat, Walker flopped into the small backseat area. Jensen quickly engaged the automatic transmission and sped out of the parking lot into the building morning traffic.

Jensen expected the worst. A quick look back confirmed her fears. The fast-approaching vehicle was the same van that had taken Gwen hostage only moments earlier, and it was soon following closely—so closely that Walker could make out many of the facial features of its Asian occupants. The man in the van's passenger seat seemed to be leaning forward, trying to help the van along as it navigated the city streets.

The chase van drove down the middle of the street, showing no sign of care for the heavy pedestrian traffic. The driver of the van was doing a better job than Kate. *No doubt he's done this before*, Kate thought to herself.

Road spray from the recent rain clouded her vision, and she did her best to turn on the wipers while running a red light. She wanted to turn the chase back toward the base, hoping to stay ahead of the bad guys just long enough to crash the gate. As she contemplated a series of quick left turns to change direction, any doubts she'd had about her pursuers' intentions vanished. An assault rifle appeared from the van's passenger side window.

A shower of bullets cracked into the car around them. One of them grazed Walker's right forearm. "I'm hit," he stated matter-of-factly. He tore off a piece of his shirt and fashioned a makeshift tourniquet for his bloody arm, reaching with his next movement for Jensen's gun and focusing its barrel on the trailing vehicle's left front tire.

The Mustang should have been able to outrun and out-maneuver the van, but the narrow streets and parade crowd offset the car's speed advantage.

"I can't believe he's shooting at us," groaned Jensen. "There are families all over the place."

"They don't seem to care. Get us a little farther away, and maybe they'll hold their shots until we get out of the downtown crowd.

Jensen swung the Mustang hard to the right, almost ejecting her backseat passenger.

"Get on the phone and try and round up the police. Tell them to try and cut off the van before it gets to the parkway. In the meantime, I'm going to make a quick exit."

"You're going to do what!" screamed Jensen.

Walker's eyes followed the almost blind driving of the van. He was amazed that none of the pedestrians had been hurt in the chase. When Jensen slowed the car to navigate an intersection, Walker made a less-than-graceful exit from the car.

He attempted to distract the van's driver as the big vehicle sped past, but the driver seemed unaware of his exit. Walker glanced up and down the street, not sure what to do next. He spotted an idling delivery truck doubled-parked about twenty yards away. Without much thought or advanced planning, Walker unceremoniously commandeered the delivery vehicle.

His bullet wound hurt more than he'd let on to Jensen, but he did his best to ignore the burning sensation in his forearm. He made his move and pulled the large, brown vehicle out into the oncoming traffic. Unlike the agile Mustang and late model van, the delivery truck moved like an albatross. It listed hard to one side as he steered into a violent U-turn.

The awkward, brown vehicle gained speed as it pulled away from the parade traffic and onto a local divided parkway. Walker could only hope that the addition of a third chase vehicle would distract the van driver. An overpass loomed ahead, but Walker paid no attention to the height restriction warning that flew by at nearly eighty miles per hour. Traffic was stopping on both sides of the parkway; pedestrian and drivers alike were dumbfounded by the odd combination of vehicles involved in the chase. A biker stopped atop the parkway overpass and chuckled at the sight, oblivious to the gunfire still emanating from the middle vehicle.

"I'm not going to fit," shouted Walker.

He looked up at the arched overpass just as the top third of his vehicle made contact with the bridge. The noise was deafening as the metal frame of the delivery truck became partially embedded in the hundred-year-old bridge. Walker braced for the worst, but it never came. The truck hardly missed a beat and exited the underpass at nearly the same speed that it had entered. Walker stole a quick moment to look into his side view mirror. The road behind him was littered with shaved metal and dozens of packages.

The 9-1-1 operators were getting reports at an alarming rate. Frantic callers from cars, homes, and office buildings were reporting similar sightings of the Mustang, van, and newly minted convertible truck speeding along the parkway. The 9-1-1 coordinator's quick chuckle faded as reports of gunfire were added.

"There're headed east toward the onramp to Route 70. Maybe the state patrol can cut them off on the highway," reported the coordinator.

Walker clung to the oversized steering wheel, trying desperately to control the vehicle against the drag created by the truck's scarred back end.

Jensen was in control of her vehicle and, now that they'd

reached the highway she'd stopped the relentless jerking of the steering wheel that had miraculously kept the shooter from hitting his target and had managed to pull away. Soon she was maintaining a safe distance ahead of the van. Unexpectedly, the van made a sharp left turn and headed off the highway into an industrial area.

By now, the state police cars had joined in the chase. The driver of the lead police car motioned for Walker to leave the parade of vehicles, but with Saunders still captive in the van he wasn't ready to comply.

Walker felt the first twinge of fear as the group raced past a series of off-airport motels. He wasn't ready to cut off the van or take any other offensive action that would risk the life of the van passenger. Hopefully, the driver of the police chase vehicle would feel the same way. There was still a very real likelihood that the van, traveling at such a high rate of speed, would crash on its own, and he wasn't ready to enhance that possibility.

A hail of bullets suddenly erupted around the delivery truck. Both of the odd-looking vehicle's front tires were shot out. The truck veered violently and flipped onto its side, skidding almost one hundred feet before coming to a stop, where it all but blocked the main entrance to Frederick Municipal Airport.

———

Doug Moon glanced back at Gwen Saunders with a business-like stare. She was trying to hold herself steady in the rear bench seat of the van. Moon returned his attention to the driver.

"Take us out to the tarmac," he commanded.

9

After local paramedics cleaned up his minor bullet wound and his other scrapes and bruises, Walker was reunited with Jensen. They were both in shock, still unable to come to grips with reality that Saunders had been captured. The police had finished protecting the crime scene and were about to transport the pair back to the police barracks for questioning.

Before they'd left the scene, Walker had gone over to the remains of the brown truck that had never quite made it to the chase's end. The amount of damage that the truck had sustained was amazing. The remaining portion of the storage compartment was now entirely disconnected from the truck frame. He couldn't begin to count the number of bullet holes in the hood and engine area.

The chase van was also a wreck. It looked much less menacing than it had a few hours earlier. The thugs had crashed it before hauling Gwen off to a waiting helicopter. The local authorities and airport officials had not yet located the aircraft. Walker moved around to the rear of the van. He expected to find it picked clean by the investigators and was surprised to find a crumpled T-shirt under a rear bench seat. The school name silk-screened onto the front of the athletic shirt was not familiar to him. He'd quietly stuck the shirt in his coat pocket and exited the van.

The questioning at the police barracks seemed to go on for an eternity. Walker finally convinced the detectives to take a break. During the break in questioning, Walker was able to get in touch with Mark Bekins. He gave the CDC virologist a brief update and asked him to be available for another debriefing in the evening.

After another hour and a half, the two detectives finally seemed satisfied that they had extracted all tidbits of information and allowed Walker to leave.

Walker found Kate Jensen asleep in one of the detective's offices. She had her feet up on the desk and looked none the worse for wear given the morning events. He had always admired her ability to nod off regardless of the surroundings. He stared at her for a moment; oddly, he had never noticed a small freckle on her right cheek and another near her collarbone. A quick tap on the shoulder, and she sprung to life.

"Let's get out of here," he murmured.

"What's next?" she asked

"You're going to call Director Pierce and let him know that you've lost his girlfriend."

Walker arranged for an army transport from Fort Detrick to Reagan National. He waited until they were safely airborne in the Bell utility helicopter before he showed the T-shirt to Kate and described how he had liberated it from the back of the van. The name on the front was partially worn off, but they were able to make out the words "Property of Ieyden" or possibly "Teyden" inscribed on the front of the shirt, just above the ubiquitous XXL marking.

"Not much to go on," stated a monotone Kate Jensen.

"Maybe not, but I don't think the shirt was wedged up under the rear seat by accident."

"You think someone hid it there?"

"I'm not sure, but we need to find out."

"I'll follow-up on the T-shirt lead once we land," commented Jensen. "You can contact Pierce and have him trace the chopper that left Fredrick Airport with Gwen and her captors on board, and maybe you can find someone at NIA headquarters who can help you analyze the data Gwen captured this morning before all hell broke out," she continued.

Director Pierce was waiting on the tarmac when the army transport landed at a remote corner of Reagan National Airport. He immediately sensed something was wrong but held his tongue until they were all in his car.

Kate was abrupt and to the point. She in no uncertain terms described Gwen's capture and her unknown whereabouts.

Pierce was silent. He kept focused on the road, but it was obvious to both Saunders and Walker that he'd been hit hard by the news. Walker offered to drive, but Pierce just shook his head and continued on course.

They were headed to Jensen's NIA office near the DC Mall. Pierce turned into an underground parking garage as if on autopilot. The silence continued as the group boarded an elevator for the ride to Jensen's fourth-floor office. Her assistant, Paris Rand, was waiting for them. Paris could best be described as having Lara Croft features. Kate made the introductions, and everybody took a chair.

Pierce spoke first, his voice visibly shaken but coherent. "I spoke with Director Baum at the CDC just prior to your arrival at Reagan National. He voiced his growing concern over the lack of any credible leads in our search for either the source of the electronic intercepts or the source of the virus. He doesn't want to sit on the discovery much longer. He suggests that we turn the data on the infections over to the Department of Defense."

"You know where that would lead," said Jensen, shaking her head.

"Yes I do, but we need to understand the pickle that Baum's in. On one hand, he wants to control the news regarding the virus, especially given Bekins's latest update. On the other hand, we need to be prudent when it comes to national security."

"I for one know exactly how it will play out if this gets turned over to DoD," Jensen remarked. "The army brass will immediately go into political protection mode and request that the president address the nation and order the CDC to start mass vaccinations. All the while knowing that the process will save zero lives and accomplish nothing, except maybe insight mass hysteria."

"How did you leave it with the Director Baum?" asked Walker.

"He agreed to hold off on any information sharing with DoD until we follow up on the information that Gwen and Kate gathered this morning outside Fort Detrick. He did stress that the report to the DoD would have to be made sooner rather than later."

There were unspoken synergies in Jensen and Walker's thoughts. They both knew it wasn't realistic to ask Pierce to sit idle while Saunders was in the hands of unknown captures. They agreed on a three-pronged attack. Jensen would try to work out the meaning of the athletic shirt recovered from the van. Walker would return to South Carolina to work on the data captured by Saunders earlier in the day, and in a parallel effort, Pierce would get out in the field and try to determine the origin and current location of the helicopter that had escaped from Fredrick Municipal, presumably with Saunders onboard.

10

The quiet of a late Saturday morning was interrupted by a knock at the door. Walker was trying to sleep in, still recovering from the late night flight from DC to Hilton Head Island, South Carolina.

The reason for his unplanned wakeup call turned out to be an overnight package from his office containing his weekly mail delivery. Walker did not like to visit headquarters. As an independent intelligence officer, he reported to Director Pierce and had no direct reports of his own. He relied instead on Pierce's assistant for his mail forwarding and a small amount of clerical support.

A short walk on the beach followed by a hot shower and Walker was ready to face the delivery from headquarters.

He dumped the contents of the package onto the coffee table and began to pick at the mess of assorted communications. He began with interagency memos. Many only received a cursory glance before floating into a nearby recycling box. A hand-written post-it note poked through from the middle of the stack. It was attached to a newspaper clipping from *The Frederick News-Post*. The front-page article featured a color photo of Brian Walker, complete with disheveled hair and torn pants, posed against the backdrop of a shattered, brown truck hull. The headline read, "Hungry Bridge Messes with Morning Commute." The story brilliantly disguised the true events of the day. It read as a light adventure story about a misguided delivery truck driver rather than a serious story of terrorism and kidnapping.

You've got to hand it to the Ft. Detrick public affairs office, Walker thought to himself.

After crashing through three-quarters of the pile, Walker stood and stretched. A nearby picture of Kate Jensen distracted him from the mail. He opened a patio slider and walked to his small pool area, which overlooked a lagoon and the aptly named Ocean golf course. *Kate has not seen enough of my home*, he thought to himself. She had visited the island on many occasions, but he had never invited her to visit on a purely social basis. They'd never traveled together for pleasure. Their travel was always for work and usually in a stressful environment. There were so many things about his life that he wanted to show her and so many things about her life that he wanted to know.

Kate often joked about taking golf lessons. He should have been happy to engage the local pro on her behalf, but he'd never made the effort to follow through on her hints.

His guilt grew, and he made a mental promise to engage Kate on a more personal level. He had been selfish, and it showed.

He reentered the climate-controlled house and continued to poke at the stack of mail. There was a copy of a fax from the Frederick County Highway Department addressed to the NIA accounting office—something about remuneration for bridge work.

The mundane task of reading through week-old mail came to

a quick stop. A single piece of folded paper, stapled and taped at the top, contained the remark "For Director Walker's eyes only, please." Inside was a typed note. Walker laid the open sheet of paper on the table and stared at the short message.

He put the note aside and poked through the rest of the pile. The pieces of mail all seemed to blur together, a meaningless pile of paper. The anonymous note seemed to float above the others, taunting him and waiting for him to come back to it.

Walker retraced his morning steps to the beach and repeated his walk. He carried the note with him, squeezing it tightly in his hand. He was oblivious to the beachcombers and surf skimmers. His thoughts were completely focused on the note. When he returned home, he went inside and flopped on the couch.

Whoever it was that had sent the note knew more about the eavesdropping than anyone in his group. He wanted to catalog likely candidates but came up empty. No starting point, no real hints, just a directive from an anonymous source.

Almost as if on cue, the phone rang. It was Kate Jensen.

"Hello, gorgeous," spoke Walker without waiting for a hello.

"Same to you. Hey, the T-shirt lead worked out. It came from Leyden Academy in Northfield, Massachusetts."

"Good job. What else did you find?" asked Walker.

"Well, I just got off the phone with the academy's headmaster, and she agreed to have someone in the school's information technology department create an account for me. I should be able to electronically walk through the student and faculty records from my office computer."

"Very good. I just received a typed message from a little birdie—most likely the same bird that sent you to the recorded message. In the note, he or she suggests that we get ourselves to Amherst, Massachusetts, before it's too late. Maybe there's a connection with your lead to Leyden Academy."

"If there is, I'll find it soon enough. Why don't you arrange to get us to Massachusetts while I poke through the school records and try and dig up a culprit."

"I'll meet you at Reagan National tomorrow at noon."

"It's a date," Jensen smiled into the phone.

Brian Walker put down the phone and stared at a pile of clothes and other clean and dirty artifacts from his recent travels. Sitting on top of the pile was the T-shirt he'd liberated from the escape van in Maryland.

11

The counter clerk at a small bookstore, just a block from Ellen Yi's house, did not acknowledge his new patron. If he had looked up from his reading, he would have been unfazed. Doug Moon didn't have the appearance of a man who had spent the better part of his adult life planning to murder millions of people. He did not have sinister features. In fact, his round face, brown hair, and matching eyes gave a mien of a pleasant, almost relaxing person. There was not, however, a pleasant person hidden behind the eyes. There was an emotionless, uncaring person who was ready to kill.

Moon circled the store collecting a few odds and ends, mostly clothing. In his haste to leave Frederick, he had accidentally abandoned his small travel bag. He was not fazed by the sea of purple and maroon athletic clothing that confronted him. It reminded him of his days at the academy, when loose-fitting sweats and ripped T-shirts had been his standard issue sleepwear.

The student clerk looked up from his book. "Are you finding everything all right?"

"Just about," responded Moon, picking up one last item, a token gift for Ellen.

Moon paid for his purchases and exited the store. He thought for a minute about getting his rental car for the short drive to Ellen's house. He decided that it would be a more prudent to leave the car at the local bed-and-breakfast rather than draw the attention of nosy neighbors by parking an unfamiliar car near Ellen's house.

The house was not what he had expected. It wasn't a rural New England cabin but, rather, a neatly kept, nondescript two-story home in a suburban setting. Bright flowers bordered the front walk, boxed geraniums decorated the first floor windows, and a trickle of water ran down the driveway from a recent lawn watering. The Kellogg Avenue house was not even close to his mental images. The neatly trimmed hedges and the pole-mounted basketball hoop gave the secret lab the look of a family home, not the drab low-profile building that he'd long pictured.

A light rain began to fall, and Doug Moon began to wonder if Ellen Yi was living a dream or was more cunning than he had imagined. Only the barred basement windows gave any indication to the activities that took place within.

He stepped up to and knocked on the windowless side entrance to Ellen's residence. There was no exterior sign of a security system. He worried that Ellen had been lax in her efforts to protect their plan.

———

Because of her dedication to work, Ellen had very few friends. There had not been any men in her life. None since a brief interlude with an associate professor in her post academy days—a fact not lost on her as she contemplated her meeting with Doug. She was certain that whatever had occurred in the past had been lost over time.

The expected visitor's knock interrupted her thoughts. She stood up from her seat on the floor in front of the fireplace, put down her notebook computer. She walked across the creaky hardwood floor toward the stairs. Her heart raced, and she braced herself as she opened the door. She waited for a reaction from her visitor.

"Ms. Yi," he stated, monotone but with a slight smile.

"Doug Moon, an honor to see you again," Ellen Yi spoke while bowing gracefully. He had put on a few pounds, she noticed. Even so, his dark eyes could still pierce through her as if reading her mind.

"I hope you'll forgive my late arrival, but I didn't want to arrive empty-handed." Doug handed her a box of maple sugar candy and a single rose.

Ellen Yi was silent; she was not prepared for Doug's offering. She had been prepared for a stone-faced businessman arriving for a meeting, not a former lover greeting her with flowers. Moon followed her up the stairway to the second-floor flat.

"Come in and sit down. Would you like a drink?"

Moon nodded.

"I can brew coffee or a cup tea. Maybe you would prefer a glass of wine?"

"Wine would be nice." he smiled again as he removed his leather jacket and sat down in a large chair near the fire.

Ellen was surprised by the response. Doug had never been much of a drinker.

"Too bad about the discovery in the Gulf," she said, trying to get her thoughts back on track.

Moon sat up straight. "A miscalculation on my part—I should

have dropped them in the water rather than risk their discovery."

"It was just an unfortunate accident. The storm was beyond your control."

"One of my communication shadows tells me that the last of our human experiments has died. Was it the third victim that was vaccinated?" asked Moon.

"Actually, all three were vaccinated, but only the third victim was vaccinated prior to infection. Keep in mind that the first two were infected with an earlier strain of the virus. So we really only have one test case so far. I need to do more human testing using the latest strain to be sure that it performs as expected."

"Okay, let's talk about more human testing."

"That's fine, but before we get to that I have a concern. I'm worried that the discovery of our test subjects could jeopardize our plan. Now that the government authorities have control of our test subjects, they also have a sample of the resistant strain. They could also have a path to your West Coast operations."

"I'm not worried. They have no evidence that ties the test subjects to any part of our operation. As for the virus, if it is truly vaccine resistant, then it's they, not us, who should worry."

Ellen stood and walked over to a wall cabinet. She uncorked two bottles of wine, one merlot and one cabernet.

"The merlot is my favorite, but it might be a little tame for your tastes," she said, trying to lighten the conversation.

"The merlot would be nice." Doug Moon put his feet up on a footstool near the fire and slouched in the chair. He relaxed for the first time in months.

12

From a coffee shop in the Savannah Airport Brian Walker checked his e-mail on a small notebook computer. There were three messages from Director Pierce, one generic message that had been sent to a distribution list, and one from Mark Bekins. He was glad the first message was an e-mail; his boss sounded aggravated, something about him pissing off a "full bird" colonel at Fort Detrick. The second message was a thank you for the same reason. A quick apology message took care of the first one; there was no need to respond to the second.

Walker ran his fingers through his unkempt hair and yawned. He quickly glanced at the generic internal e-mail, which contained an update on the mysterious helicopter take-off and subsequent disappearance at Frederick Municipal. The FAA had no idea where the abductors' helicopter had come from; nor could they give any information as to its destination.

In the fourth e-mail, Mark Bekins wrote about his daylong

battle with the virus. The third victim, as expected, had been infected with a different strain of smallpox than the other two. Bekins described victim three as "screaming hot"; what that meant Walker could only guess.

He was eating a croissant at a public table just outside the queue for airport security. The line was long, but Walker wasn't in any rush. His flight was already delayed thirty minutes. He couldn't remember the last time he'd used a commercial carrier. He almost always relied on military transportation, but this time he needed to get to Washington in a hurry. The anonymous message that he received in his mail pouch seemed to imply that time was not on their side.

Walker scanned the front-page headlines of *The Atlanta Journal-Constitution* while he waited for the security line to recede. A story just below the fold gave him a chuckle and a reason to call Kate.

He dialed the number for the electronic switchboard at the NIA in Washington. After working his way through the labyrinth of recordings, he entered J … E … N … S … and was connected to her extension. Her line was busy, and the call went straight to voice mail. He accidentally prompted out to the operator while trying to skip Kate's recorded greeting. The operator tried unsuccessfully to transfer him back to her voice mail, and two different secretaries working hastily managed no better. "The U.S. government at its best," Walker joked out loud. He hung up and tried again. This time, he found his way to Kate Jensen's assistant, Paris Rand. She put his call through to Kate.

"Kate Jensen," she answered.

"I'm going to be late," he replied.

"Good, because so am I. As you can tell," she added, "I haven't left the office, and I still need to make it back home and pack. Fat chance I'll be at the airport an hour early. I hate commercial air travel."

"That's our only option if we want to get to Massachusetts by tonight," he said.

"Maybe you can cause a stir at the gate and delay your take-off."

"Or maybe you can get your lovely rear end in gear and meet me at the airport on time," he responded.

"Then hang up and let me finish my work."

"Okay. Say hello to Paris for me," finished Walker with a tone of lust in his voice. He was referring to Jensen's rather well developed assistant.

———

After making the compulsory stop in Charlotte, Brian Walker's US Airways flight touched down in a driving rain at Reagan National. "Great. An angry and wet travel partner," whispered Walker, noting the rain-soaked wing of the Boeing 737.

They rolled slowly to gate 37 where most of the passengers stood almost the instant the plane stopped. Brian pulled his less-than-accommodating travel case up the jet way, cursing the one stubborn wheel that refused to spin. He noticed Kate sitting with her back to him one gate over. Walker moved around to get in her line of sight. It was an unnecessary tactic. Her eyes were closed.

"How about a long weekend on the beach after we get through with this trip," he said, whispering into her left ear.

"I'm one step ahead of you. My new bikini is in the bag, and not much else," she said with a reverse wink.

The estimated flying time to Hartford, Connecticut, was just over one hour. Another fifty minutes by car and they would be in Amherst, Massachusetts.

Unlike during most flights, Brian Walker never had the chance to be anxious. As soon as the wheels were up, Kate dove into a brief on her research, starting with her search of the student transcripts at Leyden Academy and ending with the one glaring target.

"So you've narrowed the search to one. You've selected your evildoer," stated Walker. "Does your bad guy have a name?"

"Ellen Yi," Kate said, thumping Walker on the shoulder. "Weren't you listening?

"You have to admit," she continued, "Yi has the profile to be a bad person. Her school records read like a timeline of escalating bad deeds. Maybe some of her extracurricular activities could be labeled as pranks, but too many of them were dangerous stunts that could have seriously injured fellow students and professors."

"You'll have to come up with a little more evidence than a twenty-year-old prep school transcript if you want to question the woman."

"I never said anything about questioning her. I just want to take a look at her current environment. Maybe a brief investigation into her life for the past dozen years or so, but nothing as invasive as a question," Jensen smirked.

"I'm not completely comfortable with your conclusions. I agree that the T-shirt that we discovered helps draw a link between Saunders's kidnapping and the school, but I don't think your brief electronic visit to the school record room is enough to start an investigation."

"Do you have a better idea? We're running out of time."

"I guess not. Are you sure you've been through the records for all the students?'

"Only the ones from the last thirty years."

"And nobody else has ever done anything wrong or been reprimanded in some way?

"Not for poisoning fellow classmates."

"What about the phone interviews with the faculty?"

"Very few were at the school during the time when our target attended. One science professor did remember the girl. He wasn't aware of her sordid past and was actually surprised by her history of trouble."

"I think this is going to turn out to be a lot of chasing around for nothing, but given that we have nothing else to go on and our invisible friend pointed us to Amherst, I'm willing to do a little digging. Why don't you call the office and see if somebody can pull together some data on the girl in the years since her graduation from the academy. In the meantime, we can both do a little scouting at her current place of employment."

13

Doug Moon left early in the morning, after spending the evening on Ellen Yi's couch. Ellen nursed her first hangover in a decade and at 11:00 a.m., she still felt terrible. She was due at the university lab in less than an hour. Ellen drank half a beer, a remedy she often heard around the university lunchroom, but she seemed immune to the cure. Ellen Yi was exhausted and still a little nauseated at noon. She slumped in her reading chair and slept for another hour.

Ellen was still yawning when she finally made it to work. She donned a lab coat and headed toward her latest project. Her favorite experiment was a genetically modified banana plant. It bore square fruit. Growers and shippers would love it, but peeling and eating the fruit was a little disconcerting.

Shiri, her co-worker, was smiling when Ellen entered the lab area.

"Didn't expect to see you at all today," she said, looking at her watch.

"It was a late night."

"I can tell."

Shiri was busy injecting a liquid into an odd-colored carrot. She replaced the carrot in a soil bed and said, "There were a couple of people poking around your experiments today." She pulled two business cards out of her coat pocket and pushed them across the table to Ellen. "It was a man and woman accompanied by a university administrator."

Ellen looked down at the small cards in front of her. She felt her heart racing. "What? Who were they? What kind of questions did they ask?"

"Simple stuff. They wanted to know what projects you were working on and the hours you kept. Stuff like that. They also asked what kind of car you drove. I told them I didn't think you owned one."

"What else did you tell them?"

"Not much. I wouldn't have given them any information at all, but they both produced government IDs so I felt obligated to give them the basics. The administrator made me give them a copy of your schedule and your current working papers. I told them you and I weren't very close and that I had no information about your life outside the lab."

Ellen blinked rapidly and her face flushed. "Did they ask anything else?"

"Not from me, but the university administrator gave them your mailing address and some other information regarding your work history at the university." Shiri paused. "Hey, are you in some kind of trouble?"

Ellen Yi didn't respond. She had expected that one day her environment would be compromised, but she always assumed it would come after an accident in her lab or during some official investigation, long after her mission was complete. Doug Moon had constantly pressed her to be prepared for an emergency escape from her private lab. She had not prepared well. Now she'd have to make some decisions on the fly.

"Hey, Shiri," Ellen said as casually as possible, "do you mind if I borrow your car for a while? I need to run an errand."

"Sure," Shiri replied. "Go ahead."

Yi accepted the keys then stood and left the lab area without a word.

Yi approached her work with the virus much like a programmer would with an active codebase. Every time she modified the virus, she created a backup copy just in case. Once a week, she labeled a small container with a date-based reference number and stored the container in the university lab freezer, and without hesitation, she moved an encrypted version of her current working notes to her private storage space on Google's servers, complete with a progression number to diary and index her work. Doug Moon would have considered the later move ridiculous, but she considered it low risk given the huge amount of semipublic storage that her data would comingle with. This archival process would ensure that at any point during the research process she could recover a previous version of the enhanced virus without losing any more than a week's worth of work. This process also ensured that Ellen could escape the Amherst area without returning to her private lab.

Satisfied that she had recovered both the original and most recently modified version of virus from the university lab freezer, Ellen steered her co-worker's Subaru Outback onto Route 9 and headed west out of Amherst and out of her former life as a quiet associate professor.

14

"This doesn't strike me as the smartest thing you've ever done," said Kate Jensen. She nervously inspected the yard of the Kellogg Ave house. "Are you sure this is a good idea. As you pointed out earlier, we have very little evidence to link this woman to any bioterrorism activity. All we really know is that she works in a genetic testing lab at the university."

"Her history of terrorizing fellow students is good enough for me. Besides, just a little while ago you were the one looking to crawl into her life. What harm can come from a little late-night, peeping Brian activity," reasoned Walker.

"What do you expect to find during your intrusion into her private home?

"I'm not sure. Maybe documents that might tell us if we're even getting warm."

Walker stood up in the back of the nondescript panel van that they had parked just down the street from Ellen Yi's house. He adjusted an oversize button on his breast pocket. Jensen leaned over a small television monitor to check the video image being captured by Walker's pocket camera.

"The image is perfect. You're good to go," she said, pointing to the back door of the van.

Walker pulled on a pair of dark gloves and pressed on his ear to be sure his communications plug wasn't dangling again. He reviewed the floor plan that he had retrieved earlier from the local town building inspector's office. The little background information he was able to gather about her tenant dentist was unremarkable. He'd check out the office just to be sure. He gave Jensen a quick poke to get her attention then flashed her a thumbs-up and exited the van.

Walker moved confidently toward the front entrance of the dentist office. Just for good measure he tried the door. It was locked. The office windows were bare. There were no shades or curtains to obstruct his view. After a brief peek in each window, he was convinced that nothing would be gained by entering the office portion of the house.

He turned his attention toward the side entrance. Staring upward, he noted a much different exterior than the open view offered in the front of the house. All of the windows were either painted opaque or concealed by interior shutters. He paused to adjust the bothersome earpiece before looking down at the barred and frosted basement windows. The basement protection seemed logical given the building's close proximity to the street. It seemed odd that the second floor would be so secluded. He was intrigued to say the least.

"I'm at the back door," he disclosed to Jensen. "Not much to see from this vantage point. I'm going to try and get through a door or a window."

"You're going in?"

"What did you expect me to do, report on the shade of paint on the side of the house?"

"That would be safer. What if she comes home?"

"I'm willing to take the risk. We're running out of options, and you know as well as I do that if we don't get a warm lead pretty soon, this whole thing is going to be out of our control."

"Okay, but try not to wake the neighbors."

Walker didn't attempt to enter the building immediately. He spent nearly five minutes circling the house looking for the best place to enter the rear living area. The house had originally been designed as a two-family residence. A second-floor fire escape was visible on the back of the house.

"Here comes a car," said Jensen, speaking quietly into Walker's right ear.

"Let me know if it slow or stops."

"Okay."

The voice in his head was disconcerting and would have been downright annoying if it had come from anyone other than Jensen. He was not used to this kind of spy work. Most of his intelligence gathering endeavors had centered around the high-end workstation in his home office.

Moving around to the side door he shined his pen-sized flash-light on the lock. He was surprised to find only a standard key lock on the doorknob. He worked on the lock with a special tool that he'd borrowed from Kate, but after about ten minutes, he gave up and re-turned to the van. He was visibly frustrated. "Okay, okay, I don't want to hear, 'I told you so.'" He reentered the van and closed the door just a little too hard.

Jensen didn't say a word. She leaned back and smirked as Walker fumbled through an oversized toolbox and removed a short-handled sledgehammer. He exited the van without saying anything.

The embarrassed Walker unceremoniously marched up the middle of the driveway and faced the side door with renewed vengeance. His second attempt was less graceful but much more productive. The knob fell away on the second strike, leaving the side door free to swing on its hinges.

Walker gently eased through the door and entered into a dark hallway, only partially illuminated by his small flashlight. Working deeper into the dark apartment, he moved down the hallway and quickly examined the staircase that led up to the second floor. He moved slowly up the stairs and found a small apartment. There were three rooms in all, a combination kitchen/living area, a bedroom, and a full bathroom. All were empty except for a few modest furnishings. His hands shaking, he checked the only visible storage areas, a chest of drawers and a utility cabinet. There was nothing special to report. A few ladies' undergarments in the bureau and miscellaneous cleaning supplies in the utility closet; the place hardly looked inhabited.

"Hey."

Walker jumped.

"Here comes another car."

He was still uneasy with Jensen in his ear.

He checked the living area one last time. Then he moved back down the stairs to the first-floor hallway. He began to second-guess his decision to enter the property.

He checked his Timex watch. It was almost 1:30 in the morning, and here he was wandering around a woman's apartment, checking her underwear drawer.

That would make for a good story in the local newspaper, he thought.

"I'm coming back out," he said aloud.

"Your camera isn't much good in the limited light. Did you find anything?"

"Nothing I'm proud of. The living area is basically empty."

"How about the basement?"

"I never made it that far. I'll give it a quick look."

He stepped on an abandoned sneaker on the third to bottom step and slid the rest of the way down. After a hurried recovery, he trained his light on the dark basement interior. The handheld light revealed two empty cages at the bottom of the stairs. Just off to the left there was a desk area and a series of hanging uniforms and suits. He moved forward and stopped. A glass wall was reflecting the beam from his light. He adjusted the angle of the light and froze. It was a haunting picture. His heart rate accelerated until it felt like a freight train was moving through the room.

Despite the initial shock, his nervous instincts worked well enough to help him make a quick exit back out into yard. He stood out on the front lawn of the residence and fought off the nausea that was swarming him.

———

The second time, Jensen and Walker went in together. There was no hiding the second arrival. They came equipped with heavy flashlights and took great care to ensure that every available light in the hallway and basement were illuminated.

This time, the view was not quite so gruesome, at least not for Walker. A body, which Walker had originally thought was human, could now easily be identified as a medium-sized monkey. It stared at them through wide, black eyes. The body looked stiff. The arms were embracing another victim of the unknown tragedy.

The face was hard to make out. The cheek and forehead areas were covered with a dark rash that blended seamlessly with the monkey's black hair. Its mouth was open as if trying to tell them to run.

The monkey's eyes seemed to be staring into the distance, almost straining to see if someone else had accompanied them into the death chamber. Kate Jensen had not spoken a word.

They stepped forwarded in unison and for the first time were able to take in the entire environment. Walker moved over to the desk area.

"I think we found what we are looking for," he remarked.

Jensen, still not ready to speak, only nodded in agreement.

"Maybe we should call Mark Bekins. I think a CDC away team should take it from here. Let's hope that the lab area is airtight."

Jensen finally diverted her eyes away from the killing scene on the other side of the insulated glass wall. "This is unbelievable. I count seven carcasses and a few odd body parts."

"And I count two notebook PCs and a dozen or so binders over here," spoke Walker, trying to redirect her attention, away from the dead animals.

Jensen helped him put the notebook PCs into a cardboard box for transport to the van.

"Unless my intuition is wrong, and it almost never is, this place has been abandoned," conjectured Jensen.

"That would seem to be the case. It's too bad, though, we were certainly getting close."

"What makes you think we're close? This place could have been abandoned weeks ago?"

"I haven't done an exhaustive search through the documents, but the top few pages are dated the day before yesterday."

"Then we should get a move on while the path is still warm."

"I agree, but first we should get the CDC team in here before any nosy neighbor or local cop starts poking around."

"The away team will have their work cut out for them. Mopping up this mess while maintaining public safety will require some very visible work."

———

Walker showered. He spent his usual thirty plus minutes soaking up the warm mist while thinking about the early morning events. Normally he would relax with an afternoon drink. Not today though. It was only 9:00 a.m. and, besides, he hadn't been able to find any open liquor store on his drive back to the hotel.

Walker dialed Bekins's number at the CDC.

"Dead monkeys, you say," said Bekins, after listening to Walker and Jensen's brief of the findings at the Kellogg Ave residence, "covered with blood and blisters on the face, hands, and feet."

"I'm not certain about the feet. I wasn't ready to go in and take a close look," muttered Walker.

"Did all the animals look the same?"

"For the most part. Some looked worse off than others. A few were covered with more blisters than others. One of the animals was swollen to the point that you couldn't make out its eyes or mouth."

"You and Kate should quietly make your way down to our site to be tested. There are no assurances that the lab you discovered was still functioning with negative pressure."

"How about if we get a member of the away team to test us here? That way we can continue to study the papers that we retrieved from the lab."

"That's okay with me, but you better make sure you see Dr. Lawrence. He's the only member of the away team that won't make you go into quarantine while you wait for the results."

"Thanks, Mark. After we get the test results, I'll accompany Kate back to Washington and then continue down to Atlanta with the data recovered from the lab."

"Sounds good. By then we should have received at least some of the animal carcasses back here in the lab. Have a safe trip, and remember, keep a low profile until you get your own test results back. I'm sure I speak for the entire greater Amherst area."

———

It seemed that the Kellogg Ave lab was very sophisticated. It was equipped with an airflow management system that rivaled anything at the CDC, and it was still operating. The CDC blessed the system within a few hours of their arrival. That was good enough for Walker and Jensen. Without wasting any time, they skipped the blood test and boarded a government transport to Washington DC. Jensen slept most of the way while Walker passed the time wandering the aisle and occasionally checking in on the pilots.

When the pair stepped off the plane at Andrews Air Force Base, it was early afternoon. Walker was unpleasantly surprised to find a freshman senator waiting to pick up Jensen. It seems Jensen had called ahead for the ride.

"Kate, you look great," the senator said as he strode toward her and took her overnight bag. He flashed a coy look in Walker's direction. The senator looked the part in every way. His precisely groomed, jet-black hair matched his designer suit. He was playing the part well, a fashion model on the streets of Washington DC. Walker knew the type, kept and fit on the outside but soft in the mind and soul. *Probably never worked a real day in his life*, he mused to himself.

Walker knew better than to play into Jensen's mental game. Instead, he smiled politely at the pair and stretched his back before boarding another government transport for the second leg of his trip into the Atlanta area.

Jensen looked back at Walker and flashed him a resigned good-bye. Her smile looked crooked. "Sorry," she mouthed. It had been a bad idea to play this trick on him. She knew it. He knew it. Walker smiled back and, with a wink, waved her off.

15

The man who was the driving force behind the plan to infect the U.S. population relaxed on a hammock in the backyard of his compound near Yakima, Washington. The retreat's name, Indigo Run, was inherited from the previous owners. He rested his eyes and tried to concentrate on his upcoming meeting with the Yis.

Doug Moon now realized that Ren was not going along with the family plans. He had firsthand evidence of Ren's betrayal. The older brother of Ellen Yi had become more belligerent during the past few weeks—so much so that, during Moon's recent visit to Massachusetts, he and Ellen had discussed the option to permanently terminate the relationship.

Moon opened his eyes, feeling little relief from the stresses of the past twenty-four hours. He scratched his unshaven chin and reached for a nearby wireless handset. He was most concerned about how to deal with Ren. He found it necessary to communicate with the

elder Yi more frequently than he wanted. The news that Ellen was retreating to the Yakima, Washington, compound was not nearly as distracting. He had planned for that event.

Ren Yi answered the phone with a hurried, "Hello." His voice
slowed noticeably when he recognized Moon's voice on the other end
of the line.

"We need to talk," spoke Moon in a nonconfrontational tone.

"I thought you weren't going to call anymore. We agreed that
my participation would be limited from this point forward."

"That's not true. You asked that we leave you out of the implementation phase, but your sister and I still need your assistance."

"What happened now? Did you accidentally leave a dying
monkey on the White House lawn?" responded Ren with a bothered
sarcasm.

"Your sister's lab has been compromised."

Yi paused. "Was there an accident? Is she all right?"

"She's fine. Two U.S. government intelligence employees
stumbled on her location."

"Is she in custody?"

"No, a co-worker at the university tipped her off before the
raid. She's on her way here to Yakima, and we need you to come over
to the compound and meet with us face-to-face."

"We've been through this before," Yi spoke firmly. "I'm not
going to continue to be sucked into your plans whenever it suits you."

"These are not my plans. They are the plans of two families,
two nations, and at one time a dedicated brother and sister. You're
going to continue to be available to us as for as long as we need you."
Moon's tone turned angry.

"I'm done. Carry on if you wish, but leave me out. I'm not
coming to Yakima, and I want this to be our last contact." Ren em-
phasized the point, not realizing the gravity of his statement.

———

A United Airlines 757 began its final approach to Sea-Tac Airport. Ellen looked out the right side of the plane at the passing Seattle skyline and wondered how her brother was managing. *Does he still live in the same house?* It was difficult to believe that he was the leak.

A few years ago, her visit to the Seattle area had been on different terms. The threesome had still enjoyed their private discussion of martyrdom, passing the evenings at a small neighborhood restaurant near Ren's Seattle house.

Her escape from the college town had been relatively uneventful. She was surprised that her only moment of remorse had come when she realized that she was abandoning her small convertible. She was fairly certain that it wouldn't be easily traced. It had never been registered under her name. She had driven the car unregistered for over five years on a set of license plates purchased via the Internet.

Ellen eased through the busy airport, skipping baggage claim. She pushed her tortoise-shell glasses more comfortably onto her nose and quickly skirted around the crowd. Her load was light. She had no luggage, only a small cell phone with an oversized battery. The idea was Doug Moon's, and it was brilliantly simple—an idea that, if it worked, would allow Ellen to transport the virus unchecked through airport security. And if a nosy security agent got too close, she had a plausible story. The battery was actually a small, fully functional power pack encased in a plastic mold that contained a hollow chamber for the virus. The encasement shell contained rows of cooling gel. She'd kept the small, mobile storage unit in the freezer at the university lab. The unit acted like a reusable ice pack.

In the end, no one had questioned the integrity of her cell phone. She still worried that it would all be for not. Without access to a liquid nitrogen freezer or a proper host, the virus would most certainly die in just a matter of hours. She wondered what surprise Moon might have in store for her when she reached his home in Yakima.

———

There was a light wind out of the northeast. Large snowflakes drifted slowly to the ground, almost playfully, against the backdrop of the Scotch Broom and Ponderosa Pine.

From his bedroom window, Doug Moon scanned the scene again. It would be the first time in over three years that he and Ellen would be together at his northwestern home. He put a small log on the fire in the corner of the room and headed to the living room area to wait for his guest. He enjoyed sitting in the living room. From an old rocking chair by a bay window, he could see the darkening evening sky above the distant mountains.

Outside, a limousine delivered Ellen Yi in front of the stone steps leading to the entrance of Moon's home. The arriving party exited the somewhat out-of-place transport with a mild sense of urgency.

Moon's peaceful moment was broken by a soft knock that told him it was time. Doug opened the door and greeted Ellen for the second time in a week.

"Good to see you," he said with a slight bow. "Come in."

"Thank you," Ellen said without expression.

Ellen and Doug spent the evening hours discussing their plan and recalling their parallel life journey. At 10:00 p.m. local time, Ellen retired for the night.

The next morning came too quickly for Ellen. She tried hard to stay in bed as long as possible then gave up. It was 5:00 a.m., eight by her internal clock. She moved through the great room at Doug Moon's secluded retreat. She was familiar with the environment, having spent many summers at Indigo Run during her years at the academy. In recent years, Ellen had been forced to stay away from Doug's house in Yakima. She and Doug had agreed not to spend any time in the same area. Her recent escape from Amherst changed all that.

Moon spared no expense when it came to building redundancies into their plan: Ellen knew this from firsthand experiences. Every time she'd thought there was a glitch in their plan, he had disclosed a viable alternative. This time it was no different. On the flight from New England, Ellen had convinced herself that the plan to distribute the virus would have to be put off for months, maybe years. She had no idea that Doug Moon had anticipated that her lab might someday be compromised.

Trying to maintain some sense of a routine, she took a long walk down the cobblestone drive that led to the Indigo Run compound. She turned onto the gravel rural route that passed by the end of the driveway and traveled to a nearby river and back. Her jaunt was four miles in total. She strolled back into the compound just before 6:30 a.m., awake and refreshed. Doug Moon greeted her halfway down the driveway.

"How was your walk?"

"Not bad. I forgot what a wonderful place this is."

"In hindsight, we should have set you up here from the beginning."

"No one could have foreseen the discovery of the lab, and don't forget that, at the time, access to the university freezer was a priority."

"Not anymore. Follow me," he said with a smile.

He handed her a cup of tea and led her around to the back of the main house. They walked about fifty yards due north toward a large barn. Doug pulled aside a large door that hung on an overhead trolley. The interior of the barn had been modernized. The barn vestibule contained two small clothes lockers; a large, surround-style desk, complete with a new Dell PC; and a shelf populated with familiar textbooks, as well as her personal research diary.

Ellen stood speechless for over a minute. "Where …? How did you get the diary?" Ellen brushed a stray tuft of hair away from her eyes.

"I sent someone back into your lab the morning after it was discovered. The government employees who entered your lab only stayed a few minutes before calling in a support group. There was at least a five-hour period between the time the lab was first discovered and the arrival of the biohazard team."

"Won't they know you were there?"

"I don't think so. Only your research diary was liberated from the lab; we left everything else. And even if they were suspicious, it really doesn't matter now. They have no idea where we are."

Moon flicked on some other lights, further illuminating the barn's entire inner space. Again Ellen was without words. He had rebuilt her entire lab environment to original spec, though most of the working areas were much larger and visibly newer. Moon stayed only long enough to show off some of the more subtle features of the new lab, including remote light controls, a high-fidelity sound system, and a small kitchenette.

Ellen spent the rest of the morning getting comfortable with her new surroundings. She had plenty of organizing to do before she could even think about rewaking the virus.

The barn vestibule felt enormous compared to her small office anteroom in her basement suite. After a quick snack from the fully stocked refrigerator, she removed her class ring and put it on the desk before working her way over to the locker area. She opened the locker on the left, the one with her name on it. Inside were three neatly folded sets of blue surgical scrubs. She moved behind a privacy curtain and removed all of her garments including underwear, before slipping into one of the neatly pressed blue uniforms.

Ellen moved across the locker area toward a sterilization chamber. Standing in her bare feet, feeling clean and refreshed, she pulled open the door. A monotone-colored world greeted her in the ultraviolet sterilization chamber. Viruses do not do well when exposed to ultraviolet rays; their genetic infrastructure comes undone making it difficult for them to prosper. Ellen was not surprised that Doug had equipped the new lab with this feature. Nothing surprised her any-more. The UV chamber was a luxury absent in her Amherst lab.

All the perks of a real lab environment, except maybe socks, she thought to herself, noting the absence of any footwear. Not a prob-lem—she had been in a blue suit barefoot before. She wiggled her toes and a slight smile formed as she reflected on the past forty-eight hours.

She pushed on through the next door into another staging area. She found a container full of latex gloves and a wheel of precut tape. In the old days, she would have been forced to tear four or more short strips of tape and stick them to the wall before donning her blue suit. This role of tape was perforated every eight inches. There was one strip for each wrist and ankle. *Such a simple invention*, she thought. Hanging on a rack in the corner were two brand new, blue space suits.

After lowering a soft plastic helmet over her head, she pulled on the zipper that ran from her navel to her throat; a series of hissing sounds followed. Her face mask began to fog, indicating that she was now airtight. Pulling on a retractable rubber hose hanging from the ceiling, she snapped it into a receptacle on her protective space suit. A cool, dry breeze immediately replaced the warm, moist interior en-vironment. The suit puffed out, and her mask cleared.

Now it was time to christen the new suit and lab. Ellen un-hooked her tethered air hose; another identical hose existed in the lab.

She moved forward into the decontamination airlock, the last line of defense before and after her time in the Level 4 environment.

The Level 4 chamber was the only place where she would allow the virus out of its cage. This was the place where her animals, and sometimes human pets, would be exposed to the virus. Outside the decontamination environment, all was supposed to be safe. The lab that Doug had designed was nearly a perfect replica of the Amherst lab with only a few exceptions. Across the room from the monkey cages was a stainless steel cylinder, a liquid nitrogen freezer. The freezer was identical to the one she'd kept her work in at the university, complete with a digital display monitoring the inside temperature and power supply.

Ellen unlatched the freezer and gently eased open the lid. A small cloud of smoke rose from the depths of the small device. She found her mobile phone alone in the frozen cell.

16

It was Saturday, and Brian Walker worked alone in his home office. After six straight hours of switching his attention back and forth between his computer and a map of the United States, Walker stood from his chair and straightened his legs. He raised his arms high above his head, rose onto the balls of his feet, and stretched toward the ceiling. Then he relaxed back into his desk chair.

He had finally been able to put together most of the information on the heavily encrypted hard drive that he and Jensen had recovered from the Amherst lab. With a little help from a friend at the FBI, he'd been able to gain access to a decryption tool on a secure IBM server in Armonk, New York. The difficult part had been the necessary task of hand-building the blocks and blocks of corrupted header information to provide the decryption program a starting point. The decryption effort itself had only taken about fifteen minutes.

Amazing, he thought, considering his first exposure to a large, data-center environment had consisted of a simple punch card program that ran on a room filling IBM 360 mainframe equipped with about 3 percent of the memory of his current desktop PC.

Using a secure line, Walker was able to copy an image of the recovered hard drive onto the server in Armonk. The returned product was more than he'd hoped for. He was staring at a list of files recovered from the hard drive. There were hundreds of files, ranging in type from word processing and spreadsheet documents to very large image files.

The directory looked clean. He hoped that the analogous files were intact. The first few image files were enormous and took some time to open. The images were extremely clear but were meaningless to Walker. He assumed that these images were from an electron microscope. They looked very similar to the images that Mark Bekins had shown them at the CDC lab. A few of them were photographs that offered scenes of disfigured monkeys, and at least one picture displayed a human victim. All the portrayed victims were demonstrating the now all-too-familiar signs of the hideous disease.

He opened one of the spreadsheets and was confronted by a series of long mathematical expressions that he had neither the interest nor the aptitude to decipher. A separate directory labeled "working papers" seemed to offer a more likely path to discovery. *Assuming they were written in English*, he thought to himself.

It didn't take long before the horrible plot began to spill onto his display. Walker shook his head and rubbed his eyes in an attempt to shut out the disturbing images. Unfortunately, they were burned into his mind.

Brian Walker's phone rang five times; then the voice mail picked up. It rang again five more times, and the routine was repeated. The phone was only a few feet away on the desk, but Walker didn't acknowledge its presence. He was lost in a trance. The bioterrorism plan was unbelievable—it couldn't be possible to pull off such a large-scale attack.

A minute later, the phone rang again. This time Walker answered it.

"Who's calling?" he asked, still distracted by the information taken from the hard drive.

The voice on the other end was firm and confident. "Is this Brian Walker of the National Intelligence Agency?"

"Yes it is. Who's calling?"

"It doesn't matter right now."

"It does to me." Walker's trance was beginning to dissipate. He didn't know the name, but he had a pretty good idea who it was on the other end of the line.

"I'm sorry about your trouble in Frederick. I had no idea that they would come after you," spoke the anonymous caller.

"Who are they?"

"They are former colleagues of mine who are brewing some bad soup. I can tell you more, but you have to promise to follow my instructions, no questions asked."

"Will I end up like the girl you abducted in Maryland?"

"The Saunders girl is due to be released tomorrow."

"You know where she is?" Walker screamed at the phone.

The caller ignored his shouting. "To learn more you need to travel alone. Leave on the morning United nonstop from Atlanta to Seattle." The caller abruptly hung up.

———

Brian Walker sat in the back row of the 10:00 a.m. flight from Atlanta to Seattle. It was Monday morning, and the United Airlines flight was packed. He was glad to have secured an aisle seat, just in case his multiple cups of coffee need an exit. Being on the aisle also gave him a little more legroom to stretch out his six-foot-three frame. An uneasy feeling began to crawl across his brain, two hours into the flight and no one on the flight had said a word to him. He had been on hundreds of commercial flights in his life, and the one constant was a chatty neighbor. Maybe the early week crowd was full of introverted technology types returning to one of the hundreds of small technology companies in the greater Seattle area.

The toilet flushed across the aisle, and the door was abruptly kicked aside. The last in an almost endless line of lavatory patrons caught Walker's eye with a smile. Through the painful aroma, he managed to smile back at the attractive female. Many minutes later, the end of the line was the front, and the female passenger was now facing away from him. He admired the short red skirt. It hung perfectly, just low enough to leave underwear to the imagination. Her hair landed in about the same place. She wore an unnatural blonde mane that had probably required more than one container of bleach to complete the job. The toilet door swung open then closed, along with his mental imagery.

A few moments later, the bright-haired patron wiggled out of the small restroom. Just as she passed to his left, a poorly feigned misstep landed her in his lap. With barely an apology, she stood and continued her way up the aisle and out of sight. Walker was sufficiently distracted by the young woman's action. He almost missed the bright white envelope protruding from the magazine pocket in front of him.

The note contained only one sentence and an address. He was instructed to make his way from Sea-Tac Airport to a hotel in Bellevue, Washington. Further instructions would be waiting for him in his hotel room.

After picking up his rental car, it took only fifteen minutes to reach the hotel. Trying to be normal in the face of unfamiliar and uncomfortable surroundings, Walker took to the Bellevue, Washington, city streets for a jog. He ran at a record pace, covering a four-mile route in less than twenty-eight minutes. When he returned to the hotel, he was not in any condition to turn in for the evening. Instead, he showered and headed back out for a quick snack and nightcap at a local brewpub.

He slept until housekeeping began knocking on the doors of the rooms around his. Checkout was at eleven, not eight, and Brian Walker knew he was safe until checkout. The maid service always left the turnover rooms for last. He showered, shaved, and then shoved his dirty laundry on top of the clean clothes in his small travel bag. He left the room and headed to the parking lot.

His rental car looked unchanged since he had parked it. The vehicle was parked in the third from last spot in the row farthest from the main entrance to the hotel. This location matched the specific orders in the last anonymous communiqué. He walked around the car twice before getting in. All seemed normal until his eyes drifted toward the ignition. A CD partially extruded from the dashboard radio. He stopped and stared at it, wondering how his anonymous informant had been able to break into his rental car without any sign of forced entry.

Though anxious to hear the contents of the CD, Walker was uncomfortable not being in control of the situation and hustled the car out into the traffic. He drove quickly along the city streets, keeping one eye on the rearview mirror. His sweaty palms tried to keep a firm grip on the steering wheel. Exiting the last in a series of hard turns, he pulled into a public parking garage at a local mall.

The voice on the CD was significantly disguised and difficult to understand, much like the earlier one sent to Kate. After listening to the short passage for the third time, Walker was fairly certain he understood the message. He was instructed to proceed to Shilshole

Bay Marina on Seaview Avenue, and the meeting would proceed from there.

The drive to the marina was about forty minutes according to a travel specialist at a roadside visitor information booth. Walker made the trip in half that time.

When Walker arrived at the marina, a large wooden gate was opened for him and closed behind him by a petite man dressed like a navy enlistee. He was directed to a nearby parking space, where another deckhand escorted him to an elaborate harbormaster facility. The marina was labeled as the premier sailing center in the Northwest. This was according to a glitzy marketing brochure that he had acquired at the roadside visitor center. A major modification to the mooring facility was nearing completion.

"The president's coming in two weeks," his young escort eagerly told him.

"Good for you," spoke Walker supportively.

Walker was directed to a waiting area just outside the club area of the harbormaster facility. A woman dressed in a nautical blue pantsuit and designer deck shoes appeared from behind a frosted glass door.

"Hello," she said, "my name is Erin." Her brunette hair was swept up into a chignon, perfectly in place. Her smile was radiant, Walker noticed, and she wore just the right amount of makeup to compliment her sparkling green eyes; she looked almost too perfect.

She led him into another, more private sitting area overlooking the harbor. The view was tremendous. A wall of glass provided a frame for the snow-covered Olympic Mountains high above the waterline.

"You know why I'm here?" asked Walker expectantly.

"Yes I do, Mr. Walker. Mr. Yi has asked me to be your hostess until he is available to meet with you. Would you like a drink?"

"Yes, please, black coffee would be fine."

"Mr. Yi?" thought Walker. He guessed that this was the missing brother.

He was starting to get aggravated with the cat and mouse game he was playing with the now less anonymous Mr. Yi.

The self-proclaimed hostess returned with the coffee. A strong aroma followed, and Walker guessed hazelnut.

"Can I wait out on the balcony?" asked Walker, displaying his trademark friendly smile.

"Most definitely." She smiled back before turning and leaving the room.

There were three sets of double French doors leading to the balcony. Walker sipped his coffee and slipped through the nearest balcony egress. A small lawn separated the building from the vast array of yachts moored just a few yards away. Everything smelled and looked new. A landscape crew on the lawn below was busy trimming hedges while another group freshened the surrounding bark mulch.

"Mr. Walker," a voice called from the clubroom. His hostess had returned. "Sorry for the delay. Mr. Yi is available now. I will take you out to see him."

She escorted him back out of the building, where an oversized golf cart was waiting. She motioned to the driver of the electric car, who responded by relinquishing his position to her. She drove carefully and deliberately along a narrow cobblestone path, past dozens of docks where small sailing vessels were docked. They stopped at the last dock, where a small motor launch waited.

"The water's a little rough today," she said apologetically. "It should take about ten minutes to reach Mr. Yi's yacht," The engines were already running, and again she motioned for the in-place driver to exit the transport.

"A Jack, or should I say Jill, of all trades," smiled Walker.

"Mr. Yi asked that I personally see to your comfort," she said. Walker smiled again.

They cast off and slowly maneuvered past more rows of small boats, then larger boats, and finally past two anchored yachts that Walker guessed to be over sixty feet each. Walker turned his head and felt the first twinge of worry as he watched the breakwater fade into the distance.

———

Anchored almost two miles from the marina in Puget Sound was the *Opium Princess*, a fifty-one foot fiberglass sailing yacht. The only visible passenger was a tall Asian man waving slowly from the deck.

"I'm glad you found your way," said Ren Yi, extending a hand to help pull the yacht and launch closer together. He bowed slightly and waved to the female escort, who quietly turned the small motorboat around and headed back toward the marina.

"Please follow me, Mr. Walker," he said, and they walked gingerly along the side of the boat to a pair of Adirondack chairs positioned on the forward deck. "What can I get you to drink?" Yi asked, searching Walker's eyes.

Suspecting that Yi was not a man who often experimented with hard liquors, Walker said, "Wine or beer would be fine."

Walker nearly jumped out of his seat when he felt a new presence on deck. Two glasses of dark red wine arrived on deck almost as if by magic. Up until now, Walker had assumed that he and Yi were the only two inhabitants of the yacht.

"Sorry if I have startled you, sir," apologized a slight Asian man dressed as a ship steward.

"How about that, an invisible butler. Do you have any other surprises stowed below deck?" asked Walker, fidgeting in his chair.

He was very uncomfortable with his current surroundings.

"I'm sorry. I guess I should have better introduced myself and the surroundings. My name is Ren Yi, and this is my server, Wat. Wat and I are the only ones on board. There won't be any other surprise visitors this evening."

Walker extended his arm and engaged Ren Yi in a hesitant handshake.

"I hope you're comfortable with the accommodations."

"Why are we meeting out here rather than at the marina club?" Walker asked.

"I'm becoming increasingly more comfortable offshore. You can clearly see both the city and the mountains from here, and I can get more accomplished here than I ever could in the office. There are no unwanted distractions. This is also where I hide. Very few people know that I own this boat."

Walker took a sip of his wine.

"How do you like it?" asked Yi.

"Very nice. A local product?"

"Yes, Washington State wines rival the best in the world. Some would argue that many are superior to California's best."

"I have only a moderate wine palate, but so far, I agree."

"Wat is going to prepare fresh salmon for dinner. Is that okay?"

"Perfect."

"And we have fresh crab also; they are always good but best this time of year."

"I went to school one state away from the home of the crab. I spent four years devouring Maryland's finest."

"I know," Yi said, looking at his watch. The sun reflected off his shiny, black hair. "Maybe we can have crab out here on the deck while we discuss business, then adjourn below for the salmon and a small show-and-tell I have put together."

Walker just nodded. He wanted to ask a million questions and wanted to ask them all at once, but considering the venue, he decided to be patient for a little while longer.

The steward reappeared, this time carrying a huge bowl with so many bony legs hanging out that Walker thought he must have slaughtered a sea monster for an appetizer.

"How did you know where I went to school?" poked Walker, trying to stimulate a meaningful dialogue.

"Just a quick search on the Internet, and there you were. Actually, I have been monitoring e-mails between my sister and her partner, and their correspondence pointed me to you. It seems that you and your team are doing a good job staying one step behind them."

"Maybe you can help me keep up. Did you say your sister?" Walker feigned ignorance.

"Yes, my sister. You remember her; you visited her in Massachusetts."

"Oh her. I did knock on her door, but no one was home. Well maybe a few dead monkeys and a virus or two, but nobody with a pulse."

Yi's eyes narrowed, and his lips flattened into a near frown. After an extended pause, Ren Yi continued. "I want to cut a deal with you."

"I'm not sure I have the authority to deal."

"It's actually a very simple exchange. I will tell you everything you need to know as long as my sister is allowed to leave the country."

"I can't go along with that. She's already broken a ton of federal laws."

"If you want to stop Mr. Moon and his elaborate plan, you'll find a way to let her out."

"I can't do that, and I'm not sure who this Mr. Moon character is. The best I can do is to give her a head start. If you give up her accomplice, I will make sure that my agency follows up on leads related to him first," Walker lied.

Yi looked lost in thought. He wasn't sure how his sister would react if she knew that he was cooperating with the government.

Yi proposed a comprise offer. "How about if we take a baby step? I have a meeting with Mr. Moon scheduled for late tonight. If I offer you a close-up glimpse of the man behind the curtain, maybe we can deal."

Walker looked out into Puget Sound. He didn't want to seem overly eager to accept the offer. He scratched the back of his left hand with his right.

"I don't know, Mr. Yi." He paused again to keep Yi off guard. "I *might* be able to go along with the proposal, but given that I won't be party to the meeting, how will I indentify Mr. Moon?"

"Trust me. You won't have any trouble picking him out in a crowd."

17

Kate Jensen had taken a few days off, now that the captured evidence had been turned over to Bekins for analysis. A perfectionist in her work and her personal life, she managed a light workout every weekday morning and participated in a yoga program on weekends. Even with her busy work schedule, she got her beauty rest. She averaged close to eight hours a night. Sleep was her outlet; almost never dreaming, she was more than capable of leaving her work behind when her head hit the pillow.

Never married, her only consistent companionship was Walker, and even that was a stretch. Considered a very eligible bachelorette by government standards, she was often seen on the arm of an administration up-and-comer, and regardless of the imagery, these were always platonic meetings. Kate silently held hope that she and Brian Walker would someday be together.

Saturdays she went to yoga class near the U.S. Capitol Building. DC was her home, and she was comfortable traveling around the city. She took the metro to the Smithsonian station and exited to the street for a brisk morning walk the rest of the length of the mall to the capitol building area. Kate moved along quickly, not realizing the amount of nervous energy she had built up inside her. She moved along a gravel path with her arms and ponytail moving in rhythm.

The sea of early morning joggers and tourists mesmerized her. She thought back to the events of the past few weeks. It seemed like an eternity ago that she and Brian had been taking in the passive South Carolina beachscape. She did not look forward to the coming week and the difficult task of convincing the CDC director that her team could stop the bioterrorists before they let the virus loose on an unprepared public. She was also bothered by the lack of any lead in the investigation of Gwen Saunders's abduction. She could only pray that Pierce could unravel the mystery before it was too late.

The CDC director was pressing to brief the Department of Defense on the virus outbreak and was prepared to ask the Department of Health and Human Services for permission to begin a massive public vaccination campaign. Jensen viewed this as nothing more than a cover-his-ass act by the CDC director. He knew as well as she that the virus they were dealing with was blind to current vaccines and would only serve to unnecessarily put the public health at risk. She also knew that, if they were to be truthful with the public and disclose the magnitude of the bioterrorist plot, the hysteria would be unmanageable.

A ray of sun broke through the clouds, exposing the morning dew on the sporadic grassy surfaces of the mall. Kate crossed 9th Street and moved to yield for an approaching jogger. As he approached, she recognized him as John Pierce.

She stopped in her tracks. He looked frightened, his face pale and gaunt. She didn't say anything at first, fighting off her own feeling of anxiety. She could tell that he had been crying. The areas under his moist eyes were red and swollen.

"If you ever want a date, just let me know," spoke Pierce, eyeing Kate and trying to hide his emotions.

Jensen stared unwavering; she knew he was upset but needed to know what was going on.

"You didn't hike all the way out here to laud my yoga outfit."

Pierce embraced her; she could feel his body shivering, and it was not from the air temperature.

"What's happened?" She spoke gently.

Pierce pulled back and looked at Kate. "They found her; they found Gwen."

"Is she all right?"

"They used her as a test subject, just like the ones we recovered from the Gulf."

"How can you be sure?"

"She told the team that recovered her that she had been injected with the virus. They took her straight to Atlanta and are running tests on her now."

"Maybe her captors were testing a different virus, something less lethal?"

"Do you really believe that, Kate?"

She looked down. "Not really, but let's not jump to any negative conclusions until we hear from Bekins at the CDC."

She put her arm around the waist of the slumping Pierce. She had never seen this side of him before. He seemed beaten, almost heartbroken.

18

The nightclub was a short walk from Seahawks Stadium. It was housed in a turn-of-the-century building that had once been a club for the city's elite. In more recent years, a much younger crowd, sporting rainbow-colored hair and pierced tongues had replaced the blue-haired elite. The late night crowd spilled into the city street, all but blocking the view to the club entrance.

Ren Yi looked through the one-way window of his town car at the strange outfits and over-the-top hairdos and took them in stride. They were not that dissimilar to the styles worn by many of his employees. Ren Yi's black town car deposited him at the front of the large evening queue. The doorman, who had previously been tipped off to Yi's arrival, spotted the car before its wheels came to a complete stop.

The driver stood at attention as Yi exited the rear door of his ride and bypassed the waiting crowd. Yi and Moon often met at the offbeat club. Ren Yi was glad tonight would be the last such meeting. He planned to give Moon another final ultimatum. He scanned the pulsing crowd and was disappointed that Moon was not on site. He did catch a glimpse of Brian Walker standing by himself in a poorly lit corner of the club.

Walker had also managed to skip the waiting line. He'd greased the palm of a security guard standing his post at the rear entrance. During the earlier meeting on the *Opium Princess*, Yi had agreed to let Walker spy on his late-evening meeting with Doug Moon. Walker had arrived almost a full hour early and had spent the time taking in the odd gyrations on the dance floor.

Walker had promised not to interfere. He was only after a glimpse of the now infamous Doug Moon. With a visual image to go along with a name, Walker felt he would have enough to get his agency started on an investigation into the whereabouts of Moon and the younger Yi sibling. He hoped that it was not too late.

Walker stood by himself in the dark corner and scanned the club for Yi's former classmate. He casually munched on pistachio nuts. He noticed nothing out of the ordinary, if you consider a sea of bodies throbbing up and down in unison ordinary. He was dressed in casual beachwear, consisting of a T-shirt from a local brewpub, chino shorts, and leather Tevas. Walker wanted to be ignored. He had bought a Seattle Mariners cap from a gift shop and pulled it low over his forehead.

Yi seemed oblivious to the local dress code, wearing a poplin business suit, a bright tie, and wingtips. He would not be ignored.

Shortly after midnight, with the crowd on the dance floor slowing a bit, the door to the club opened widely, and Doug Moon strode in. His suit was darker than Yi's, but the general motif was similar, right down to the wingtips. Moon and Yi greeted each other with a handshake and a long embrace. The friendly meeting, combined with their almost perfectly coordinated attire worried Walker. He thought for a moment that this might be a setup. There were no fellow NIA agents to back him up. In fact, nobody except Ren Yi and Kate Jensen even knew he was in Seattle. He could feel the moisture building on his palms and, for a brief second, toyed with an unceremonious exit through the rear door. He nervously tossed two pistachios in his month. Then three. Then four.

Walker never had a chance to react. He recognized the extended tube barrel of the silencer as soon as it appeared from behind Moon's lapel. With bold deference to the surrounding crowd, Moon raised the gun and leveled it at Yi's temple. The attack was quick and visually brutal. Moon fired two times. Walker watched the event in slow motion as Yi's head lurched sideways then backward before almost recovering to normal. His hands and arms twitched, and an almost confused look came over his face just before his legs gave way. The attack was over in a matter of seconds.

Moon's shirtsleeve bore the red cells of Ren Yi. He was not one to admire his handiwork. He turned, dropped the weapon, and walked casually past the bouncers, through the front door, and out onto the city street. Walker's legs were obviously not taking orders from his brain. He quickly made a path for the rear entrance, exited the club into the alleyway, and charged toward the street. Moon was walking away from him and toward a waiting taxi when Walker called his name. Moon paused briefly and turned, exposing a broad smile.

The smile faded quickly. Both men stood frozen. In the brightly lit street, Walker was able to get his first clean glimpse of Moon. They had met before. The taxi driver emerged from the vehicle, and he was also a familiar face. Moon's smile returned—a smile devoid of friendliness. Moon and his driver, Tung, had been together for the infamous, bullet-ridden car, van, and truck chase in Frederick, Maryland.

"Hello, Mr. Walker."

"Hello, Mr. Moon."

Moon gestured toward the larger-than-life silhouette of a man standing beside him.

"Mr. Tung, meet Brian Walker. He's the one responsible for the hole in your arm."

"Sorry about your arm. I meant to blow your head off."

Without a word, the giant man moved toward him. Walker moved away quickly. The crowd mulling outside the club saw them both coming, and most hustled out of the way. The oversized thug kept coming. He plowed through the crowd just a few yards behind Walker.

Walker raced down the sidewalk, past a closed gas station, and out into the middle of street. Walker yelled back to the nightclub crowd. "Call the police."

Mr. Tung was still coming.

Even in the wee hours of the morning, the sight of a large man wearing a designer suit chasing a tourist down the middle of Madison Street caused a commotion. The Seattle city streets are full of all kinds, but this combination was quite unique. Walker turned off the street and into a nearby hotel lobby. There was a loud crash behind him. Tung had slipped trying to negotiate the only unlocked lobby door. Walker made a dash for the front desk. Thinking only about self-preservation, he leaped over the high desk wall and cowered behind the deserted check-in counter.

Tung's own misstep infuriated him. He looked feverishly for Walker and moved spastically around the lobby area. Walker could hear him knocking over chairs and yanking open doors in his search. Walker knew it would only be a matter of seconds before he was discovered. Then, strangely, he heard nothing.

Walker managed a quick peek when silence became the norm.

Tung was moving quickly, skipping steps as he ran up a two-story escalator to a second-floor lobby area and open-air bar. At almost the same instant, Walker caught a glimpse of a slow moving police car out on the street and made his move.

Brian Walker's exit from the check-in desk was less than graceful; his trailing leg got stuck on the business side of the desk, and he crashed to the lobby floor. The loud thump echoed through the quiet hotel lobby. A grunt from the large pursuer was the only stimulus necessary for Walker to continue. He sprinted out of the lobby and hailed the passing police car.

———

The worst of an overnight storm brushed Seattle proper before drifting southeast toward the airport. The winds dropped precipitously as the storm moved farther inland, but a steady rain continued for almost three more hours. Brian Walker's previously warm and inviting downtown hotel room was now dark and felt like a cell.

Apart from a small bruise on his forehead and a sore left buttock, he felt reasonably healthy given the trials of the previous evening. Walker lay on the large hotel bed and stared at the mosaic of paisley decorating the bedside wall. He summoned images of the evening before: dinner on the exotic yacht, the colorful nightclub patrons, a slow motion murder, and a foot chase that had left him with a bruised ego.

Stretching under the soft bed sheets, he groaned, feeling the pain in his legs and back. He rolled out of bed and swung his feet to the floor. He sat upright for many minutes before his bladder changed his focus to the bathroom door. Twenty-five minutes later, he emerged from the steamy room with a less-than-thirsty hotel towel covering his broad shoulders. He went to the pile of folded clothes on a nearby chair and found a pair of olive slacks and a Cavaliers Lacrosse T-shirt. A pair of upside-down running sneakers served as a paperweight for the stack of clean clothes. He finished dressing, shaved and arranged his dirty clothes into two piles, those that were either soiled or wrinkled beyond repair and those with some life left.

Shortly after leaving the hotel lobby, he indulged in his favorite morning ceremony by visiting a local coffee shop. He stole a full thirty minutes to enjoy a vanilla latté and a sugar-encrusted corn something while eyeing the soggy Seattle foot traffic.

A colleague at NIA had already profiled Ren Yi's company. His primary office was only a few miles from the coffee shop. Walker marked time, waiting almost an hour for an NIA investigator by the name of Tyler Newton to arrive at the corporate headquarters of Putuo Development, Inc. Putuo was the budding software concern founded by the deceased Ren Yi.

According to the NIA brief that greeted Walker at Regatta Peninsula, Ren Yi was the fifty-first richest person in the state. His death was a newsworthy event. A local cable station profiled Yi and his extravagant but charitable lifestyle, giving no mention of the *Opium Princess* or his younger sister, Ellen. He was portrayed as an unintended victim of a gang shootout—a surprising outcome given that only two shots had been fired and nobody else in the club had been injured.

Walker spent the next three hours in the company of NIA field investigator Newton. They scoured every inch of Yi's office. They searched for any shred of evidence that might help lead them to Doug Moon or Ellen Yi. They found nothing exceptional.

They were interrupted when another NIA agent arrived with lunch. Walker thanked the young agent and asked him to leave the bag on the large, black desk in the middle of the room. Walker knelt to pick up a plastic spoon that fell out of the lunch delivery. He noticed a large space underneath the desk. There was a one-inch gap between the oversized surface and the underlying support. The top of the large desk seemed to float unsupported.

"What do you make of this?" Walker asked Newton, pointing to the gap in the desk.

"There must be some kind of concealed support system. Maybe it's an aesthetic design feature."

"I don't think so. Give me a hand with this," prompted Walker.

Mirroring Walker's motions at the other end, Newton grabbed the wide desktop with two hands. The top lifted slowly, with a motion similar to a piston-driven storm door. The top stopped, and there was an audible click as the desktop locked in place, ninety-degrees from its original position.

"Well, look what we found," said Walker. The interior area of the desk looked like a frozen black pool. Walker studied the blackness just long enough to declare the unit suspicious. He did this without speaking, but Newton was still able to nod in agreement. It took them another ten minutes to negotiate the touch screen remote control attached to the underneath side of the desk lid. The dark pool came to life.

After an hour of poking at the remote, the pair agreed that the visual show-and-tell had run its course. Few of the images had added to Walker's mental database. Except for a short series of images detailing the construction of the peninsula office complex, he had seen it all before. The 3-D images were a rerun of the still images retrieved from the notebook PC in Amherst lab. There were no new hints embedded in the images, no date or timeline labels, no exact locations, only a U.S. map dotted with graphic icons.

"What do you make of these images?"

"I'm not sure," answered a disgruntled Walker, shaking his head. He had no interest in disclosing his intimate relationship with the bioterrorism investigation to a junior NIA agent.

Walker did come away from the search with one unexpected benefit. He had quietly lifted an elaborate, hand-addressed envelope from Ren Yi's inbox. It was an invitation to a gala at the Chinese Embassy in San Francisco.

———

Just a few hours' drive to the east, Ellen Yi completed the final-stage testing of her rewakened recipe. It was the last step before she began the arduous and repetitive task of mass-producing the enhanced virus stock. As a rule, a virus does not survive long outside its host, and Ellen and Doug both worried that the strain transferred from Amherst might not have survived the journey. Her last-stage testing had put those worries to rest. All that was left now was the destruction of the latest test subjects. There were six in all, two monkeys, a rodent, and two male humans.

19

Mark Bekins realized that Gwen Saunders was carrying a highly contagious virus and that it was probably airborne. Bekins vaguely recalled a textbook story about a smallpox outbreak in the early 1970s.
An infected patient quarantined in a European hospital had infected
over twenty others. None of them had ever stepped foot inside the
hospital quarantine wing. Smallpox particles have a disposition to
drift a long distance, and in this textbook case, the patient was a
smoker and kept his window open for ventilation. The viral particles
traveled outside the hospital walls and infected many of the patients
on the upper floors.

Bekins returned his attention to Saunders. He had all he could
do to communicate with the girl through the mobile bio gear that he
was required to wear in the quarantine unit. The relatively lightweight
suit was a mobile version of the blue suit that he wore in the lab. The
mobile suit managed airflow via a scuba-like tank strapped to the in-

side of the suit.

Saunders did not show any visible signs of infection. She paced the small room with her arms across her chest. As she had not been allowed to shower, her sand-colored locks hung limply to her shoulders. Her eyes revealed the exhaustion she must have felt.

"How are you feeling, Ms. Saunders?" Bekins asked from his blue bio suit.

"Like crap," she snapped. "And my throat is burning."

"Please sit down and try to relax," Bekins urged. "Tell me as much as you can remember after you were abducted."

She began with a short synopsis of the chase at Fort Detrick and the hasty helicopter retreat.

> At some point during the helicopter ride, she heard a soft pop and an accompanying pain in her thigh. The last thing she remembered was sitting in her seat unable to move.
>
> She awoke alone in a windowless room about eight-foot square with a small sink basin and toilet in the corner. She wasn't sure how long she had been there or how she'd gotten there but was certain that it was some kind of cell. The only sign of life was the occasional passage of food through a locking mailbox device on the bottom of her door. She had no concept of time during her stay in the room. She could only guess by her body hair that it had been a number of days.
>
> At some point during her captivity, she was awakened by a new sound. Her cell door had been opened, but there was no sign of life on the other side. The door opened into a windowless hallway that led

to another open door at the end of a long corridor.

Through this door, she discovered another detainee. He was standing motionless in a room about three times the size of the room she had been kept in. There was a brief exchange. The other captive's story was almost identical to hers. He said his name was Kevin. There were a few remarkable differences though. Kevin's room had a narrow row of opaque windows, and he complained of a soreness and swelling in his upper left arm. Neither could muster a credible theory for why they were being kept in this place.

It wasn't long after the meeting that Kevin complained of body aches and a fever. In the evening, his fever spiked, and it was apparent that he was very sick and needed medical attention. She settled in and tried her best to care for the young man but had very little to offer other than kind words. Much to her surprise, the aches and fever were short-lived, and in a matter of hours, he was feeling better.

A few days passed, and they were getting along as reasonably as could be expected under the circumstances. It was sometime in the afternoon or early evening when she noticed a distinct change in the young man. He had been exhibiting a mild cough through the day, but it wasn't until evening that Gwen noticed red areas on his face and exposed arms.

The next day, the areas of red had spread. The areas were bumpy and looked like a bad rash, much like what you would see in a bad case of poison ivy. The rash turned to pimples. These pimple heads were

*not small like acne but were large, marble-sized blis-
ters. They seemed to be rising all over his body. The
blisters were breaking out everywhere. He had blisters
inside his mouth and ears. You could tell by his actions that the blisters and sores were extremely
painful. It seemed as if everything was happening in
fast motion. It wasn't long before a new fever broke
out. Kevin was very aware of his condition, so much
so it seemed that the affliction had heightened his
senses. The burning sensation had become unbear-
able. He began to scream and move around violently.*

*What happened next seemed unbelievable. To-
tally unexpectedly, a spacesuit-clad character carrying a stainless gun entered the room. In the moments
before darkness, Gwen remembered thinking that the
unknown visitor's spacesuit seemed remarkably high
tech. It was not the generic suit that you see on TV
worn by those at the scene of a chemical spill. This
suit looked more like something an astronaut would
wear. The intruder shot her in the arm with the gun-
like device. That was her last memory from the room.*

With a distant stare, her dissertation came to an end. She
turned her focus back to Bekins and coughed. Only then did she notice
the onset of her second fever in as many days.

————

Every building at the CDC had a story. Veterans working at the main
campus could tell stories of countless deadly animal viruses that were
examined at the facility, but few had come face-to-face with a deadly

human disease. The newer workers and transient employees were to-tally unaware that the secret campus south of the city existed. When John Pierce had first traveled to the off-campus Level 4 facilities at the CDC, he'd been uncomfortable. He was certain that no man-made infrastructure was capable of preventing a microscopic virus from es-caping. After his last visit, he'd vowed never to return. However, when he received word that Gwen Saunders had been recovered and trans-ported to the CDC facility at Cedar Grove, he couldn't get there fast enough.

When his flight landed at Hartsfield Airport, it was a sunny but chilly day in Atlanta. John Pierce took in the endless rows of Geor-gia Pines that lined both sides of the rural landscape as he drove to-ward the Cedar Grove CDC lab. He was trying to mentally drift away and ease his building sense of anxiety. He tried to dwell on the mem-ories of his weekend in New Orleans and his subsequent romantic en-counters with Gwen Saunders. He thought back to the intelligent and charming woman that he'd first met in New Orleans. His images of Gwen were still clean, but he worried that, in less than an hour, his mental images would be replaced by terrifying images that would haunt him for the rest of his life.

The rural and mental tours ended when the lead vehicle and its driver bid farewell and directed Pierce's car through the second se-curity gate and into the lifeless tunnel beyond. His car moved slowly through the brightly lit tunnel that led to the subterranean CDC lab and conference facility.

Some of Pierce's anxiousness was forced away by his need to stay strong and supportive of Gwen. Regardless of the evil that might disguise her external beauty, he wanted to be energetic and positive when he saw her. He parked the car and walked the last few feet to the facility's underground entrance. One last security check, and he was admitted.

He was escorted to a private conference facility where he endured a short reintroduction to Mark Bekins. After that, he dove in with a series of questions.

"What is the longevity for someone infected with smallpox?" he asked. He held his breath and waited for the answer.

"There is no fixed end point. The general prognosis from this point in the infection is ten to sixteen days," answered Mark Bekins, with whom Gwen Saunders's fate rested. "Keep in mind that not all cases are terminal. Historically, only 30 percent of the cases have been fatal."

Pierce closed his eyes for a moment then opened them. "Have any of your animals recovered?"

Bekins shook his head. "None yet, but remember, we've only had an animal model of the virus for about two weeks now."

"This is not a documented strain of the virus, is it?" pressed Pierce.

"No, it's not like anything we have cataloged or anything we can match from our reference strains in the freezer."

———

While Mark Bekins flailed away in the lab, Brian Walker chased anything that smelled funny in the Seattle area. Neither party was having any success. The only certainty was that time was running out.

20

The political infighting grew worse as the days wore on. A week passed with no headway in the chase to find Doug Moon, Ellen Yi, and their secret location. With the nation's safety in jeopardy, Director Pierce was ready to tell all. The pressure from Director Baum at the Centers for Disease Control had reached a climax.

The director for the Department of Health and Human Services was the only person outside the inner circle who knew that there had been domestic smallpox casualties. His subordinate, Deputy Director Andres Garcia, hadn't been brought into the inner circle yet. Garcia had spent the previous seven years working in Washington DC in the Labor Department as the associate director for labor statistics. He now played the same role for the Department of Health and Human Services. His subtitle was associate director for international statistics.

In regular times, communications between the CDC, NIA, and

HHS was a slow process. The organizations exchanged highly secure e-mail and an occasional secure phone call. In the days since Saunders's rescue, the communication traffic increased dramatically. It was like a game of musical chairs and nobody, including NIA Director Pierce, wanted to be left standing if all hell broke loose. Judging from the rhetoric in the most recent e-mail from the CDC director, the boiling point was near.

———

Director John Pierce put down the latest intelligence file. He decided not to wait any longer. At the earliest possible time, whenever it was convenient for the other department heads, he would brief them on the full sequence of events, beginning with the discovery in the Gulf and ending with Brian Walker's trials in Seattle.

No one really expected the various department heads to agree on where to meet. Each department head contended that the problem fell squarely in his department's domain and insisted that the summit be held at his headquarters. The fact that the trio had agreed to get together at all, on short notice, was itself remarkable.

So they agreed to meet at three different venues simultaneously.

———

At 4:00 a.m., the pager on Andres Garcia's nightstand went off. He silenced it and tried to roll over to kiss his wife on the cheek. It was not to be this morning; his four-year-old son had managed to unceremoniously squeeze his way into their bed during the overnight. Andres rolled back the other way and exited the bed the same way he had entered it only a few hours earlier.

Garcia headed down to the kitchen in his boxers to return the message. He recognized the number; the message was always the same. He was not concerned. Alerts like this had become commonplace in the years since the September 11 attack. As the deputy director of Health and Human Services, it was his job to follow the progression of any Level 4 viral outbreak or, as had been the case to date, supposed Level 4 outbreak.

He languished in the shower and then dressed. Peering into his closet, he picked out a dark gray business suit and chose a white shirt and blue tie. While adjusting his tie in the mirror, he noticed another gray hair and plucked it from his full head of dark hair. He didn't think he was old and certainly didn't want to appear that way. Back in the kitchen, he left a note on the counter for his wife.

> *I came home last night, I really did! Everything's cool.*
> *I need to run to the office to show my face, probably*
> *another thirty-five-year-old with a bad case of the*
> *chicken pox or something. I'll call later. xooxxxo*

While he was backing his car out of the garage there was another page, this time from his contact at the CDC. *Par for the course*, he thought. *As soon as I'm out of the house, the false alarm sound comes in.* He stopped at the end of the driveway and thought about going back in the house for a few more hours of sleep.

Garcia gazed back over the roof of his Washington townhouse at the bright orange sky. He thought about how his attitude had changed over the past year. All his achievements and efforts in the field of statistics seemed to be for not. He had eagerly accepted the position as deputy director, believing that such an appointment at his young age would jumpstart his career. He'd never imagined that he would become a glorified secretary for his less-than-exciting boss.

He backed his ubiquitous government issue Ford Taurus onto the street and headed south towards the Capitol. His pager went off again; this time it was from a number at the White House. The text message that accompanied the page requested that he immediately proceed to the White House. The director would meet him there. Garcia had only been to the White House twice before, once with a small gathering of family and friends for his lightly attended swearing in ceremony. The other time was during a department show of force for newly passed Medicare legislation, a program that he was sure would not be around long enough to benefit his generation.

By 5:45 a.m., the DC traffic began to build, and it was well past 6:15 by the time Andres Garcia pulled up to the White House gate. The security procedure at the facility was painfully inefficient; it was a full hour before the gate was opened and he was allowed through on to the facility grounds.

As Garcia exited his car, a secret service agent walked up to him and said, "This way, sir."

Garcia wondered, *What's going on? Did I do something wrong?* His shirt felt a bit damp.

The agent escorted him through a doorway into a section of the White House that he had not seen before. The entrance was like an oversized hatchway, similar to the kind found leading into the basement of a house. The pair entered a short hallway that was barren of windows. Garcia's escort opened a password-protected door and gestured down a long corridor toward a group mulling outside a meeting room. Andres Garcia recognized one of the assembled and joined the group.

After a series of inquisitions, to which Andres had no answers, the group was corralled into the meeting room. The important people were already seated. The sight of the other participants in the conference room momentarily stopped Garcia and his colleagues. Garcia recognized one of the three as the vice president of the United States. The newcomers were invited to sit. A brief but very formal round of introductions followed; it included the vice president, a few cabinet members, the director of the CDC, members of various intelligence and counterterrorism departments, a group via satellite at the NIA headquarters across town, a CDC virologist via satellite in Atlanta, most of the joint chiefs, and a gaggle of army brass.

When the doors were closed on all three meeting sites, there were close to forty people, including Bekins at the CDC via videophone. Many attendees felt charged to bring along a lackey. Pierce was in no position to fight the broad-based attendance. Any meeting in Washington was subject to leaks, and this one would be no different. It was only a matter of time before the rumors began to fly.

The vice president stood and walked to the end of the table; in a pensive trance, he looked down at the conference table.

"Four weeks ago, three army medical officers were rescued by a coast guard cutter from an abandoned oil platform in the Gulf of Mexico. The rescued parties were flown via helicopter to a civilian hospital in Mobile, Alabama. Fortunately, a perceptive ER physician refused the cargo and, instead, accompanied the group, who were redirected to a dormant naval facility in another part of the city. The physician suspected smallpox and contacted the CDC for advice.

"Within ten hours, a CDC away team arrived in Alabama, quarantined the naval facility, and provided secure transportation to Atlanta for one living and two deceased victims, as well as two exposed coast guard pilots and the ER physician." The vice president paused.

Garcia looked around the room. Everyone was silent. *Remarkable*, he thought, *for a town where everybody wanted to be heard.*

The vice president turned the meeting over to an extremely quiet and nervous Mark Bekins, whose larger-than-life image was displayed on a wall-sized monitor at the far end of the table.

Bekins started by outlining the dangerous situation. He stated that the results of three separate tests had confirmed the existence of smallpox in the three victims. Additionally, he noted that the pilots and physician were infection free.

Bekins quoted the U.S. secretary of Health and Human Services:

> *Bioterrorism presents unique challenges since it differs dramatically from other forms of terrorism and national emergencies. While explosions or chemical attacks cause immediate and visible casualties, an intentional release of a biological weapon will unfold over the course of days or weeks, potentially culminating in a major epidemic. Until sufficient numbers of people arrive in emergency rooms, doctors' offices, and health clinics with similar illnesses, there may be no sign that a bioterrorist attack has taken place. Individuals with symptoms may be at considerable distance from the site of initial exposure, both in terms of onset of disease and geographic location. Moreover, the bioweapons most likely to be used are pathogens not routinely seen by health care providers. Medical providers generally are not familiar with the diagnosis and treatment of these disorders and may even fail initially to recognize symptoms and signs. These scenarios underscore the importance of preparing for the possibility of biological terrorism.*

"We were not prepared in this case, only lucky. To date, there have been no other reports of infection," finished Bekins. He made no mention of Gwen Saunders.

21

On the sixth day after Gwen Saunders's recovery, Mark Bekins arrived at the CDC Cedar Grove facility before sunrise. He was already exhausted but anxious to get to work. He'd spent the entire evening with a stack of epidemiology textbooks, and he had new ideas. His eyes ached from straining to read the small print in the reference material. He needed coffee.

Bekins's lab hours had varied greatly in recent weeks. In the time since he'd been blessed to work in the Level 4 lab, his weekly lab time had ranged from just over thirteen hours per week to the almost thirty hours he'd spent in the blue suit last week. His skin was dry and chafed, not just in the usual places but all over his body. The cool, dry air in the suit excited the eczema on his torso and extremities. Only his hands and feet seemed immune.

Mark Bekins was not into the thrill of victory. He relied on his mental faculties, a regimen of disciplined work habits, and structured, logic-based processes rather than the trial-and-error efforts often implemented by others in his field. Three times a week, he would take in a yoga session on the campus of nearby Emory University. Today, he would skip the yoga session. He was ready for a full-day session in the lab.

Bekins was ready to give his latest idea a go. He entered the Level 4 lab at 8:00 a.m. He wasn't feeling particularly well. His head was aching, his throat was aching, and the rest of him was just exhausted. He wasn't sure if he had come down with something or if he was just overly tired from a long night of reading.

Bekins would be working alone this morning. He thought it best not expose his new ideas to too many eyes. He pulled on a salmon-colored set of surgical scrubs. It was a new color for the lab. The old ones had been washed and sterilized so many times that they were literally falling apart. The socks were new also, but they were the same color as the old ones. He carried the socks in his left hand and moved into the bland light of the ultraviolet chamber. After his session in the chamber, he put on his blue suit and entered the Level 4 lab environment.

In the Level 4 lab, his blue suit hung limp over his shoulders. He pulled down on one of the air hoses and plugged in. There was a rush of air, and his suit filled. The cool air felt good on his face, but the noise generated by the rushing air didn't help his headache. He spent the next hour setting up his new experiment.

The Level 4 lab was symmetrical, in the shape of a rectangle. It was thirty-five feet long and twenty feet on the ends. There were three animal cages mounted on the wall at the far end of the room. Two were vacant. The middle cage contained a monkey from Southeast Asia. Bekins had installed a rotary-style padlock on the cage door. Some of the earlier inhabitants had figured out the latch system, and he wasn't going to take chances with this guy. This monkey was not the friendliest character; with light brown fur and large fangs he would probably give a pit bull a run for its money.

Bekins was almost ready to bring the monkey out. He made one last movement with the virus. He was going to use the strain of the virus retrieved from Gwen Saunders. There were two vials sitting alone on a shelf on the long wall to the right, and both were labeled "GS strain." He opened one of the vials and transferred the liquid into a syringe. His hands were sweating. He was holding enough of the virus to infect an entire New York borough. Bekins moved slowly, acting as if the vials and the syringe contained nitroglycerin. He gently put the full syringe back on the shelf next to the vials of smallpox stock from Saunders.

The lone animal was quiet. Bekins had given him a tranquilizer shot in the thigh. The animal was still awake but looked ready to go out at any moment. He waited a few more minutes, and the monkey was ready. Bekins unlocked and opened the latch on the middle cage and carefully lifted the animal out. He carried the monkey facing away from him with a hand under each of the animals armpits. He didn't want the long-toothed animal to be facing him if it happened to wake up.

The scheduled morning procedure was simple. He injected the monkey with millions of particles of the GS strain before slowly pulling the needle out of the animal's leg. Just as he was about to put down the used syringe, one the animal's legs jerked and bumped his left arm, the same arm that was holding the smallpox-riddled syringe. The worst result came true. Bekins's arm was knocked back against his own body, and the dirty needle penetrated his blue suit just above his waist.

Bekins didn't panic. He slowly rolled the monkey over onto its side and carried it back to his cage. Bekins's mind remained clear. He moved through the next ten minutes as if on autopilot. He threw

out the syringe in a biohazard container built into the wall and began
to clean up his workspace.

He suddenly felt more anxious about his brush with the virus.
He sighed heavily and swallowed hard. Had he just made a pinhole
in his suit, or was the penetration more invasive? Bekins decided not
to stay in the lab. He spent seven long minutes in the Lysol decontamination shower before he moved to the transition area and peeled
off his blue suit. He quickly moved to the deserted locker room. In
the warm shower, he examined the area just below and to the left of
his belly button. The lighting was not good in the shower area. He
thought there might be a small red spot, but he couldn't be sure. His
fair skin was littered with irregularities. He dressed and moved
through the brightly lit passageway leading away from the lab area
and into the conference facility. He hoped to get a better view of his
abdomen in the brightly lit conference room.

John Pierce blocked his way. He was milling around outside
the conference facility when Bekins came from the lab area.

Oh great, thought Bekins. He tried to move the other way. He
was not interested in stopping to talk to Pierce, but the decision was
being made for him. Pierce had already started in his direction. Bekins
saw determination in Pierce's eyes and knew that avoiding him was
not an option.

"How's she doing today?" he asked, confronting Bekins in
the corridor.

Pierce had not been allowed to enter the quarantine area to
visit Saunders. His only view of Saunders was via a wide-angle shot
from a closed-circuit monitor in the nurses' area.

Bekins did not want to hang around. He kept walking as he
answered the barrage of questions coming from Pierce. "She's doing
surprisingly well, all things considered. The virus doesn't seem to be
taking a strong hold on her. She should be past the highly contagious

stage of the disease. Would you like to go in and visit today? You can, provided you wear a surgical mask and scrubs."

"I'd very much like that. What's your best guess on her prognosis?" responded Pierce.

Bekins stopped. Pierce had hold of his arm. "I'm not going to promise anything, but she does seem to be handling the disease better than anyone here expected. I am concerned about her energy level. She has been in and out of consciousness for three days, and I can't figure out why. Most smallpox victims become increasingly sober and more aware of their condition as the disease progresses. The one wild card with Gwen is her internal organs. The quarantine area does not have any high-end imaging equipment, so we haven't been able to get a clear image of her internal organs."

Bekins excused himself and returned to the lab area. He had his own welfare to attend to.

———

A quiet nurse nudged John Pierce out of the conference room and through a series of hallways. They stopped near a break room just outside the isolation ward. The nurse instructed him on the finer art of dressing in scrubs and how to enter and exit Gwen's zero flow room.

There was no sign of life in the corridor that led to the quarantine ward. The entire wing had been deserted. The nurses' station appeared to have been abandoned in a hurry. Only an old gurney left askew in the hallway gave evidence that patients had inhabited the area.

The entrance to Gwen's room was blocked by a series of hanging plastic sheets—nothing as sophisticated as he had imagined, but rather plain plastic sheeting. It was the kind of sheeting that might be used to line a backyard ice rink or control dust during a home-remodeling project. He had envisioned a series of airlock doors, but Gwen was being kept in a new zero flow room that restricted the air circulation to a controlled environment. The plastic sheets were to prevent outside air from being sucked into the quarantine area. There wasn't any risk of air escaping into the rest of the facility.

Memories began to wash over him as he made his way through the simple air barrier. He tried to close his eyes and conjure a picture of Gwen the way she was when they had last met, but continuing waves of guilt clouded his vision. He should have been there to protect her. He should have insisted that he accompany her on the counter-eavesdropping mission.

John Pierce took a deep breath and pushed the last plastic sheet aside. He stepped inside and waited for the shock, but it never came. He had expected to be confronted by a disfigured and unrecognizable face. After all, he had seen pictures of it all week. But the sleeping face seemed more angelic than ever. Her face was a bit pale and drawn, but the features were still splendidly innocent.

Gwen seemed to be asleep.

Pierce walked slowly around the bed and took a good look at his fallen friend. She needed her rest, so he stood and stared. He was exhilarated by her peaceful condition. He was not in any rush and enjoyed the peaceful time with her. He carefully lowered himself into a seated position at the end of her bed.

After what seemed like only a few minutes, he looked at his watch. It had been over twenty minutes since he had first entered her room. He stood and moved toward the head of her bed. He rubbed her arm, but she didn't move, and for many minutes, he stood over her frozen, not wanting to disturb her but at the same time feeling a little like a trespasser.

Gwen wore comfortable-looking flannel sleepwear garnished with a silk collar and matching waistband. She'd lost weight, but other than that she looked wonderful. Her sandy blonde hair was clean and in perfect order, but something else seemed wrong.

Under the failing evening light, John moved closer to the bed. He began to realize that Gwen Saunders was not breathing. He caught on slowly at first. He shook his head and spoke softly to her, but there was no response. He leaned over her and touched her exposed wrist. It was cold. There wasn't a pulse.

Gwen Saunders was dead.

There were two chairs in Gwen's sparsely decorated room. Pierce backed into the one by the window and, for a long time, he sat there across from the bed—waiting for his friend to awaken. But Gwen lay motionless. The only sound in the room was his heavy breathing and rapid heartbeat. He stared at her small breasts and waited from them to rise, even just slightly. *Up and down—just enough to start the blood pumping*, he thought. But nothing happened.

His intimate friend was dead. She lay comfortably in her pajamas with a relaxed look on her face. She seemed to know that her sleep would be eternal. His lips quivered, and he rushed the bed and embraced her. Where were the doctors? Where was the nurse? Where was Bekins? Not that any of them could help.

Alone with Gwen, the tears flowed easily, and he thought back to his own demons. *Why hadn't he been there when she was abducted? Why hadn't he found her sooner?* The list would go on, probably for the rest of his life.

He knelt beside her and put his head on her chest, and he whispered, "I love you. Please wake up."

22

An evening on the town with Kate Jensen was all that Brian Walker could think of. The ride from the San Francisco Airport rental car agency seemed to take forever. With Ren Yi's personalized invitation in his Tuxedo pocket, Walker rang the doorbell at the Lombard Street address Kate had e-mailed to him. On the second ring, the voluptuous Paris Rand came to the door. The presence of Kate's late twentysomething assistant was an unexpected plus on Walker's adventure to San Francisco. Paris stood in the doorway wearing a tight-fitting, short sleeve cardigan sweater over a short, black lace evening dress. Walker noticed that a cascade of shimmering curls had replaced her normally conservative hairstyle, and her always-remarkable lips were a much brighter red than usual. Boldly, she looked him up and down with a confidant grin.

She smiled, obviously enjoying the surprised look on Walker's face.

"Brian Walker in the flesh, as I live and breathe," she said sarcastically.

"I was expecting Kate, but I guess you'll do," he said with a little apprehension in his voice.

"Not so fast," called a familiar voice from the hallway. Kate Jensen walked briskly toward the front door. She wore a classic black dress with a plunging neckline and pearls. At the moment, she was also wearing fleece-lined Crocs.

After recovering from a short-lived dream, Walker forced himself past Paris and followed Kate into the living room. Walker made his best potato imitation and flopped onto the couch.

"I'm sorry that you were forced to go out of your way to pick me up. A college friend offered me use of her house, and you know how I hate hotels," said Jensen.

"How come Ms. Rand is here?"

"Paris has never been to San Francisco, so I offered to let her tag along. I'm sure she brought some work with her to justify the trip," Kate said with a shrug.

"Is she joining us this evening?"

"Over my dead body. I saw the way you greeted her at the door."

"I don't remember saying anything that could be considered out of line!"

"That's the problem. You didn't say anything. You just stood and drooled."

"Sorry."

"I guess it proves that you're human."

Paris skirted by the room and blew a kiss in the general direction of the couple. She headed out the door to a waiting taxi.

Walker looked at his watch impatiently.

"Okay, I get the hint. I just need to get my purse."

Jensen returned a minute later, pushing a small handgun into her open purse.

"You won't get very far with that thing. I'm sure the guards at the Chinese embassy have screening equipment staged at the entrances," stated a bothered Walker. He was not a fan of guns, and she knew it.

"I plan on leaving the purse in the car. Just a little added protection," she said, quietly reminding him of their last car ride together in Maryland. Kate kicked off her Crocs and stepped into a pair of high heel dress shows by the door.

Walker stood and held out his hand. "Your chariot awaits." He led her out the front door and down the sidewalk to the behemoth parked at the street corner. She stared in disappointment at the huge box on wheels—a gaudy yellow, no less.

"What possessed you to drive this thing?"

"It was either this or a Crown Victoria. You can stay for the shootout. I prefer a safe escape vehicle," he said with a laugh.

"I've never had the pleasure to ride in one that wasn't the color of vomit." She was referring to the camouflaged U.S. Army Humvee that they'd ridden in during their visit to the CDC in Atlanta.

"This is an H2, not the standard issue armed forces Humvee. This one has a fuel-injected, six liter V8 and a much more street savvy suspension. Plus a triple-sealed acoustical panel system, just in case you decide to test out all nine speakers at the same time."

Jensen decided to ignore the less-than-elegant vehicle and relaxed into the oversized leather seat. Walker turned the car downhill and away from the crooked part of Lombard Street to the intersection of Laguna. He turned left onto Laguna and moved the car smartly through the city traffic.

Parking anywhere near the embassy compound proved futile. Walker found a spot a few blocks away, though dangerously near a hydrant. He stepped off what he decided was about eleven feet of curb before returning to the car to retrieve his date.

The debriefing derby began almost as soon as she got out of the car. Walker had not been forthcoming when he'd first invited her out to the coast for a party.

"What do you want me to do while we're here?" she asked.

"I'm not sure," Walker said. "Try to enjoy the party."

"Are we meeting anyone in particular? Do you have a solid lead?" Jensen wanted to know.

"Um … no, and maybe," Walker said vaguely.

"Are other agencies involved?"

"Probably not."

"Uggh!" Jensen said in frustration. She suspected he was either flying blind or following one of his famous hunches. Walker didn't attend these kinds of events for pleasure. The prospect of spending hours in a room crowded with politicians and lawyers was almost revolting to him. Jensen stayed quiet for the remainder of the walk to the embassy. The cool early evening air felt good, and she was glad to be out alone with Walker.

Four of San Francisco's finest were on patrol outside the embassy compound. Two comrades wearing Chinese dress military uniforms were checking bags and politely bowing to guests just inside the gate. The pair paused at the checkpoint while a guard checked their IDs against the guest list. There was a little commotion inside the guardhouse. A guard emerged holding their IDs in one hand and a copy of the guest list in the other. In a strong but amiable tone, he told them that he couldn't find them on the list. Using a previously prepared speech, Walker explained how the late Ren Yi's personal assistant had asked them to attend, even after his tragic death. The guard was not interested in the diatribe.

Jensen pushed Walker aside. She spoke a few words to the

guard in his native language.

"Have a good evening," the guard said, granting the pair access to the party with a slight bow.

A skeptical Walker returned the bow and followed Kate Jensen to the gate and on through an ornate garden path to the main house.

Walker stayed silent for many minutes before turning to a smiling Jensen. "What was that about? I knew you could speak a little Chinese, but I had no idea that you could fib in the language."

"It wasn't much of a lie. The first thing I said to him was true. I do have to go to the bathroom badly. I lied about you stealing your traveling boss's invitation to try and impress me and get lucky."

"And that worked?"

"It did when I told him that you weren't going to succeed."

"Very funny. You were able to communicate all that with just a few sounds?"

Kate just nodded and offered a wide, albeit smug smile. Walker took her by the arm and led her through the embassy house front door. Bypassing the receiving line, she headed straight to the restroom. Walker stood guard outside the powder room, and with his arms crossed, he took in the party scene. The large lobby and accompanying ballroom reminded him of the lobby and ballroom at the Mark Hopkins hotel just a few blocks away. The embassy shared its combination French chateau and Spanish Renaissance-style architecture with the hotel. Both buildings had been erected in the mid '20s.

A few minutes later, the couple passed back through the lobby and into the capacious ballroom. The focal point of the three-story high cathedral ceiling was the enormous chandelier that hung seemingly from a small thread. Walker surveyed the ballroom landscape. The environment was reminiscent of the Washington power meetings that Kate would often force him to attend. It was an endless parade of fit woman on the arms of overweight lawyers or CEOs.

An army of caterers stood ready to serve. Fine California wines and local seafood were the fare for the evening. They moved across the crowded room to the bar, where Walker ordered a whiskey on one cube for himself and a draft beer from a local brewery for Jensen. At Walker's prodding, they continued the tour by stopping beside a young woman holding an offering of raw seafood.

"Precisely what are we looking for?" asked Kate as she chewed on a sesame cracker covered with raw tuna and too much wasabi.

"I'm not sure. Maybe an evil villain dressed in black or maybe nothing at all."

"I shouldn't have asked."

"Maybe we should interview the beautiful Asian woman standing alone in the corner," she offered.

"Walker glanced at the woman who Jensen was referring to. That's a smashing idea. Maybe you should stay here while I go over and interrogate her."

"And leave me alone, I don't think so."

"Then lead the way." Walker stood at attention with his arm outstretched.

"You're serious."

"We need to mix with the crowd. We don't want to stand out. After all, we *are* crashing the party."

Dutiful, Jensen followed Walker across the room toward the solitary woman. They stood a few feet away for many minutes before Walker approached her.

"Are you here alone?" he asked. He could feel Jensen's heat-seeking eyes burning a hole in the back of his head.

The woman nervously glanced to her left and right and then looked back down at the drink in her hand. She looked up again, but made no effort to speak. Walker thought she was going to turn and run.

"No, I'm meeting someone here," she said with a soft, diminutive tone, her eyes lowered further toward the floor.

Jensen leaned into the conversation. "We didn't mean to intrude. We just wanted to introduce ourselves. My name is Kate Jensen, and my bold friend is Brian Walker."

"Hello," she said with a slight bow. "My name is Ellen Yi."

Walker paused. It took Jensen another minute to catch on. When she did, there was an audible sound as she drew in her breath. There was no emotional outburst and no excited body language. The woman obviously was not familiar with either Walker or Jensen. Walker's only response was a slight increase in his heart rate and a quick look around to see if anyone was watching them. Jensen, on the other hand, stood horrified. She was staring into the face of a murderer, and it looked nothing like she envisioned. The woman's face was soft with a warm and gentle smile. There was no hint of evil or coldness. She stood with a grace and dignity that seemed impossible, knowing her history.

Walker seemed to be enjoying the meeting, but Jensen was becoming increasingly agitated and was on the verge of screaming at Ms. Yi. Walker wanted to step in and break up the inevitable, but before he could even come up with an exit strategy, the unthinkable happened.

Ellen Yi introduced a new arrival. "May I offer Doug Moon. Doug, this is Kate Jensen and Brian Walker."

For a moment, nothing was said. Walker took a small step backward. Jensen thought Walker was about to make an exit, but instead he held his composure and remained courteous. "We've already met," added Walker.

Ellen Yi blinked and her eyes shifted from Moon to Walker

and back again. "You ... you've met?" she stammered. She had no knowledge of Moon's escapades at the Seattle nightclub and Fort Detrick in Maryland.

Doug Moon looked past Jensen and stared directly into Walker's eyes. "Your government estimates that an outbreak could grow from fifteen hundred to fifteen thousand in a matter of weeks. I think the number is more like one hundred fifty thousand. What do you think?"

Walker, Jensen, and Ellen Yi were all caught off guard by Moon's comments. Ellen stepped back, nearly spilling the drink she was holding. She looked to Moon for direction. Walker was dumbfounded by Moon's blunt admission of guilt. He said nothing.

Moon was blind to the unspoken response. "The widespread infection forecast is not as farfetched as you think. Consider the number of mobile business travelers there are today. The large number of domestic and international flights that take off each day from U.S. airports would make the source of the infection and geographic spread impossible to track."

Ellen Yi began to pull nervously on Moon's sleeve.

"An interesting model," said Walker. "But meaningless against a vaccinated public."

"A clever comeback, but I happen to know firsthand that your man in Atlanta, or should I be more precise, Cedar Grove, has his own private battle to fight. I don't think he'll be offering a remedy to the virus anytime soon."

"I'm not sure I follow you?"

"Mark Bekins is keeping a secret from you, a deadly secret that is going to squash any hopes you have in our little battle."

Moon obviously had the upper hand. Ellen Yi was completely lost and wanted nothing more than to escape back to the Yakima compound. Kate Jensen was looking for an escape also, but Walker wanted to keep the conversation alive for as long as possible. There was already a fairly fertile information flow, and he wanted more.

"How do you propose to infect the public?"

Moon backed down. He could tell from Yi's expression that he was out of line. He snapped his fingers twice.

"I have a mutual friend I want to reintroduce to you."

Walker immediately sensed trouble. "I think it's time for us to go," he said to Jensen.

"I agree," spoke a large Asian man that Walker immediately recognized as the infamous Mr. Tung.

Acknowledging the diplomatic position of strength, Walker backed down. The embassy facility gave Moon and Yi all the protection they needed.

If Doug Moon or his rough sidekick Mr. Tung planned any offensive maneuver, they would certainly hold their attack until Walker and Jensen were safely out of the embassy facility and out of earshot of the guests.

The pair made a quick retreat from the embassy campus. They covered the two short blocks to the parked H2 in less than half the time of their earlier trip.

Walker was silent as he moved the large vehicle away from the curb and away from the Chinese embassy.

"So how do we deal with your friend and his female companion?" asked Kate Jensen.

"We ignore them until they slip. We need to find out where their base of operations is. Ellen Yi must still be in business, and that means that the enhanced virus is alive and well. I'm willing to bet its somewhere in the western United States."

"Great job narrowing the field of search," she said sarcastically. "Where do we start?"

"We start by asking Doug Moon's friend, Mr. Tung."

———

The assassins came to the Lombard Street home before light. They came in sets of two and surrounded the block in a well-coordinated attack. Mr. Tung spoke confidently into his hands-free communicator, making fine adjustments to his team members' positions.

"Do not fail," Tung warned them. "Mr. Moon will be very unhappy if you do."

Mr. Tung was not new to the game. He was a practiced urban sleuth who had used deadly force on more than a few occasions. He was prepared for an all-out war. This morning's prey had eluded him more than once, and he vowed to emerge victorious this time. He liked the odds. There were no outside lights on at the house, and the inside was equally dark.

His team of seven men, one woman, and four vehicles were in position. One team was positioned at each street corner, and another in an alleyway behind the house. Mr. Tung was the passenger in the fourth vehicle. The female driver moved the command vehicle into place just behind Walker's parked H2. A member of Tung's team moved toward the house. He moved from window to window, reporting his view from every angle.

The first man in called through his headset for support. Two men dressed in dark jumpsuits moved from the back of a nearby vehicle and rushed toward the front door of the house. The first to arrive at the door knelt beside the lock, and in less than a minute, had the door swinging freely. The other figure standing by the door pulled on night goggles and slid through the doorway.

Mr. Tung could hear his man inside breathing heavily as he moved through the house.

"Which room, which room?" asked Tung through this headset.

"Room one empty, room two empty," a pause, "room three empty, no sign of a target."

"Keep looking. Their vehicle is still here. I'm staring at it."

Tung looked up. At first he thought his eyes were playing a trick on him. The H2 seemed to be slowly rolling away from him. He watched for a full ten seconds before he realized what was happening. The large vehicle's engine sprung to life, and its tires screeched as it accelerated down the street toward team two at the intersection of Lombard and Fillmore. The H2 was traveling at nearly 60 miles per hour when it sideswiped the Mercedes SUV that partially blocked the intersection.

———

Walker took a quick look at the side view mirror and at the trailing parade of Mercedes. He recognized the lead car as a CL600 coupe. The occupants were virtually invisible. They were cloaked behind the heavy tint on the front window. The V12 that propelled the sleek car could easily overtake the H2.

The driver was good. He or she was obviously experienced at traversing the wet San Francisco pavement. The trailing vehicle was moving up quickly, trying to find a spot to overtake the H2 on the narrow city streets. Walker was thankful for the sparse weekend morning traffic. Both sides of the street were crammed with parked cars. There was hardly room for the H2 to navigate, let alone room for passing.

Walker slipped down low. He moved to grab Jensen and force her down, but she was busy aiming her small pistol at the trailing traffic.

The H2 was still gaining speed. Walker hung on to the steering wheel as the vehicle jumped a nearly two-foot rock wall on the corner of Marina Green Drive.

"Let's see them try that one," he yelled excitedly to no one in particular.

"How come they aren't shooting at us?" asked Jensen. "They're certainly within range. I've unloaded two clips, and I'm certain I've poked a hole or two in their windshield."

The H2 careened down the muddy grass on the Marina green. The truck's huge 315-millimeter-wide tires left an unmistakable path.

Tung instructed most of the trailing motorcade to fall back. He wanted his group to disperse before the inevitable police barricade appeared. As if on cue, a line of San Francisco patrol cars pulled onto the street just as the H2 exited the Marina Park.

Walker showed the same respect for the line of police cars that he did for the pristine Marina green and plowed through the line of cars, leaving a gaping hole for the trailing Mercedes. The Mercedes slowed to a stop, and Tung exited the vehicle carrying an automatic rifle. He casually put down a line of fire, knocking out the tires on the surviving police cars. Tung nonchalantly dropped the expended weapon and slipped back into the waiting vehicle. The female driver easily caught the H2 as it rounded a sharp corner on Route 101 North and sped past a sign for the Golden Gate Bridge toll plaza.

Unlike the crowded city streets, the relatively wide breath of the long bridge gave the chase vehicle ample time to pull alongside Walker and Jensen.

"We have visitors," spoke Jensen, pointing out the driver side window.

Without corroborating, Walker turned the truck hard to the left, and hit the Mercedes broadside. The Mercedes bounced off but kept pace. Walker's second attempt to throw the chase vehicle off course was less successful. The H2 spun sideways just as the pair of vehicles exited the north side of the bridge. The large tires caught the pavement like a pair of track shoes, causing the H2 to flip on to its roof and skip across Highway 101.

The coupe stopped alongside the wounded giant. Tung exited the car and walked toward the H2. Both passengers were unconscious.

23

The property at Indigo Run was a forty-nine acre compound. It was not an overly large property for the area, but it was secluded and peaceful. Its borders were protected by a moderate sized body of water to the north and west and a rural country route to the south and east

Unlike his deceased contemporary, Ren Yi, Doug Moon did not indulge in many of life's finer offerings. His only vice was the Yakima, Washington, property. He'd taken over the property from an unknown benefactor shortly after graduating from the academy in Massachusetts. His first project had been to create a relaxing vacation retreat for himself and the Yis.

He hadn't stopped there. He'd built a year-round fortress that was both off the beaten path and not too far from Ren Yi's base of operations in Seattle. The main house, in addition to Moon's living quarters, contained his working and planning suite.

There were three special-function outbuildings surrounding

the main house. One was the recently converted barn, now home to Ellen Yi's work. Another served as garage and storage center for the compound. Six weeks' worth of supplies was always on hand. The building farthest from the main house was a secure storage center and underground disposal area.

Kate Jensen slowly came to life in the Indigo Run storage building. She had no idea how long she had been asleep. Her last memory was of the strange car chase that had ended on the Golden Gate Bridge. Her mental fog slowly diminished, and she became increasingly aware of her surroundings. Her clothes were gone, replaced by a set of blue surgical scrubs, and a thin pair of socks, no shoes. Across the room, she noticed a still unconscious Brian Walker in a similar predicament. The only remnant of their previous wardrobe was an odd sock and Walker's belt.

Jensen picked up the black leather belt. She used the hard metal tongue of the belt as a pry to remove the oversize hinge pins on the large barn door. Little by little, she worked the tongue under the first pin and pushed upward. The hinges were rusty. They looked to be about a hundred years old. She stubbed her fingers over and over, but she kept trying. That door was their only way out. After what seemed like forever, the first pin popped out and clanged on the floor. Kate fell backward, exhausted. She looked at her fingers; they were bleeding. She wiped them on her clothes and kept at it. What I wouldn't give for a crowbar, she thought.

Jensen spent the next thirty minutes trying to stir Walker. The effect was minimal. Walker occasionally moaned and once made an attempt to roll over, but he was not all there. Jensen worried that he might be suffering a more serious effect to their obvious drugging.

There were only three hours of darkness left when Jensen and a still very groggy Walker exited the storage building at Indigo Run. "Here, lean on me," she told Walker. Putting her arm around his waist, she helped him turn the corner of the building. She stopped. Had she heard something?

She peeked around the building to check. She saw no one. She held her breath. *Voices, about fifty yards away*. In the distance, she heard a dog barking. She looked to her right and saw a storage building with lights on. She thought she saw a person inside. To her left, she saw another building, this one unlighted. "This way," she whispered to Walker.

In coordinated steps, they navigated about seventy yards to an area of dense brush.

Walker sat quietly on a rock while Jensen worked her way to a nearby building. She moved back and forth between two side windows. She nodded in Walker's direction before boldly moving to the side door. She tried the handle. It didn't move. Kate grimaced and tried again, this time with both hands. The door finally swung open, making a loud scraping noise. Kate stopped, waiting for someone with a gun to appear. When no one did, she slipped inside. Walker's calm became excited anxiousness as he watched her disappear into the dark building. He wanted to follow, but his unsteady legs and a dizzy head made his doing so impossible.

Jensen condensed her frame as she entered the building. Her eyes swept back and forth, trying to adjust to the darkness. The room seemed familiar to her. She felt as though she had been there before. All at once, her eyes adjusted to the new surroundings. The area was almost an exact duplicate of the space she and Walker had visited in the basement of the house in Amherst. Her first instinct was to turn and run. The memories of the grotesque scene were still etched clearly in her mind.

The next few minutes revealed a desk area, locker area, and a clear floor-to-ceiling wall that exposed the lab. She forced a smile. The work area of the lab was void of life.

Just to the left of the locker area was another door. *It's probably a closet or storage locker*, she thought to herself. The handle turned with ease, but the door itself was difficult to pull open. A more aggressive tug and Jensen felt a hiss and escape of air. She stood frozen. Momentary disbelief shrouded her mind.

The room was brighter now, thanks to the increasing illumination of the young morning. The first few feet of space in the storage room was separated from the main compartment by a series of overlapped plastic sheets. She stared in horror as she took in the scene. The room was littered with human bodies, all dressed in the same surgical scrubs that she and Walker were wearing. The bodies were stacked two and three deep across the ten-foot-wide room. There must have been ten or more bodies that she could immediately make out. They were all amassed parallel to the doorway. Some heads were turned toward the door. She could make out a variety of emotions on the stricken—surprise, anguish, and even one or two with a look of content resignation.

An awful thought came to her. She could only make out the first few stacks of bodies. The light did not penetrate far enough into the room for her to begin to estimate the extent of the carnage.
A cold tingle in her spine brought her back to reality but only momentarily. Strangely, her eyes were drawn back to the ungodly space. The distressing environment took on a new level of wickedness. She saw a number of children dispersed amidst the sea of dead. The bodies on the top layers of the pile seemed restful, but there were increasing signs of decay on the bodies farther down the pile. Jensen had seen enough.

Suddenly, Jensen realized why their hosts had not killed them. Anxiety and anger swept over her as the reality of the situation hit. They were intended as guinea pigs for the virus. *Have we already been exposed?* She did not recall any external residual sensation from an injection. *Maybe we've been breathing in the virus.* The thoughts were coming too fast. She exited the necropolis.

Jensen found Walker at the exact spot where she had left him. In faltering words, she told him what she had seen.

Walker's face did not hide his thoughts. He'd obviously come to the same disturbing conclusion about their predicament.

"I'm sorry, Kate, but I think we might ..."

Jensen broke in mid-sentence. "I've already thought about the possibility that we may have been exposed to the virus. My guess is that they haven't gotten around to us yet."

"How do you come to that conclusion?" asked Walker.

"I don't recognize any of the telltale signs of an injection. No soreness or visible marks that ..."

It was Walkers turn to interrupt. "Why don't you let me look around at your backside. Maybe they poked you someplace in the gluteus." Walker feigned a smile and then stopped, looking deep into Kate's sad, brown eyes. "Kate," he said, "if we've been infected, I want you to know ..."

The sound of a car on gravel interrupted him. He never finished the thought.

A car drove along a gravel drive about fifty yards from their location.

"Do you think it's coming or going?" asked Jensen.

"I'm not sure. Let's find out."

"How do you plan to navigate? You can barely walk."

Walker stood and hopped three times on one foot in an effort to demonstrate his rapidly improving balance. "How's that for a quick recovery."

The car stopped near the main building, and three large men armed with assault rifles got out. "Let's go!" Kate whispered hoarsely at Walker.

"Do you think they saw us?"

"I don't want to hang around and find out," Kate said. She helped Walker hobble toward the cover of the woods.

Walker and Jensen were both committed to stopping Doug Moon, whatever the consequences. Each would kill him if the occasion presented itself. For a while both thought about turning toward the main building and rushing the place, but in silent agreement, the pair moved away from the building and into the woods. Reaching civilization and getting in touch with colleagues seemed the only sensible next step.

24

As his latest experiment ran its course, Bekins began to feel desperate. The army boys were finally clued in to the smallpox discoveries and were massing in Frederick. He could see them now, an overzealous mob of lightly trained biologists looking to make history. They were probably gearing up now, getting ready to board an army transport and charge down to Atlanta to take over for the pathetic, overworked, and understaffed team at the CDC. There would be dozens of them. They would be all dressed in army fatigues and carrying very important-looking but nearly empty titanium briefcases. They were coming to rescue him from his own ineptness.

How could the intelligence people allow them back in? thought Bekins. It was the army idiots who had let the virus out of the can in the first place.

At lunchtime, Bekins went back in again. He donned his scrubs, gingerly pulling his left arm through the sleeve. He felt an

ache stemming from the site of a recent self-inflicted smallpox refresher immunization. After his earlier brush with the tainted needle,
he was taking all available precautions. He had still not told anyone
that he may have stuck himself. *No need yet*, he figured.

Almost a week had passed since the monkey in the middle
cage had been infected with the GS strain of the virus. The monkey
seemed listless but externally healthy. He was sitting in the cage. This
was a signal that all was not well. Monkeys do not generally sit down
in the presence of humans. This victim didn't seem to care. The pri-
mate was groggy, not unlike the Saunders girl during Bekins's final
visit with her. As Bekins stared into the monkey's eyes, he entered
data at breakneck speed into a wireless device. The army team was
scheduled to arrive soon, and Bekins needed to make the most of his
remaining time alone in the lab.

———

The next afternoon, the monkey in the middle cage was dead. Bekins
went over to the cage and looked at the huddled monkey. Feeling
somewhat anxious, he stuck his gloved finger through the cage and
poked the animal just to be sure. He needed to cut into the corpse
sooner rather than later because time was running out.

*Is it possible that this animal's body coincidentally reacted to
the virus the same way as Gwen Saunders's, or is there something new
and different about the GS strain?* He opened the latch on the cage
and rolled the monkey so that he could look into its eyes. To his surprise, almost shock, the animal's eyes were wide open, locked in a
stare.

Bekins decided to eat lunch and reenergize himself before cut-
ting into the monkey. He carried the monkey to a stainless steel table
and laid the animal flat. A surge of dizziness moved through his head.

There was a pain in the back of his eyes, and they momentarily went out of focus. "I need some food," he whispered to himself.

In the community cafeteria, Bekins met up with a very tired and solemn John Pierce. Today was autopsy day two, and Bekins could see the pain in Pierce's eyes.

"Any news?" asked Bekins.

"None yet. The last update was three hours ago. Your colleague, Dr. Martin, said he was almost finished for the day."

"Maybe you should get a change of scenery. You should go back to work or visit your family."

"I *am* at work. Jensen and Walker are on the west coast, so I've decided to remain here and report in if anything comes from Gwen's autopsy or from your work in the animal lab."

Wow, he must be one tough cookie, Bekins thought. *How can he hang around at a medical facility and wait for the outcome of his lover's autopsy?*

"I should be finished today," he said. "The army team is due to arrive in days, if not hours, and I'm certain the environment and the agenda will change." He balled up his sandwich wrapper and excused himself.

"Let me know how it turns out. I'd like to put a report together tonight," spoke a bland John Pierce.

Failure and doom seemed to be hanging everywhere. Time and fatigue were winning out. Bekins placed his lunch tray on top of the trash container. He was going back into the lab for the second time this hour.

Bekins carried a small, round metal stool to the side of the autopsy table. His back had now joined his eyes, both aching and vying for his attention. He spread the skin tight on the animal's abdomen making a long incision and being very careful to cut away from his own body. He wondered how the army team would handle this very situation. In this sequence, smallpox would be streaming out of the animal carcass and directly into the air. He was certain that none of the army biologist were experienced with smallpox. The only experienced ones were all dead now. This group would be working face-to-face with an airborne disease that was seeking a human incubator.

Nearby containers were beginning to fill with monkey parts. The entire spleen, both kidneys, and heart were arranged in a sequence on the lab table, and all looked normal. The only major organ missing from the parts buffet was the liver. This animal's liver was unnaturally crimson and speckled with blemishes over the entire visible surface. It was the only organ that looked the part for a smallpox victim. Unfortunately, it was also filled with blood and broke open before Bekins could remove it from the body cavity.

Why did the GS strain attack the liver with such vengeance? It seemed to ignore the rest of the anatomy.

Bekins needed to finish; his eyesight was becoming increasingly clouded, and the pain in his back was increasing also. He could feel a slight trickle of sweat forming on his temple, not an easy accomplishment given the cool, arid atmosphere of the blue suit.

He left the lab in a hurry. He wanted to compare his findings with those of Dr. Martin's autopsy on Gwen Saunders.

Dr. Martin's findings were amazingly similar to Bekins's monkey results. Both victims seemed to have expired from a total system shutdown that stemmed from a destroyed liver. The livers of both victims were nearly liquefied.

Bekins's head was spinning, not from the pain behind his eyes but from all the new ideas that were swirling in his head. One idea in particular stood out, but before floating the idea by his colleagues at the CDC, or for that matter to any of the arriving army biologists, he wanted a second opinion. He sent an urgent e-mail to Dr. Gauthier, an epidemiology professor and his former mentor at Johns Hopkins.

After one more hour in the lab, Bekins was done. He shook his head in a resigned disbelief. The pain in his eyes shot down through his spine and into his abdomen. *Damn. I'm sick.* He pulled an arm into the body of his blue suit and wiped sweat from his forehead. *This is not the flu*, he thought to himself.

Bekins exited the lab and picked up a phone receiver in the locker room area. He called John Pierce.

Pierce picked up the phone on the first ring and immediately acknowledged the lack of energy in Mark Bekins voice. "I need a little assistance."

"Are you okay?" asked Pierce.

He shook his head as he spoke into the phone. "No, I'm sick. I've managed to accidentally infect myself." His voice was grave, and his throat was sore.

"Are you sure?"

"Not 100 percent, but I'm willing to bet that I have the virus."

"Have you had a recent immunization?"

"Yes. But I'm certain that it is useless against this strain. I need you to do two things for me. First, get in touch with CDC Director Baum and ask him to come down to the lab anteroom and call me on the locker room phone. Second, make sure that no one else tries to enter this lab. I need to stay quarantined in here so that I can continue my work."

Bekins hung up the phone and moved gingerly to the locker room couch. He kept his head as still as possible. The slightest motion felt like he was going to jog his eyeballs out of their sockets. The clock on the wall seemed to be moving in fast motion. An occasional beep emanated from a nearby personal computer. He heard the sound, but he didn't care. His head was throbbing, and his brain felt loose in his skull. The body aches were like nothing he had experienced before, and he was getting warmer. The fever was gaining momentum.

The phone rang. It rang again. A crowd grew outside the lab facility. For over twenty minutes, Pierce and Director Baum tried in tandem to call and sound noises on the exterior wall of the lab area. They knew that Bekins was better off asleep or unconscious, but that didn't stop them from trying to get him to stir.

———

Bekins came to. He heard the pounding and faint voices outside the lab walls. He tried to respond. His eyes were swollen, and his throat was raw, but he managed to signal Pierce to call again.

"Can you hear me, Mark?" said Pierce through the phone.

"Yes," returned Bekins hoarsely.

"What can I do to help?" asked Pierce.

"Nothing, nothing yet, anyway. The fever and pain will die down in about twelve hours or so. Just leave me alone until then." Bekins tried to hang up the phone but missed the cradle on the wall by a full six inches. Consciousness came and went. Twelve hours came and went. The fever didn't die.

An hour after the expected relief time had passed, Bekins checked his forehead and didn't need a thermometer to know that his temperature was raging. His face was burning. He curled into a ball on the couch. Nearly unconscious and mumbling incoherent ideas, he poured a glass of water over his head and face.

———

Dr. Martin, the CDC pathologist who was working with Saunders's body, passed by the chaotic scene just outside the Level 4 lab area. Director Baum and John Pierce were standing alone in a corner of the anteroom. The curious pathologist studied the scene before engaging the director.

"What's all the commotion about?"

"Mark Bekins seems to be sick," responded Director Baum, pointing at the glass wall that separated them from the comatose Bekins.

"Do you want me to go in and see if I can give him a hand?" asked the aging Martin in a calm voice. His gray hair was disheveled, and he pushed his eyeglasses on top of his head.

"How can you do that? The entire area inside the lab suite has been imperiled."

"It won't be a clean solution, but we can use this anteroom as a zero flow space and treat the site as a mobile hazard site. Anyone entering the space will need to wear a mobile self-contained suit."

"Go to it," said Baum.

It took less than an hour to set up the zero flow barrier outside Mark Bekins's contaminated lab and less than ten minutes for the pathologist to suit up and go in.

Bekins mumbled something to his visitor, but it had nothing to do with the present situation. His eyes were caked shut; he was dripping with sweat. If not for his physical size, he could have easily been mistaken for any one of the other infected animals in the lab.

"His fever is extremely high," the pathologist said through his headset. He's trying to communicate, but I can't make any sense out of his speech. I'll start an IV to hydrate him."

Working carefully in the awkward mobile biohazard suit, Martin poked at Bekins's arm. He found a vein and started an IV.

The pathologist checked Bekins's temperature again a few minutes later. "It seems to be falling." He passed this information to whoever was listening on the other end of the wireless connection.

———

Professor Gauthier of Johns Hopkins was shopping for a twenty-fifth wedding anniversary present for his wife when his mobile phone chimed, signifying a text message had arrived. He was a novice with his new mobile phone. It took him over a minute to navigate to the point where he could read the inbound text message. He scratched at his gray-flecked beard. He was certain that responding would take all evening.

The message was short and to the point. He understood it and was anxious to get in touch with Bekins. It sounded like he was into some exciting stuff in the CDC lab. The message made no mention of Bekins's deteriorating health.

Professor Gauthier fumbled with his new phone for a few minutes before he closed the device and opened another more familiar, albeit much larger, device to complete the job.

His call to Atlanta went through a few bureaucratic phone trees and a series of human blockers before it found its way to Bekins's line. Bekins's phone was on a hard call forward and rang almost immediately in the lab locker area. Neither Mark Bekins nor his attending physician was in a position to take the call.

The phone rang again. This time it was answered from a remote extension.

"This is Director Baum."

"Good afternoon, Joe," the caller spoke in a friendly tone.

"Gauthier? Boy we could sure use you down here right now."

"I know. I received an e-mail from our mutual friend, Mark Bekins."

"You did? When?" spoke a surprised Director Baum.

"The original message came in early this morning. It was almost sundown by the time I figured out how to retrieve it from my phone," laughed Gauthier.

"Your student is sick," said a matter-of-fact Baum.

Gauthier was silent. When a virologist gets sick enough to garner attention from the director of the CDC, it's usually a very bad thing.

"What's the matter with him?" asked Gauthier, not really wanting to hear the response.

"He seems to have contracted smallpox."

This time the professor was silent for a much longer period of time. It took another minute for him to grasp the obvious. Smallpox was awake at the CDC.

"I'll skip the twenty questions."

"Good," replied the director.

"When was his immunization last refreshed?"

"Twice in the last month. Yesterday in fact," spoke Baum.

"How sick is he?"

"Very sick."

"How is that possible? Even if the last refresher was a year ago, he should still be covered," spoke the confused professor.

"There's a lot going on right now, and I'm not at liberty to tell all. I hope you understand."

"I don't even want to know, but now I'm beginning to understand why he sent me this e-mail." Gauthier paused. "Can I speak with him?"

"I wish you could, but he crashed with a fever over ten hours ago."

"Where is he now?"

"He quarantined himself in a locker room adjacent to one of our Level 4 lab suites. We have another employee, a pathologist familiar with the problem, in with him now."

"Do they have access to outside e-mail in the lab suite?" asked the Professor.

"I think we can get a message through."

"Okay. I'm going to hightail it over to the school and send a response to Bekins's original request. Maybe the pathologist can take

Bekins's experiment to the next step."

———

A third IV bag emptied into Bekins's arm. He woke up. His head had cleared, but his vision was still fuzzy. His entire body ached, but there was no sign of the fever. He felt down his arm, and without lifting his head, he slowly eased the needle out of his arm.

He rubbed his eyes hard and slowly managed to readjust his sight to the fluorescent lighting in the lab locker area. Two legs caught his attention. They were cast in yellow. He wanted to get up and tell the person to run. Bekins tried to lift his head and say something. His head never left the couch.

"Welcome back," spoke a muffled voice from inside a yellow space suit.

Bekins recognized the face and managed a smile. The pathologist briefly updated Bekins on the happenings of the last half day.

Bekins rolled onto his side, moaned, and then sat up. He felt like gravity had increased threefold overnight.

The pathologist was extremely happy to see that Bekins was up. He had spent the better part of the early morning hours trying to put together the strands of information relayed to him by Professor Gauthier at Johns Hopkins. The subject matter was way over his head. He needed Bekins help in order to continue the experiment.

With a little help from his yellow friend, Bekins managed to hoist his large butt onto a rolling stool. The pathologist pushed him over to a computer monitor. Both sat quietly while Bekins attempted to focus on the screen. There was a long pause; then Bekins's face wrinkled up into a small grin as he took in the e-mail from the Johns Hopkins professor. He poked out a series of instructions on the keyboard and asked his colleague to complete experiment number three following the typed guide.

Bekins transferred the last of his energy to his feet and pushed his stool in the general direction of the couch. Three minutes later, he was unconscious.

25

Jensen whirled at a sound behind her. "What's that?" she said.

"It's nothing. Come on," Walker said.

"I think they're behind us," she said.

"If you don't hurry up, we'll never get out of here," urged Walker.

They decided to take a chance and walk on the road to make better time. Soon, an old pickup truck approached them. "You folks need a lift?" asked the driver, rolling down the window.

Walker looked at Jensen, who was shaking her head no.

"We sure do." He hustled Kate into the passenger side and got in next to her. "Thanks," he told the man as he slammed the door.

"No problem," said the young man. Walker figured their driver was only a local redneck, not a bioterrorist. He looked the part. He was dressed in dungaree overalls minus the shirt, a worn baseball cap, and army boots. The only thing missing was a gun rack in the rear window of his pickup truck. They traveled with the man for about twenty minutes—just long enough to feel they were a safe distance from the long grasp of Doug Moon, but a little too long to feel comfortable with the pickup truck driver.

When the pickup truck left them on the side of the road, and as the last sound of its rough engine died away, they stood alone. They both felt naked in their matching surgical gowns.

Walker's back still hurt from the impact of the crash on the Golden Gate Bridge. He squatted down and tried to stretch away the pain.

There was pain for Kate Jensen too. She wore the pain on her face. The stacks of human bodies in the storage chamber at Indigo Run were etched permanently in her mind. She prayed that the images would lose clarity over time.

Her attention was diverted by a series of cracking sounds emanating from Walker's ankle as he rolled it in a circular motion in an attempt to expel a newfound pain. They journeyed about a mile before stopping at a path the led to a secluded bed-and-breakfast.

The Cascade House was a charming Victorian-style home that looked like it had been recently renovated. Dark green pillars on either side of the front steps met the disheveled couple. As soon as she was under the front porch, Jensen began to feel safe from the torments of the past few days and nights. She realized that they were not finished with Doug Moon, but the cold sense of bewilderment and pending doom that was following her was pushed into the background. In its place crept the furor of revenge.

Her eyes scanned the roomy and inviting space of the Cascade House entrance hall. A huge woman rotated down the stairs to greet them. Flushed and breathing hard, she sat down on the second to bottom step.

"Welcome to the Cascade House," she puffed. "I'm Joan Carter." She shook hands with Walker and then with Jensen. "Halloween's not for a few weeks yet," she smiled at their odd outfits.

"Can we use your phone?" asked Walker.

"The phone is for paying guests only," Joan said, taking her pleasant demeanor down a notch.

"We plan on staying for a night or two," said Jensen, smiling at Joan.

"In that case, you can use the extension in the parlor."

Walker moved with haste toward the elegant room just off the front hallway. He contacted Pierce in Atlanta and quickly briefed him on the situation. Their discussion carried on for a full half an hour.

It was a therapeutic half hour for Kate Jensen. The wonderful chatter that rolled off Joan Carter's lips was the perfect diversion for her tired mind. She was just getting to the end of a story about a local adulterous millionaire who runs a swine fertility clinic when Walker reemerged from the parlor.

"We're almost done here," said Jensen with a big grin.

Walker was curious but not so curious to interrupt. The smile on Jensen's face was enough for him.

A few hours later, the freshly showered guests made their way downstairs to the dining room. It was nearly seven when their hostess waddled in to preside over dinner. Kate Jensen was still chuckling at the pig fertility story. Walker smiled also; his cavalry was on the way.

———

The overnight at the Cascade House was Walker and Jensen's first real sleep in three days. It was five o'clock in the morning when Walker stirred. The day was starting off cooler than normal, and for the next forty-five minutes, he lay silent, not wanting to disturb his sleeping companion. He watched the ceiling fan move in slow, counterclockwise circles. The beginning of the day was sneaking in around the bedroom shades. The coral-colored room glowed with the intruding light, and the dark cherry wood furnishings glistened the color of cabernet. A breeze poured into the room carrying a fragrance not familiar to his East Coast-trained sense of smell.

Kate Jensen stirred slightly. As she turned toward him, her dark hair fell across her face. Her complexion was flawless, except for that tiny freckle on her cheek. Even that seemed flawless to him now. He brushed a few strands of Kate's hair aside and stroked her cheek.

Staring at his bedside companion, it seemed strange to him that when they had first met, she had not seemed attractive. In their early training days, he'd watched her come and go and had never given her a second thought. But ever since that evening over ten years ago when they'd spent their first private time working on a project, he had loved her. It was that simple.

She had been assigned to his project. He could still picture the moment as if it was just yesterday. She'd exited the elevator on the fifteenth floor, home to her division's secure technology center. He could recall every aspect of her outfit, how the bright flowers were set on her summer dress, how wonderful her tan legs looked, and how she smiled when he greeted her.

Their partial night's sleep at the remote bed-and-breakfast was nearing a conclusion. During the previous evening, they had turned in their surgical scrubs for a matching pair of khaki shorts and generic polo-style tops at a nearby clothing store. They were ready for the new day.

———

It happened slowly at first. Then with increased furor, the news of the Indigo Run discovery spread through the intelligence circles. The army was organized to go in with a special bioterrorism team. The army dispatched its team from a local army training facility in Yakima.

Just over twenty-four hours after Walker and Jensen's escape from Indigo Run, the combined army and NIA team was ready to go back in.

26

There was no moon at Indigo Run, but the trees still glistened with predawn moisture. There was still the glint of a star in the sky when the first of two vans arrived at the compound. The prevailing wind had shifted from the south and was now pressing hard from the east. The North Korean and Chinese flags stood at attention atop the storage barn and lab barn at the compound. Doug Moon had waited long for this day. He'd never imagined the swell of patriotism and pride that was produced by the sight of his native flag flying at his Yakima home.

Ellen Yi stood beside Moon on the front porch. Today, she wore black slacks; a short, black jacket; and a crisp, white blouse. She had let her hair grow out in recent months, and it fell softly to her shoulders. Despite her tailored appearance, Ellen felt hollow inside. She would never win a prize for her work—she did not deserve one—but she closed her eyes and envisioned herself as a chief of staff at a college medical facility. Tears came to her eyes for the first time in years. Her family tree would end soon.

The night chill was no longer in the air. Moon and Yi no longer felt as though they were struggling against time to succeed. Their few moments of silence in the morning air disarmed the seriousness of the day to come. Ellen reached out and touched Doug Moon on the hand. He took her hand in return.

"Both vans have arrived," he said.

"Let's stay here another few minutes," requested Yi.

"Okay." Moon turned and smiled, looking Ellen in the eyes. It was not a look of passion. It was a look of admiration and pride.

———

Members of the organized NIA infiltration team gathered at a hastily installed mobile field office only two miles from the entrance to Indigo Run. The group, including Jensen, Walker, various members of the sheriff's department SWAT team, and a handful of NIA agents were to go in first. A second, more complex mobile vehicle made up of members of the U.S. Army's Biological Containment division would follow when prompted. By using a combination of aerial photos and ground surveillance, the NIA and army away teams were able to follow every move at the Indigo Run compound.

A member of the NIA surveillance team, holding a handheld transmitter, reported from woods behind Ellen Yi's converted barn laboratory. The team was careful not to use the compromised communication devices.

"Two light-colored vans are parked near the main house," spoke the camouflaged NIA scout.

Walker turned to Jensen for advice. She was more experienced in the field and could probably anticipate the next move. "Okay, what do we do now?"

Jensen didn't respond. She was slouched in a corner chair half asleep. He couldn't believe she was asleep. His palms were sweaty and his heart rate had almost doubled in the last two minutes. *How can she be sleeping with all this commotion going on around her?* With a look of exasperation, he poked her hard in the ribs with his index finger.

Walker briefly updated the yawning Jensen and then repeated the question. "What happens next?"

"That depends on what we hear."

"Hear from whom?"

"Our listeners. We have two camouflaged listening devices less than twenty yards from the house," said Jensen.

Almost as if on cue, an NIA field agent lifted his left arm and turned the knob clockwise on an overheard radio receiver. The fidelity was perfect. You could hear the echo of footsteps on the tile atrium floor as twelve guests shuffled into the main house at Indigo Run.

———

The morning gathering belonged to Doug Moon, known as Mr. Brown, to the group gathered in the great room. With Moon as the only external face to the project, Ellen Yi was only a curious backdrop. Each participant, or drone, as Moon and Yi often referred to them, had been carefully selected from a base of over five hundred applicants.

Yi and Moon knew—or at least assumed—that time was *not* of the essence. The incubation period of the virus would be days, not minutes or hours. Unlike the September 11 terrorist attacks, this initiative did not need to be based on calibrated watches; for that matter, the attacks didn't even have to occur on the same week.

Even so, they'd planned the attacks so that they would occur in parallel. It would reduce the risk that an astute official or civilian would be able to send out an alert.

As a professor turned business evangelist, then in the background as a coordinator and planner, and now as a spirited evangelist again, Moon had spent many hours speaking to groups of young disciples. All eyes were focused on him. He moved and talked with a mild sense of urgency. His speech was not nervous, but it was energetic and excited. His neat but casual dress was out of character. He wore stone-washed blue jeans, a rumpled white shirt with the sleeves rolled over twice, and deck shoes without socks. Today, he would be one of them—one of fourteen sent out into America to change the nation forever.

He stepped forward and leaned into the assembled group. He knew each seated individual well, even though, for many, this was only his or her second face-to-face with Moon. He had studied their backgrounds and pedigrees. They came from rich families and poor. They were orphans and only children. Each participant eagerly anticipated the event. Unfortunately, none in attendance actually understood the true mission ahead.

Three months ago, each participant had answered an ad for the local chapter of Indoor Air America, a fictitious environmental group founded by Moon. The story was simple. On a specified day, the group would fan out across domestic airports with environmental test equipment hidden in their carry-on travel bags. The data collected by the devices would be used in a class-action suit against the government and local municipalities.

"Can we all agree that our government is doing little to stop indoor pollution?" asked Moon.

He watched as all twelve heads plus Ellen Yi nodded enthusiastically.

"Since we're all on the same page regarding the lax attitude of the government toward indoor air pollution, can we all agree that the airport system is a good place to expose the problem?"

Another round of nods ensued. Moon studied the faces. He paid particular attention to a young man seated in the second row. The face belonged to Peter Lundi. His large, gray eyes darted from side to side with suspicion. His scraggly, unkempt hair and beard were black as night. He rubbed the back of his neck repeatedly and tapped a pencil on the arm of his chair.

"There is one more very important question," Moon stated slowly, his words resounding through the large room. With an outstretched arm, he rigidly pointed at the group and said, "Is there a single person here who doesn't believe that our government is ignoring the health consequences of indoor air pollution?"

He paused and scanned the room. The nods were horizontal now. Peter Lundi stood in the second row and cheered.

Moon introduced Ellen Yi. She stepped forward, pulling a ubiquitous black travel bag behind her. In a short rehearsed speech and a parallel show-and-tell, Yi discussed the technology behind the air-monitoring device.

"The device is easy to use," she said, demonstrating. "All you need to do is set up the device in the most suitable location." Each recruit was given a terminal map of his or her target airport. "The best place," she continued, showing a photo of a sample terminal, "is near the security check for departing passengers." She went back to demonstrating the device. "The device is simple to engage," she said. "When you tug on this Velcro porthole, a small, electric internal airflow motor will start automatically." She showed her audience how the device worked. "The device needs to remain motionless for approximately sixty minutes." She bowed and stepped aside.

Moon stepped back into the spotlight and asked if there were any questions.

"What are the targets?" asked a female college student in the front row.

"Everybody will be leaving from Sea-Tac sometime today. All flights ultimately terminate to major airports around the country. Those of you headed to the eastern or central time zones will be waiting for the morning airport foot traffic while the others will be setting up their devices as soon as they land. The top fourteen airports by traffic volume will be covered by our study."

The college student raised her hand.

"You don't have to raise your hand," spoke Ellen Yi supportively from the back of the room.

"I was just wondering why the foot traffic is so important. Wouldn't it be easier for us to collect the air samples when the airport is less busy?"

Ellen Yi went pale.

Doug Moon quickly replied. "There are two main reasons for the timing. First, we believe that much of the indoor air health risk comes from the pedestrian traffic. The thousands of travelers breathe out carbon dioxide, and we believe this is a major component of the poor indoor air quality. We also believe that this foot traffic stirs contaminants on the floor and other flat surfaces. Second, we have run a few tests, and it is much easier for a mock traveler to hang around airport security areas unchecked during busier times than it is during light travel times."

There were no more questions.

The meeting ended. Everyone seemed ready for his or her personal adventure. A handful of caterers emerged from the kitchen and opened a set of boxed gourmet breakfasts for the trip to the airport.

Just after 7:00 a.m., Ellen Yi, Doug Moon, Peter Lundi, and eleven others prepared to leave for the airport.

It didn't take a brain surgeon to realize that this was it. The opening speech by Moon and a refresher training session delivered by Yi was more than enough to move on.

"The twelve disciples don't have any idea what they are getting into," stated Jensen matter-of-factly after listening to the speeches.

"I guess not. How do our guys handle this? Will they be able to protect the unknowing participants during the raid on the compound?" asked Walker.

"I doubt it. Our team is about to storm into an unfamiliar building, a facility containing over a dozen suitcases full of a deadly biological powder. Anyone who gets in the way will be in trouble."

Walker's brain cataloged two distinct emotions—fear that the NIA and SWAT teams would not be able to safely separate the unknowing participants from the evil ringleaders and a deep urge to strike revenge against the killing team of Moon and Yi. He found it painful to recall the killing. The trail of death was long. Three army virologists, Gwen Saunders, Ren Yi, and the dozens of others rotting in a storage building only a few miles away were the victims he knew about.

Squatting behind a scrub bush on the perimeter of the compound, Walker ran awkwardly behind Kate Jensen and between a small army of heavily armed field agents. He had not accepted the Glock thrust at him just before they'd exited the field office. He almost never used a gun and didn't think this would be a good time to start. His hands were sweating profusely, and he could imagine bullets exiting the muzzle of his pistol in every direction.

Jensen and Walker followed the NIA and SWAT team for

nearly two hundred yards before exiting the human train and taking up shelter behind a Volkswagen-sized rock. They were in view of the main house but out of the firing line. A hundred feet lay between the team of two NIA agents and four members of the SWAT team. Sudden movements would more than likely draw the attention of the assembled group in the house. One step at a time, with mirrored movements, the group of six approached the main house.

Ten curved granite steps led up to the door overhang. In less than a few seconds, the oversized pair of oak doors were knocked opened. The three lead members of the SWAT team fell symmetrically onto the large atrium floor. The fourth moved in behind with a sweeping motion back and forth scanning the large arched entryway to the great room. Two large ceramic containers stood at attention on either side of the entry. An overhead fan swirled slowly in the distance, momentarily distracting the SWAT team.

The infiltration team stood prone, ready to move forward, but Moon was ready for them. Moon's faithful thug, Mr. Tung, and another oversized assassin materialized from their ceramic holding chambers. Within seconds three of the four members of the SWAT team were down.

"Our guys are shooting at them," yelled Walker, listening to the action through his earpiece. But before he could start another sentence, their NIA colleagues stumbled back down the granite steps followed closely by a single, blood-spattered member of the SWAT team. The three unscathed members of the infiltration team found temporary safety behind a knee-high rock landscape wall. Jensen and Walker shrunk farther behind their own rock protection.

Tung and his partner hid behind the broken doors and fired at the infiltration team with automatic rifles. The team fired back.

The team leader yelled, "Put down your weapons!"

The response was a round of gunfire from Tung. Tung and his

thug crouched and ran for the statuary in front of the busted doors. The infiltration team fired at them but missed. They saw Tung stand up and hurl an object toward them.

"Down!" yelled the team leader.

A grenade exploded only a few yards from them. The firing from Tung stopped. The team leader had his men spread out. In the next second, they saw Tung and his cohort charge from the house toward the woods. The hasty chase was Tung's final undoing. The NIA surveillance scout hiding in the woods pulled off two quick shots, silencing Mr. Tung and his colleague forever.

While Tung and the NIA infiltration team were engaged in a shootout, the recruits cowered behind an overturned table in the great room. Moon, Ellen, and Peter Lundi dove under the head table at the front of the room.

"Now what?!" Ellen shouted at Moon.

Only Ellen Yi and Peter Lundi could see the cold stare and hatred emanating from Doug Moon's eyes.

Moon realized that his trusted protector, Tung, was no longer. He grabbed Ellen Yi, and they each grabbed one of the black travel bags and ducked behind a false bookcase. A scared but energized Lundi copied their movements.

———

The large table in the great room was covered with airline tickets, box meals, and half-full teacups. Four hours had passed since the infiltration at Indigo Run. It was midday, and eleven of the twelve recruits were now in custody. One by one, the recruits gave their statements to the onsite NIA team.

After thirty minutes of hunting, Jensen and Walker discovered a secret tunnel leading from the house to the woods. They tracked the escaping trio of Moon, Yi, and Lundi to a moderate-sized stream deep in the brush behind the house.

"How far do you think they took the river?" asked Jensen, breathing heavily

"I don't think they traveled by water at all," responded Walker.

"What brings you to that conclusion? A small boat slip with dangling ropes would certainly indicate that a boat was tied up here."

"That's what they wanted us to think. They wouldn't have gotten very far on the water. Our guys would have spotted them before the second turn. My guess is that the river scene is a setup and they took some other transportation in or near the water."

Jensen stood next to Walker and gazed at the slow-moving river against the backdrop of jagged hills. The virus dispersing team was now less than one quarter its original size, but it was still lethal.

27

During the evening, the visiting Dr. Gauthier replaced the CDC pathologist attending to Bekins and his experiments. Bekins was weak and sweating again, but he was determined to stand and greet the visiting professor.

Gauthier smiled. "No, no, please, Mark, stay still." He tried gently to push Bekins back down onto the couch. Bekins waved him off.

"But I need to get up," he insisted. Grunting mightily, Bekins rose to his feet with one arm out for support.

The professor turned for a moment to acknowledge a message on a nearby monitor. He didn't see Bekins hit the floor, but he heard and felt the shock wave. He quickly grabbed Bekins under the arms and pulled him back onto the couch.

Bekins stirred and without opening his eyes, asked "What happened?"

"You passed out and dropped like a rock."

Bekins tried to roll out off the couch, but this time Gauthier was more forceful.

"There is nothing you can do right now except stay alive."

"Thanks for the advice," Bekins mouthed, a barely audible response.

"Just take it easy for awhile. I'll go check on the experiment."

Bekins's fever returned during the evening, heating his face and torso. A line of sweat dripped into his left eye, a forbearer of things to come. This time, the fever did not simmer to a slow boil. It sent quakes through his body. This time, even his eyeballs showed the sign of fever, glowing crimson red where they were supposed to be white. The small couch creaked each time a new wave of chills passed through his body. His temperature passed through 104 °F and he was on the verge of going into shock. There was nothing that the attending Gauthier could do for the young man, except wait.

At seven o'clock, Gauthier could wait no longer. He phoned Director Baum and made a radical request.

"Hi, Joe. We need to use the boy as a host for experiment three."

"I can't authorize that."

"I know you can't. I just wanted to tell someone else what I was up to before I took on the responsibility myself. Joe, the boy is dying. I don't think he'll make it through the night."

"How can his experiment help?"

"I don't think it will do him any good at all, but it's an opportunity to test the therapy on a living human." Gauthier looked down at the floor. He wasn't proud of the idea, but he suspected that the end result of the experiment might help take the smallpox therapy to the next level.

"Joe, you need to level with me. Is there any chance that this strain of the virus is out in the real world?"

Director Baum was silent.

"I'll take your answer from the silence. You need this therapy, and Mark Bekins is a perfect human trial subject. Maybe if we're lucky, he will live long enough for us to get some useable results."

Baum put down the receiver without a comment.

Gauthier moved over to the quivering patient. He removed the IV needle from his arm and inserted a syringe.

Dr. Gauthier left the lab suite just before 10:00 p.m. No one would spend the night with Mark Bekins. Gauthier hoped that, when he returned in the early hours of the next morning, Bekins would still be alive.

Gauthier spent the evening and most of the overnight in the company of CDC Director Baum and NIA Director Pierce. Baum finally let his guard down and came clean with respect to the bioterrorist plot.

The professor was a little surprised by the ingenuity of the unnamed terrorists. Just the idea of working in and around the smallpox virus gave him pause. But to think that this virulent supervirus had been developed and grown in a makeshift lab was beyond his comprehension.

He was intrigued but not surprised by the story of interagency espionage between the CDC and the army biologists. Gauthier was more than familiar with the methods of the army's infectious disease group and was fairly certain that there were many other microorganisms awake in the army lab in Maryland.

———

In the dark, contaminated lab, a shadow appeared and moved to the edge of Bekins's couch. He sat by the couch for twenty minutes and watched Bekins twitch. Occasionally, his eyes would blink. He touched Bekins forehead with the gloved hand. He could feel the heat through the latex.

The professor was startled when Bekins stirred.

"Are you God?" Bekins murmured.

"No, I only wish I were right now," responded Gauthier, still a little shocked that Bekins was conscious.

"I'm going to draw some blood from your arm," he whispered. Gauthier reach down and tied a large rubber hose around Bekins's arm.

"I'm ready now," spoke Bekins in a clear but hushed tone.

Gauthier wasn't sure whether he was referring to the bloodletting or if maybe he thought he was still talking to God. Those were Bekins's last words for the early morning.

The blood sample showed no remarkable activity. The blood was visibly littered with smallpox bricks. The images portrayed on the overhead display looked no different than the textbook images that the professor had studied many years ago.

He left the lab suite at 3:00 a.m., armed with the knowledge that Bekins was still breathing.

28

Jensen and Walker boarded an afternoon flight from Seattle to Baltimore. Walker was exhausted from the three days of hell in and around Indigo Run and wanted nothing more than to join Kate Jensen for an in-flight nap. Instead, he managed to get in touch with Director Pierce for an update.

Walker was silent as Pierce recalled the day's events. NIA field agents in Seattle, Chicago, Las Vegas, and Detroit had reported in. Pierce was justifiably dismayed by the news that three members of the SWAT team had been killed and another seriously injured. Equally high on the Director's list of disappointments was the disappearance of Yi, Moon, and their travel companion.

There was some good news.

"The interrogation team at Indigo Run has mapped out a pretty good picture of the planned bio attack," Pierce told Walker on the in-flight phone. "We know the timeline and the target airports."

"Great!" Walker said. "What else?"

"Based on information obtained from the eleven recruits and their unused airline tickets, we've been able to narrow the search for Moon to Chicago's O'Hare airport. Yi and the still unidentified, at-large recruit were destined for either Las Vegas or Detroit. We've got a problem, though."

"And that is?" asked Walker.

"No one can ID Moon or his rouge disciple," Pierce spoke.

"Yeah, big problem," said Walker.

"The lone missing recruit is a wild card," Pierce said. "No one on the NIA team could say with assurance that he was a willing participant or not."

The plane bounced, and Kate Jensen woke from her abbreviated nap. She came to life just in time to receive an abridged update from Walker.

Without saying a word to Walker, she ordered the pilot to divert the army transport to Chicago. She wanted to be in the chase. Ellen Yi aside, Walker and Jensen were the only two living people who could visually identify Doug Moon.

———

The O'Hare tower was unusually quiet. An early-season storm had all but shut down the airport. The last outbound flight had left the Chicago airspace over two hours ago. Inbound air traffic lasted only for another half hour after that. The last few flight arrivals were still waiting for an open gate at the terminal.

"They'll be playing with fire trying to land in this weather." The matter-of-fact statement came from the control tower supervisor, Craig Rehnquist. He was referring to the government charter that was coming in from the west. "Visibility is nearly zero, and the wind is blowing as hard as I've ever seen it here."

The others in the tower could tell that Rehnquist was nervous. For the first time in the four years since smoking had been declared off limits at the airport facility, he lit up. In fact, he sucked hard on the cigarette, and in a matter of minutes, he was done. The entire staff watched as he unhinged his thumb and sent the butt somersaulting through the air and onto the floor.

"They'd stand a better chance of putting down safely if they circled around and headed back toward the storm," spoke a control tower staff worker.

"Wouldn't make that much difference if they did. The wind is swirling from a thousand different directions," responded Rehnquist. "The way I see it, the pilots must have extremely low IQ scores or a gun to their head if they want to land at this airport. Who gave the okay for these guys to land?"

There was no response, and everyone in the tower was silent. Streaks of lighting lit up the sky, and it began to hail. The tower chief grabbed a headset and updated the incoming flight. "An ice cube on hot pavement stands a better chance of survival than you do. Call off your approach and go around."

The reply from the plane was military-like. "The person in charge up here wants to thank you for worrying about our safety and acknowledges your concern."

"It's not their safety I'm worried about. There is a distinct possibility that you will take out a ground crew or even an entire terminal."

Caught in a frozen stare, the tower crew watched and waited for a glimpse of the suicidal flight. The bland-colored DC-9 didn't appear until just a few second before touchdown. Though the wind was blowing hard, it was in the pilot's face for the approach, and he somehow managed a relatively benign landing.

The plane had barely come to a stop when the cabin door was flung open and an emergency escape rope ladder was tossed into the wind and rain.

"That was some kind of landing," whispered Rehnquist. "Let's see if they can exit the plane as gracefully."

The entire staff of the tower went silent. Two long and shapely legs appeared and easily navigated the dangling ladder. "This must be some kind of joke," said Rehnquist.

"Either that or the flight was a drag queen transport," joked a member of the tower crew.

Walker followed Jensen down the rope ladder, and the pair sprinted across the barren tarmac to a waiting luggage tractor. Walker was ready to lay into Jensen for risking his life, her life, and the lives of the pilots, but he could see the anger in her eyes. She was still dealing with the demons from the storage facility at Indigo Run, and Doug Moon was target number one.

The tense moments during and after the landing were behind them. In front of them was a sea of monitors in the airport security facility.

"The last flight from Seattle landed over five hours ago, but chances are Moon took a connecting flight through any one of a dozen other locations," noted Walker, reading from an arrival log. "My guess is that we need to go through recent security tapes to find him."

Jensen was silent. She didn't acknowledge Walker's comments. Her eyes were fixed on a monitor displaying images from the baggage claim area at terminal one.

"Where did this plane come in from?" she demanded, pointing to a Boeing 757 parked at terminal 1.

Brian Walker looked down at a fresh FAA printout. "That flight came in from San Francisco; it landed almost three hours ago."

"The plane has been sitting on the tarmac waiting for a gate.

It only began unloading about ten minutes ago," added an FAA official.

Kate Jensen's eyes remained fixed on one of the security monitors. It was displaying images of pedestrian traffic from the arriving San Francisco flight. Her eyes were locked onto something or someone. In the next second, she flipped open her cell phone and called Pierce."

They began tracking Doug Moon as he exited baggage claim. He moved between terminals 1 and 2. NIA agents followed him until the foot traffic thinned enough to allow the eye in the sky to monitor his movements. The woman behind the invisible eye called ahead to waiting agents at each of three security check areas. Kate Jensen was near her boiling point and wanted to go after Moon personally.

Each NIA group was told to remain in the background. There was a plan to apprehend Moon, but the decision to move had not yet been made. There was a problem. He didn't have any luggage.

———

Another team of NIA field agents moved around McCarran Airport in Las Vegas, blindly searching for Moon's young recruit. They were unaware that their surveillance effort had already failed. Peter Lundi had already opened the second flap on his black travel case.

The timer on the bottom of the travel case delayed fifteen seconds, just long enough for the natural air draw to begin.

First a small capacitor was charged and then discharged to break the seal on the aerosol virus container. Next, two low-voltage fans began to spin. One fan gently cycled the dust out of the lower storage chamber and into a modified, high-efficiency particulate air filter. The second fan enhanced the natural air draw, pulling air through the case via the two exposed portholes.

The virus-laden dust reached the filter at about the same time that the filter dry washing began—a technique similar to the process introduced by riverbed gold prospectors during the early 1920s. The dry washing model implemented in the travel case was a very basic operation. Room temperature air was forced through a rapidly vibrating filtration device. The aerosol filtration system ensured that only the lightest particles were released into the atmosphere.

The draw, filter, and dry wash procedure would last for approximately sixty minutes before the reserve was emptied. After that, the relatively large particles would stay in the air for eight to fifteen hours, depending on the foot traffic and air circulation in the building.

The final act came from a device called the sweeper. By closing the dormant air intake flap on the travel case, a fourth and final operation was triggered. A plastic comb device scratched against the side of the particulate air filter, and the exhaust fan was spun up to full capacity. This ensured that every available particle was ejected into the air supply—a process designed to mimic the concept of licking the bowl after frosting a cake.

Peter Lundi stayed leaning against the wall for a few moments longer. He was done with his tour of duty, but he wanted to wait for another few minutes to be sure. The hidden device gave no visual or audible signal that it was empty. Lundi scratched his face, deciding to buy a razor and shave his itchy beard when he got home.

Most airport terminals were a sprawling maze of hallways; escalators; and various, odd people-mover contraptions. The chance of infecting the entire population of any given airport facility was slim. Moon and Yi understood that the asymmetrical design of most airport facilities would limit the exposure to a particular terminal, lobby, or gate area.

This was not the case at McCarran International. The facility in Las Vegas was a structural anomaly when it came to airport design.

It was a relatively new facility, and growth was designed in. There was a method to the facility's long-term build out.

There was only one main concourse at the heavily trafficked airport. It was built around a large, multistory lobby that was encircled by a second-story balcony. An air bridge provided traffic distribution between the two terminals.

As luck would have it, Peter Lundi set up shop on the air bridge. From his vantage, Lundi could watch the arriving traffic form long queues at the check-in desks while just a head swivel away was the mammoth baggage claim area. It was not by design, but this was a perfect location for Ellen Yi's device. The exhaust from the dry wash unit would float down from its perch on the air bridge and infiltrate the airspace surrounding both the arriving crowd and departing travelers.

A crowd formed outside a nearby bar, distracting Lundi for a moment. He watched a man consume a quart of beer in one gulp. Lundi was ready for his own beer. He buttoned the remaining open flap on his travel case, and the job was complete.

Lundi stopped by the airport lounge to see what all the commotion was about. CNN was running a breaking news story. The terror alert status was raised to Red for the first time since the threat indicator was put into effect following the 9/11 tragedy. The story switched between images of the Indigo Run compound in Yakima and an NIA briefing in Seattle.

Lundi stood silent. The news anchor told the story in broken sentences, stopping frequently for new information being pumped to his left ear. A black travel case identical to his was shown in a small window to the left side of the screen. No one knew exactly what was in the case, but NIA officials implored the public to stay away from the bags if they came across one. Lundi turned away from the lounge and gazed at the throng of late-day business shuttlers and colorful

Vegas patrons.

He tore through the now familiar concourse looking for anybody who might vaguely represent a figure of authority. He engaged a National Guard soldier stationed near the air bridge. The guardsman directed him to the facility administration offices on the third floor. It took a total of seven minutes for Lundi to move from his station at the main concourse to the entrance to the wing of offices that housed the airport administration offices.

He realized that there were personal risks to his pending disclosure, and he stopped dead in his tracks. What was he thinking? Was he crazy? Lundi laced his fingers behind his head and took deep breaths. He avoided eye contact with a passing group of pilots and flight attendants. Maybe he was wrong to think his secret mission was related to the CNN story. *What if the story was a hoax?* He would expose himself and his team before they had even analyzed the air sample.

Maybe it wasn't a good idea to tell anybody about his mission and his disguised air filter.

He turned away from the office area of the airport and moved back to the abandoned travel case. It was still leaning against the railing on the concourse balcony. Contrary to the repetitive loudspeaker message, the airport security detail did not dispose of lone travel bags.

The crowd at the lounge had increased fivefold since the last time he passed by. Some of the patrons grabbed their luggage and ran from the lounge. Others stood transfixed by the CNN story and the accompanying local news warnings that were streaming as text across the bottom of the screen.

This is ridiculous, he thought to himself. *There's nothing illegal about what I'm doing, and even if this bag does contain a banned agent, I was not aware of it at the time I brought it onto the airplane.*

He did a U-turn in place and headed back to the wing of the

airport that housed the administrative staff.

He stepped into a small corridor off the concourse balcony. The third door on the left was labeled, "Las Vegas Police Department."

Peter Lundi swallowed hard and knocked on the door. No one answered, so he opened the door. The interior office area was an open space with four desks facing a windowed wall looking out on the tarmac. Two uniformed officers stood in the corner monitoring the same CNN broadcast that was being shown in the airport lounge.

Lundi cleared his throat.

"Can we help you?" asked one of the officers.

"I think so. I want to speak with someone about the story you're watching."

"You and everyone else in the airport," he said, unfazed.

"I think you want to hear me out," Lundi said softly.

"Oh you do," the officer said, still more interested in the breaking news story than the visitor.

"I have one of the black bags," blurted Lundi.

Both officers turned and glared at him. "What's your name?" asked the now interested officer.

"Uh, Peter Lundi." Lundi felt faint and asked if he could sit down.

The officers moved over to the chair and began to ask questions. Lundi held out his hand to stop the questions. He took control of the meeting.

The story took ten minutes beginning to end with just a few interruptions by the airport police officers. Lundi skipped parts, unimportant pieces of information that would only prolong his anxiety. They broke for soda and coffee while one of the officers conferred with an unknown party on the other end of his two-way radio. The disinterested officers were now fully engaged in the story and were no longer patronizing the visitor.

A team of three more police officers joined them, one uniformed and two others who introduced themselves as detectives from the Las Vegas Metropolitan Police Department.

Lundi told the story again, talking with his hands and pausing only to scratch his itchy beard. Just like the first time through the story, the only details he withheld were the ones describing his personal enthusiasm for the original plan to meter the indoor air quality at the airport. As the story unfolded, it became clear to the detectives that this guy was not fooling. This was not the face of a deranged local who'd stumbled in to wreak havoc on the airport.

The officers and detectives huddled in the corner of the room. When they emerged, all five looked scared. Lundi was sorry to have dropped this in their lap, but how bad could it be? After the third call in as many minutes, one of the detectives stood up and told everyone to follow him into another office.

———

Jensen and Walker slouched in their chairs, each frowning. Around the O'Hare airport security room, four fellow NIA officers and five airport police officers paced and mumbled to no one in particular. Fatigue had overtaken Walker and Jensen. Their prey had been purposely allowed to escape. Jensen felt especially dejected.

News of exposure in Las Vegas broke the teams' morale. The uncertainty surrounding the integrity of the air supply at O'Hare made the damp afternoon even soggier. No one in the office wanted to say a word. It was all too awful to think about. A crowded airport, one full of tourists and convention travelers, was being exposed to one of the more ghastly diseases of the last two centuries.

An airport luggage train made a series of wild turns to navigate through a minefield of dormant planes and assorted ground vehicles at O'Hare. The airport was still closed and, pending a decision from the boys in the tower, it would remain that way. It was almost dusk when the driver of the luggage train screeched to an unceremonious stop just short of the only retracted jet way at terminal 1. Bounding up the steel grate steps, he opened the secure door with a special cardkey and sprinted up the jet way into the crowded terminal. The young man was excited. He had found the infamous black case. Why it was so important was beyond him, but he had found it and wanted to be sure that everyone knew it was his diligent work that had uncovered the precious cargo. He didn't bother to knock.

"I found it," stammered the young airport employee while gasping for air.

"Where is it?" snapped the closest NIA agent.

"It's still on the plane. I found it in an overhead compartment surround by folded blankets."

"Take me out to the plane," ordered the NIA agent.

The next few minutes seemed like an eternity to the group assembled in the airport security room. Fifteen minutes later, the package was declared intact, and the agents trailing Doug Moon were told to move in.

29

Professor Gauthier found his former student drooling on himself on the locker room floor. His patient had obviously fallen off the couch during the early morning. He glanced at the empty IV bag still attached to Bekins's arm. Gauthier moved clumsily in his yellow, air-locked suit. With his gloved hand, he touched Bekins's face. It was still visibly damp, but the fever was certainly lower; he could no longer feel the elevated temperature through his glove.

"Mark," he said quietly through his protective visor. He cleared the matted hair off the young man's forehead.

On the second try, Mark Bekins groaned a few words. "I'm still here," he said in a low-key but triumphant tone. The body aches and fever were noticeably milder, but the pain in his head and behind his eyes was certainly going strong.

"I think your idea is working," whispered Gauthier.

"How can you be sure? Did the monkey recover?"

"I found a human subject."

Bekins eyes moved from quarter to half-mast. "You what?"

"You are living proof that experiment three works."

"Let's hope that we don't have to try it on anyone else."

"It's too late for that thought. We are already manufacturing your therapy in limited quantities. It's being shipped to Nevada tonight."

Bekins's eyes opened all the way. "Why ...? Who ...? How ...?" he stammered. He didn't need an answer. He could tell by the look on Gauthier's face that there had been an exposure.

———

By the time news of the quarantine at the Las Vegas airport had spread to all three major networks, plus FOX, CNN, and MSNBC, the trouble had already started. The Army Hot Team was doing everything in its power to contain the situation, but without any real evidence and no visible sign of the contamination, the crowd in the airport was quickly growing unruly. They were not told the real reason for the quarantine, but a few of the trapped travelers had spied a news story on a forgotten TV in one of the airline club rooms. All other media broadcasts had been cut off to protect against mass hysteria.

A convoy of bodies approached the airport on foot. Each participant came with a story of a friend or a relative who was trapped inside the airport. After approaching the usually busy arrival and departure roads, the foot traffic was directed back out toward the strip. After three trips around the airport perimeter, many gave up. Others, those with relatives inside, stood outside the windowed baggage claim area hoping to get a glimpse of a loved one.

For the first time in over twenty years, the outside temperature at Las Vegas's McCarran Airport reached 120 °F. There were no clouds to protect the gathered throngs from the sun's fierce rays, no breeze to dull the searing heat. Over one hundred people were being treated for dehydration at a hastily assembled first aid tent just outside the departure terminal.

The crowd continued to grow. Some just wanted a glimpse of the action; others were genuinely distraught.

———

With Brian Williams on assignment somewhere in Afghanistan, Tom Brokaw was found … who knows where. He was put on the air. He started with a brief history of the disease. Vaccination everywhere had ceased twenty or more years ago, and there existed in every country a large population that had never been exposed to either smallpox or its antigen. Moreover, some substantial portion of those vaccinated before 1980 were now susceptible to smallpox because of waning immunity. Thus, the potential for a rapidly spreading epidemic was great. A large-scale vaccination would be required to control the spread of the disease. Half or more would be first-time vaccinations. Three percent of those would succumb from the vaccine itself.

Reports of infection were coming in from all over the Las Vegas area. While all these reports were false, there were enough of them for a team at the CDC to begin to map probable infection patterns, just in case. In all, over one hundred cases had been reported so far. New cases were being reported at about two per hour. The press had done a good job educating the public about smallpox, its history, and the public's lack of immunity, but unfortunately, no one had told the public that symptoms of the disease were days, if not weeks, away.

"Yesterday, America's worst terrorism dreams came true. It started for each individual at a different time—when you turned on your computer, TV, or radio; when you answered the phone or just stepped outside." Those were the words a BBC reporter used to describe the day's events.

The images that haunted the country were surreal television broadcasts from helicopters or via fixed cameras. Many reporters were too afraid to get close to the source. The really ominous images were not the exposed trapped inside the airport facility but those of the family members who were not allowed in. The story would be the same in New York, Chicago, or Los Angeles.

The first national health alert was broadcast in the Las Vegas area just before 5:00 p.m. The director of Health and Human Services had engaged the Emergency Broadcast System. The system's ubiquitous tone, a throwback to the cold war, was followed by information on where to tune for information and updates.

It was not until evening that the White House was able to organize a press conference, and deliver up-to-date details of the bioterrorism plot.

30

Doug Moon stepped onto the L in Chicago just before 4:00 p.m. He moved toward the front of the of the commuter railcar. He stared straight ahead, his head and eyes focused only on his next step. Moon was not the anxious type—he almost never worried about past events—but today he was concerned. Neither Ellen Yi nor Peter Lundi had checked in.

A tall, slender, fair-skinned woman sat down next to him. She joined Moon in his lifeless stare out the window. Her face broke into a smile at the next stop. "My family," she said proudly, pointing at a gathering of no less than five children and a short, bald man who Moon assumed was the husband. Moon returned the smile and nodded to the waiting throng.

The doors on the L closed again, and for the next twenty minutes, he sat still, trying not to think about his own failure and hoping, praying, that Ellen and Peter Lundi had been more successful in their endeavors.

———

In the back of the car, NIA Agents Smith and Jones sat quietly, pretending to be bored commuters.

Smith, heavyset with a receding hairline, turned to his partner and said, "If we lose him, we might as well kiss our promotions goodbye."

"If we lose him we might as well not go back to work tomorrow," responded Jones. He was tall and well built, wearing a dress shirt but no tie.

———

Five minutes later, Jones was on the phone to his command officer at the makeshift NIA field office in O'Hare. "The target is missing,' he said.

"He's what?" screamed the NIA officer in charge. "How could you lose him?"

Field agent Jones went red. "Our instructions were to hold back and follow him until he stopped moving."

"I can't believe you lost him," repeated the officer. "What the hell happened?"

"He just disappeared. When the train stopped at Clinton, a huge number of people entered the train. When the doors closed, he was gone."

"That's just great, son. How long ago did this happen?"

"About six to ten minutes ago."

"Where are you now?"

"We exited the train at the Racine station, and now we're waiting for an inbound train back to the Clinton station."

"Okay, listen to me carefully. We need to find this guy soon. He cannot get away. I'll call the Chicago Police Department and get a description of him out on the street. In the meantime … find him or else."

———

Doug Moon's secret Chicago condominium was a two-story townhouse in a converted, turn-of-the-century factory building.

The factory had been renovated during a Chicagoland real estate boom in the early '80s. Moon had purchased the unit ten years after the boom.

Moon had only been to the secret location three times in the last dozen years. He didn't care much for Chicago or the condo, but right now it offered a short window of safe time while he regrouped and tried to figure out what had happened to Yi and Lundi.

Moon moved toward a lone chair framed by a twelve-foot-high, exposed brick wall. He collapsed into the oversized chair and let out a sigh. The only visible technology in the room was a television set on a steel table in the middle of the room. Moon stood and walked over to the set. He had no idea if there was a remote control for the decade-old device, and even if it had originally been equipped with one, he had no idea where it might be now.

He didn't need to stand by the set for very long. The second channel he tuned to was an all news station, and it was broadcasting a dual image, split between Las Vegas and Chicago. Moon was pleased by the scenes of disorder in Las Vegas but was puzzled by the lack of any news from Ellen's efforts in Detroit. He paced like a big cat, trying to calm his nerves. After twenty minutes of fearing the worst, he stretched his tired, aching arms toward the ceiling.

"Sleep. I need to sleep," he said aloud to the empty room.

Moon set his wristwatch alarm and promised himself two hours of sleep, nothing more. Maybe by that time, there would be news from Detroit.

At precisely 4:00 p.m., Moon was stirred into consciousness by the chime on his watch. He pushed a small button on the face of the watch to silence the annoying tone. He stood up from the chair and repeated his previous steps to the television.

There was more news from Chicago. A grainy image of a face appeared in a small window next to the anchor's head. Moon did not need to strain his eyes to make out the image. The familiar image, probably from an airport security camera, was unmistakably his. He was immediately shaken by the image, and a cold shiver went through his body. He needed to get away from Chicago. Too many people would be looking for him.

He made no attempt to disguise himself; just a turned up collar on his overcoat would suffice. He needed to assume another identity—not one he had used before, but one from a traveler with similar facial characteristics. *Not an easy task in this part of downtown Chicago*, he thought to himself.

He donned his overcoat, turned off the television, and quickly moved back out into the Chicago evening. This time he would skip public transportation and walk the five long blocks to the American Airlines ticket office on the edge of Chicago's Chinatown.

Moon sat idly just outside the ticket office waiting for a clone. He continued to watch for an appropriate candidate for another hour, but no one came. The ticket office was due to close at 7:00 p.m. He had one hour left.

Two small families, a set of newlyweds, and three single women later, he found his target. A tall, visibly Asian male entered the ticket office. Moon moved into the facility and took up a space in line behind the target. Fortunately, only one queue was left opened.

Moon did his best to memorize as much about the transaction as possible. He ignored the flight details and only retained two facts about the patron stationed in front of him: his destination, Boston, tonight at ten-thirty and his local contact information, Sheraton Towers, room 715. Moon feigned disgust at the long transaction in front of him and quickly exited the airline ticket office.

He wasted no time finding a cab. He was no longer interested in trying to dodge the public. His fear of being recognized was a distant memory, and now his only real concern was beating his future identity back to the Sheraton Towers.

Moon looked the part of a traveling businessman back from a full day of meetings as he worked his way through the lobby foot traffic and toward a bank of elevators. He looked respectable, still wearing the same neat but casual garb that he'd had on during the escape from Indigo Run.

There was no answer at room 715. If someone had come to the door, he would have apologized for bothering them and explained that he was off by one floor. It didn't open. He knocked again for good measure and waited only a few seconds before he worked a paper-thin extension rod under the door. He worked the rod up the other side of the door and poked around until he found the inside door handle. Within a minute, he was inside.

His new identity was a very neat individual. The only visible sign of life in the tower hotel suite was a set of clothes laid out on the far bed. A solid blue, button-down shirt; khakis; underwear; and socks were laid out in their appropriate anatomical positions. Moon took a quick look around before moving into his listening station on the closet floor.

His closet floor rest was not long. The prey returned much earlier than Moon had expected. He was clearly either planning to go out for a final meal in Chicago, or he was planning on waiting out his departure at the airline clubroom. He could hear the target cuss in the hallway as he fumbled with the stubborn cardkey lock. The man entered the room. Moon peered through a crack in the closet door. His target was a little bigger around the middle than he had realized. He was glad that his own clothes were still reasonably clean.

The target did not turn on the lights when he entered the room. That was his first mistake. The room stayed dark, while he moved toward the closet to hang up his coat. That was his last mistake.

Moon struck like a cobra, lashing out from his dark prison like a mad man. He kicked his stunned prey in the groin. The man groaned and fell to his knees. Moon grabbed the phone and ripped it from the desk. He used the cord to twist the life out of his confused prey, giving the term identity theft a whole new meaning.

With a little luck, the housekeeping crew would stay away from room 715 until Moon was safely on the ground in Boston.

———

Agents Jones and Smith were called back in. An observant valet at the Sheraton Towers had observed a man fitting Moon's description entering the hotel forty minutes earlier. Smith was anxious to arrive at the hotel. He hadn't expected to get a second shot at capturing Doug Moon.

Jones and Smith and a squad of four other NIA agents arrived at the hotel just before eight o'clock. Jones waited in a commandeered taxicab, hoping that he could pick up Moon's fare. Smith stood on a nearby corner snapping orders into an invisible receiver. Nothing short of a capture or a kill would suit him now. He didn't know Doug Moon; he was not aware of the atrocities in and around Indigo Run, but he loathed the man anyway. Moon had escaped his surveillance and made a fool of him in front of his boss, and that really pissed him off. He wanted the team to be patient, though; there would be no slip ups this time. One agent was stationed at each ground floor egress.

It took only a matter of minutes for things to heat up. The NIA spotter stationed inside the hotel at the atrium bar reported a man fitting Moon's description crossing the lobby. Agent Jones stood straight and waited for the target to exit the hotel. In a prearranged move, Agent Smith pulled his cab to the front of the line and waited for the signal to move in. The signal never came. It never came because Moon walked quickly across the circular valet area to a waiting limousine.

The limousine was an unexpected perk. Moon's new identity included a Massachusetts driver's license, first-class tickets for the trip to Boston, and limousine transportation to and from O'Hare and Logan Airport in Boston.

The limousine moved efficiently through the downtown traffic. It was dark, and Moon poked through his new belongings with the aid of an overhead reading light.

"Crazy day, huh," remarked the livery driver, trying to spark conversation with his new passenger.

"Busy day for you?" replied Moon.

"I mean the news—the mess in Las Vegas and all, pretty crazy stuff. I wouldn't want to be out there now. I'm just glad it didn't happen here."

"Is there any new information?"

"There was just a report that Denver's airport and the airport facility in San Diego have been quarantined."

Ellen was flying through Denver on her way to Detroit. Maybe she needed to change the venue for her attack, and the San Diego news was probably one of the many expected false alarms, thought Moon.

They rode in silence and watched the passing traffic on the inbound Eisenhower Expressway. The traffic in their direction was moving slowly.

"Time to move in," spoke agent Smith into his radio. They were safely out of the city and away from the densely populated hotel area. In a perfect world, they would wait until the limousine exited the expressway and force it off onto the shoulder of the road, but this time, they weren't going to take any chances. They were going to move in now while he and his transportation were trapped.

A glimmer in the sea of headlights caught Moon's driver's eye.

"Check this out. There are three guys out of their car marching between the traffic. I've seen it worse than this. They must be really late for their flight," said the driver.

"Move it!" screamed Moon at the driver.

"Hey, cool it," the driver said. "Can't you see the traffic's backed up?"

Moon pressed a pistol at the driver's temple. "Get this car moving, or you're dead," he threatened.

The driver gunned the limo and rammed into the car in front of him.

"Damn!" cursed Moon.

The sound of the idling traffic flew in the rear passenger side door as Moon exited the vehicle. He knew that the men moving on foot were not late for a flight. They were coming for him.

NIA agent Smith made his move. He calmly aimed his 9mm revolver at Moon and squeezed the trigger. A stream of bullets jumped from the end of the gun. Moon could hear popcorn sounds as the bullets lodged into the sheet metal around him. One entered his arm just above the elbow.

The late rush-hour nightmare, illuminated by the headlights of the stopped traffic, became a frenzied panic of bodies as travelers viewing the shooting jumped out of their vehicles. One man put up the hood of his car and tried to force his family behind it for protection. The area immediately around the scene was choked with humanity.

Jones was ready to empty another clip in the general direction of Moon when a fat black man, sweat trickling down his forehead, moved in front of Moon.

"Oh God," he screamed when he realized his position.

Moon grabbed the man and used him as a human shield. Moon and his shield moved across the stalled outbound lanes to the expressway median. Inbound traffic was still moving in the opposite direction at nearly fifty miles per hour.

With great determination and willpower, Moon said a quick

prayer and turned his attention away from the NIA pursuers and began running through the inbound expressway traffic. Only three lanes of traffic separated him from a getaway. Never once did he look back. His vision and mind were set on navigating across the passing expressway traffic.

———

Doug Moon never made it the full way. In the middle lane he and the black man were swallowed in a tidal wave of limbs and blood. Both the black man and Moon were hit with such sensational force that they never really knew what happened.

31

Ellen Yi was the first passenger off the plane in San Diego. She spent an hour sitting idle at the gate, purposely missing her connecting flight to Detroit. She made two phone calls as soon as her scheduled flight to Detroit had safely departed the gate. The first call went out to Doug Moon. There was no answer. Then she dialed a number sent to her by her brother on the eve of his murder.

"Kate Jensen here," said the voice on the other end.

"My name is Ellen Yi," she said. "Follow my instructions and do not talk." Ellen glanced around to see if anyone was listening.

"Where are you?" Kate asked.

"I said do not talk," Ellen ordered, stomping her foot out of frustration. "Do nothing. Stay back for two hours, and all will be well." There was an uncomfortable pause. "What is your fax number?" Ellen asked.

Jensen had barely finished dictating the last digit of the fax number when Yi hung up.

Ellen Yi walked with purpose toward the nearest rental car counter and used her credit card to pay for a three-day rental. She listed her local contact information as a downtown San Diego hotel.

The drive from San Diego to the airport in Orange County was a straight shot up Highway 5 with a short stint on the 805 near the end of the drive. The alone time gave Ellen Yi time to think. The compound at Indigo Run seemed a lifetime away. She had often wondered how life would feel with Doug Moon and their plans out of her life. It felt good.

An hour and a half later, she pulled into a short-term parking lot at John Wayne Airport. Yi abandoned her newly rented car and moved quickly into the airport terminal. She blended in with the other travelers by wearing casual slacks, a loose-fitting top, tennis sneakers, and a hoodie. Her only luggage was a maroon overnight bag and a satchel. She walked to the United Airline ticket counter and charged a one-way ticket to San Francisco. Then she found the America West counter and paid cash for a first-class ticket to Phoenix. After looking around, she found the business traveler's kiosk and pulled some sheets of paper out of her satchel. It took just a few minutes to feed the sheets into the public fax machine.

She waited around the gate for the United flight only long enough to be sure that she was recorded on the security cameras. She roamed the short-term parking lot for about forty-five minutes, and at the last possible moment, she went back into the terminal and boarded the flight to Phoenix.

The flight attendant came down the aisle, and Ellen ordered a vodka cranberry. It was her first drink since the hangover in Amherst. This time she was not going to get drunk, but she was edgy, and one or two drinks might help.

If Doug Moon knew what she was up to, he would go berserk. He probably already had some inkling that she was out. She was more worried that the NIA team would find her. They were probably receiving her facsimile right now.

———

Kate Jensen went into the airport copy center for the fourth time in as many minutes. This time an image was re-rendering itself onto a piece of paper. The entire document was three pages long.

Dear Ms. Jensen,

Please forgive my method of communication, but it took some time for me to come to grips with the moment and to ruminate on the wisdom of passing you this information. As you know from recent experiences, it is a very unsteady environment we live in.

Ms. Jensen, please heed what I say here. I have tried to communicate to you all the facts as I know them, and I believe them all to be true. I urge you and your government to work with other bodies around the world to better protect, if not destroy, all stockpiles of synthetic, mutated, and artificially maintained biological agents. If it were not for the U.S. government, the current predicament would probably never have occurred. The technology and science to design and build a supervirus is all in the public domain, and the Internet is the carrier. The world's only protection is renewed diligence.

Most of my efforts to create an engineered virus would not have been possible just a decade ago. When I first ventured to build a Level 4 lab, I was surprised to find that the technology was only an overnight delivery away. What would have required millions of dollars in the late twentieth century is now affordable to many.

Just recently, my brother was killed. In a direct way, my ignorance contributed to his death. This same ignorance has shielded me from my true feelings toward your country. A childhood drama concealed my families' true intentions for their country and fueled my brothers and my own blind ambition for revenge. My brother was able to see through the blinders and tried to prevent a misguided tragedy. My blinders have only recently come off.

I am sure you are aware of the chaos at some of your airports. Rest assured that no one in any U.S. or international airport has been infected. After years of firsthand experience with the virus, during which time I experienced the killing power of the virus both in animal and human subjects, I have concluded that my mission should not continue. There have been enough lives lost during this personal battle of ours.

There was a time when I could not differentiate between the killing of ten or one hundred. Perverted as it may seem, I can put my past actions behind me and start again. I have made peace with my misdeeds, as my recent actions will prevent the deaths of thousands if not millions of U.S. residents, and that is good enough for me.

You will find that all fourteen of the travel devices are loaded with an inert substance. The traveling public is not in danger of exposure.

*Please don't try and find me. I am going to do some
good for a change.*

*Please stay diligent and aware. The energy of a mis-
guided few can be too costly to ignore.*

Ellen Yi

Kate Jensen did not skim the transmission; instead, she read from the document verbatim, only pausing to gasp once.

It took Brian Walker's muddied mind a few seconds to clear. He didn't say anything for many minutes. Neither did anyone else in the room. No one was left standing; all available chairs and floor space were occupied. It felt like all the oxygen had been drawn out of the room. Walker's mind began to visualize the calming scene in Las Vegas.

Kate Jensen was the first to speak. Calmly, with a slight smile, she asked one of her NIA colleagues to get in touch with the army medical team in Yakima.

"Tell them to test the packages!"

———

Ellen Yi retreated from the Phoenix airport. She went through the baggage area but claimed nothing. She left the airport grounds in the back seat of a minivan turned taxi. Her mind was numb from the events leading up to and following the dramatic escape from Indigo Run.

At some undefined point in the last week, haunted by the dead, she had slowly gained some level of shame. She had killed innocent people without the slightest twinge of remorse, until now. Something about her latest group of victims had changed her view on her life long program of revenge. The latest group was the first group to include children, and the vision of the dead and dying young victims had changed her. They were not party to her country's hardship and should not be part of the retaliation.

Ellen was ashamed. She would accept the ramifications of her crimes, but she would not seek the punishment. She had pity for Doug Moon, but she would not seek him either.

At dinnertime, the taxi deposited her beneath a neon sign in the desert.

The first light of morning brought a realization of the previous day's events. Ellen spent the night in a ratty motel on the New Mexico border. The morning clouds were missing, and the day's heat was building quickly. She dug into her overnight bag and pulled out a fresh, white T-shirt and a pair of khaki shorts. She washed her face, applied just a hint of blush and mascara, and combed her dark hair, which she had let grow longer in recent weeks.

Breakfast was in the form of a small box stuffed with dried fruit, lemon cake, assorted pastries, and a day-old, egg-battered sandwich that she quickly discarded. She ate slowly, curious more than worried that this might be her last meal as a free soul.

She wandered around the small motel room for another hour before getting the nerve up to venture outside. The only sound she could hear emanated from the room next door. It sounded as if a newlywed battle was brewing. There were family slanders and a personal feud that almost made Ellen feel as if she'd led a good life.

She drifted out of the room and toward the front desk to checkout. There was a short moment of uncomfortable silence when Ellen thought she was done for. The front desk was void of life. Relief flooded in when the same young man that had taken her one hundred and eight dollars the evening before reappeared from behind a closed door.

"Have a good night?" he asked.

"Very nice, thank you," responded Ellen.

"I know that the original deal was for two nights, but I'm going to move on."

The young man frowned.

"You can keep the money. I just wanted to return the key and thank you for the hospitality."

A smile returned to the boy's face.

Ellen had paid the clerk in cash, no questions asked.

"How far to the reservation?" asked Ellen.

"It's just a few miles down the road. Do you need a lift?"

"Yes, please. Can you call a taxi for me?"

"No, but I can take you there myself. I live on the reservation," said the handsome young man. "Do you have business with the tribe?"

"I'm here to volunteer at the pediatric clinic."

"Then we're headed the same direction. My mother is the Havasupai reservation pediatrician. I also work at the clinic," he said with a smile.

With a quick shout to an invisible co-worker, Ellen Yi's livery driver moved around the barren desk and politely guided her through the front door and out into the parking lot to a well-used Toyota pickup truck.

It was less than fifteen minutes later when the newly acquainted couple walked through the front door of the Havasupai children's clinic. Ellen relaxed her shoulders. The tightness in her stomach lessened.

She saw the children immediately; some seemed happy but most looked undernourished and in fair to poor health. At first, the children retreated into their mother's arms. They were not sure what to make of the foreigner. The young man tried to calm the children.

None had ever seen an Asian woman before.

After a few minutes of seemingly repetitive words and hand gestures, the crowd of children and parents in the room seemed to calm.

The young man looked at Ellen.

"Japanese?" he asked her.

"Chinese, Chinese-American," she responded.

A sophisticated-looking woman with a pleasant face and soft demeanor entered the waiting room. She placed a hand on her son's shoulder and smiled at Ellen. The mother-son pair conversed in English. Ellen could hear every word. She smiled at the young boy and his mother.

Ellen was handed a white lab coat, no questions asked.

32

After two weeks in the sun, Jensen's skin had turned a dark brown. She felt no remorse for the lazy lifestyle that had facilitated her condition. The last few weeks represented the longest contiguous period of time that she and Walker had ever spent together. She'd spent the first week under the tutelage of Hilton Head's premier golf teacher. The second week had been less productive. Each day had started with a long walk on the beach and ended in the arms of her companion.

I could grow accustomed to this lifestyle, she thought to herself.

It was late afternoon when Brian Walker came to a stop just northwest of her beach chair. He was just completing his daily beach run. His body was also tanned, and his calf muscles had become taut again from his daily workout. He wore his new Nike running shoes, the ones with the embedded iPod adapter; shorts; and a tie-dyed lacrosse T-shirt. He removed his shirt and walked toward the ocean to cool off his overheated feet. This was his favorite time of year. The subtropical island climate was not near its peak. The water was an enterable seventy-two degrees, and the air still cooled to the 60s over night.

"You were gone a long time," she said, looking at her naked wrist out of habit. There was no sign of a tan line where her watch had once lived.

"I needed to run an errand. No pun intended."

She didn't press any further. He didn't elaborate.

"How about a dinner out tonight?" he offered.

"Sounds great. How much time do I have to get ready?"

"About five minutes," he said gesturing to the small craft being dragged through the surf.

"You expect me to go out half caked in salt and sand? You're probably a little salty from your run."

"Not a problem; we can clean up and change once we're on board."

"I'm not changing my clothes on that thing," she said, looking distastefully at the small boat launch.

"No one is asking you to," he responded, pointing out to a large yacht with a uniformed crew of three standing at attention along the side rail.

"Am I to assume that my evening wear is already on board?"

"Correct you are, my lady. Now let's get aboard," he said, racing down ahead of her to the surf launch in an unchivalrous fashion.

Kate jumped up from her beach chair and ran after him, laughing. They stepped into the launch and were whisked away to the yacht.

The boat was just the right size—not too big or too small. The crew of three included a cook, a server, and most importantly, a captain. The forty-eight-foot Sea Ray's twin diesel engines were hardly noticeable as Jensen took a turn in the elaborate stateroom shower.

The yacht's master stateroom was a sea of cherry wood with glimmering stone trim. She collapsed into an oversized, soft leather reading chair. For a brief minute, she thought about staying there for an hour. Only Walker's presence topside drew her out of the cocoon.

Brian Walker studied her as she emerged through the aft cabin door. He stared at her as if he was seeing her for the first time. She wore leather sandals; a short, black skirt with a hint of gold trim; and a loose-fitting linen shirt that barely exposed her midriff. She also wore a soft, beautiful smile. Her face was enchanting.

She lowered her head slightly, smiled again, and appeared to be blushing.

"I feel like I'm on a first date," she said.

"There is nothing wrong with that."

A soft and slightly cool breeze came across the water. It was almost 7:00 p.m. He reached behind the galley door and produced a white cardigan for her shoulders. She saw him glance at the digital clock on the wall.

"I hear that the service is good here. We should move aft for cocktails," he suggested. He wore a pair of navy Dockers, a beige polo shirt, and comfortable loafers. "My dear," he said, bending slightly at the waist to present his arm. She took it, and the two of them strolled along the deck.

Their proximity to Calibogue Sound made for a smooth ride. The boat moved gently past the harbor entrance, and the small crowd gathered near the lighthouse. It was a perfect spot to watch the sunset over a neighboring island.

Just north of the harbor entrance, the engines stopped and the ship dropped anchor.

"This seems as good a place as any for dinner and stargazing," concluded Walker, stopping at a linen-covered table for two. He pulled out a chair for Kate and helped her get seated before taking a seat across from her.

Kate smiled as Brian sat down.

Their server appeared with drinks and two plates of appetizers.

The eating went on for over an hour. Nothing important was said during the meal, just comfortable conversation about life, dreams, and a shared interest in staying away from the real world for as long as possible. They only had ten days left.

Just before nine, they climbed off the large yacht and back into the boat launch they'd used to start the evening. The launch transferred the pair to a ramp a few feet from the base of the island's famous lighthouse.

"How about a stroll through the shops," he suggested.

She silently agreed and held out her hand.

Most of the quaint stores were closed. Only a combination ice cream store/gift shop was still accepting customers. They passed the jewelry store, and Kate looked wistfully at the storefront display. A pair of vacant rockers just steps from the harbor wall interrupted the quiet walk.

Walker sat first and motioned her to follow.

"How long can you stay here?" he asked, with a twinge of hidden anxiousness.

"How long do you want me?"

He paused. It seemed like an eternity before he responded.

He stood and faced her. "Forever," he said, holding out a small box.